The Miracle

Previous Visionary Fiction by Michael Gurian

An American Mystic

The Miracle

A Visionary Novel

Michael Gurian

ATRIA BOOKS
New York London Toronto Sydney Singapore

1230 Avenue of the Americas
New York, NY 10020

This book is a work of fiction. Names, characters, places and incidents are products of the author's imagination or are used fictitiously. Any resemblance to actual events or locales or persons living or dead is entirely coincidental.

For information address Atria Books, 1230 Avenue of the Americas, New York, NY 10020

ISBN: 0-7434-4850-2

First Atria Books trade paperback edition May 2003

10 9 8 7 6 5 4 3 2 1

For information regarding special discounts for bulk purchases, please contact Simon & Schuster Special Sales at 1-800-456-6798 or business@simonandschuster.com

Manufactured in the United States of America

For Gail, Gabrielle, and Davita

Acknowledgments

My thanks to Brenda Copeland for her beautiful editing, Tracy Behar and Judith Curr for their support, and Candice Fuhrman for believing in my work.

My thanks also to everyone who is writing and reading profound, visionary fiction. The human story is expanding every day. I would love to hear *your* story, and urge you to visit me and others interested in visionary fiction at www.visionaryfiction.org.

Contents

"There is a Light that shines beyond all things on earth, beyond us all, beyond the heavens, beyond the highest heaven; that Light shines also in our world."

–CHANDOGYA UPANISHAD

"The kingdom of earth awaits the arrival of the new human."

–ST. TERESA OF AVILA

"Where there is good, there will be evil. Where there is evil, let there be good."

–THE HOLY QUR'AN

The Miracle

Prologue

The Spokane River stretches a long, winding green through the city of Spokane, in the eastern portion of Washington State, toward the larger Columbia River and the Pacific Ocean. North of the city, the river follows a shallow gorge, lined by pine trees, where squirrels and osprey, the hawk, the red-winged blackbird, the rabbit, the deer, and the gray mouse all live in a kind of wildlife refuge. At the margin of this refuge stands Lucia Court, a subdivision on the land east of the river gorge and south of a low dam. Its residents provide a small scent of human companionship.

From the time the Spokane Indians left due to the city expansion of the late 1980s, no humans have lived in this area. When the Lucia Court subdevelopment arrived in 1987, it came like a growing organism, rumbling on bulldozers that dug holes with a badger's ferocity, buried power lines like packrats, and built human nests out of plaster, wood, and steel.

The air near the river, accustomed for so long to its cycle of quiet breathing, adapted to the breathing of the new families moving one by one into houses that remained unlandscaped for a year or more for lack of time, interest, or money.

The Romers were among the first to move into Lucia, with their son Jeffrey, not yet two. Others came soon, knowing one another not at all until the wind broke a pine tree from Sarbaugh's yard to McDonald's, the earth broke a cable under both the Svobodas' and Basses' yards, and the thunder scared the children of two homes, who hid together in sudden community. Slowly, the people in Lucia came to know their neighbors, first by face, then name, then handshake, an embrace or two, and even, between two adolescent children on a winter night, a kiss of the richest quality. And then the most dramatic event.

Jeffrey Romer was six years old. He had no hair. The chemotherapy had removed his blond hair along with about one-third of his body weight. Despite spending large parts of many days in hospitals, he knew his alphabet, and knew how to sign his name. He loved to be read to, something his mother, Marti, and his father, Landry, did as often as possible. He liked stories from the Bible, and from other religious epics, Western and Eastern. He loved listening to stories of people who possessed exceptional gifts, people like Edgar Cayce and Nostradamus. Jeffrey's eyes gazed into the middle distance as he listened to these stories, his face alert with a kind of laconic recognition.

Jeffrey spent about half his time in bed, about a quarter of his time in a wheelchair, and about a quarter of his time trying to walk. Sometimes he could be seen crawling from one spot to another, rarely ashamed of his weakness, mainly determined. Once, Marti saw him get down out of his wheelchair and crawl toward a butterfly that, wing-wounded, could not rise. Marti had learned not to interrupt Jeffrey's concentrations—with doctors and parents poking at him so often, his concentrations were some of his only privacies. She watched him lift the brown, black, and gold monarch butterfly onto his finger and caress it, and she watched it pause upon him for breath then, healed, fly away. Turning back to his mother, Jeffrey grinned with the pleasure of being so close to the immensely delicate and beautiful. And he allowed her to help him back to his chair.

Jeffrey had become a kind of young legend in Lucia Court. Many of the neighbors baby-sat him or just came over to sit with his parents as they looked at the sun setting over the river. Twice Jeffrey had looked at neighbors and told them something extraordinary about themselves. He told Mrs. Greta Sarbaugh that she had grown up "in a town with one tall building in the middle that went up to a point, but not a cross." Greta, seventy-five, had indeed been born and raised, until seven, in a tiny town near Maribor, in Slovenia, in which the tallest structure was a mosque with a single minaret pointing up toward heaven. When Greta asked Jeffrey to tell her what else he "saw," he said, "There is an old woman by your house who is blind like your sister Trudy." Greta, an anthropologist who had been all over the world and seen just about everything, nonetheless found herself teary-eyed. The old woman in Jeffrey's vision was her blind grandmother, long gone, the woman who had raised her and her sister after their parents died.

On another occasion, Jeffrey told his mother, "Our house is going to shake during the night." He advised her to take an expensive vase down from the top of the china cabinet. When she questioned him for more detail, he couldn't provide it. He said, "It has already happened in my head." Marti tucked him in, became distracted by other chores, and neglected to prepare the house for the quake of her son's vision. At 2:04 A.M., the eastern part of Washington State did indeed experience a 4.8 earthquake. Marti's china was disturbed but unharmed. The Japanese vase, however, an heirloom from her mother, fell onto the hard wood floor and broke into pieces.

In a small neighborhood the gifts of a gentle child who had been diagnosed with cancer at twenty-two months of age can hardly be hidden. And because Jeffrey radiated a kind of grace, a quietness, and a lack of desperation that was the envy of most adults, he quickly became news—first as a feature article in Spokane's newspaper, and then in a brief Family Life spot on *CNN Sunday Morning.* Marti and Landry had hoped to keep the extent of their son's paranormal abilities hidden, but he spilled the whole can of beans.

"You have three sons," Jeffrey told the CNN cameraman. "Two are older than me and the other one is my age." He said it as matter-of-factly as only a child can speak, and the cameraman stopped in his tracks.

"You're right," he said to Jeffrey, "how did you know?"

"I can see them," Jeffrey said. "You carry their picture in your wallet and I can see the picture in my head." The man's wallet was well concealed in his pants pocket.

"Can you see anything else?" the man asked.

Jeffrey shook his head. "Just the picture."

The episode with CNN only added to the neighborhood's sense that Jeffrey Romer was a special child. His cancer, spreading first from lymph nodes to lungs, then into the bone, became the community's cancer. When the Romers had to drive to Seattle for bone marrow transplants, their house became the charge of their neighbors, and when their stay in Seattle lasted two months, and Landry, a police officer, had to return to Spokane to resume work, the elderly Svobodas drove to Seattle to help Marti move into a studio apartment just near the Seattle hospital. When Jeffrey returned to Lucia Court, the neighbors were all there within hours, bringing food and news and comfort. Jeffrey would live a long time, they all promised one another. He would become very important one day, a great thinker or an amazing teacher of some kind.

It was as if the community willed him to keep on living. They adored this boy, so emaciated, eyes deep brown and incapable of despair, his long arms almost like transparent sticks. With Annie, herself crippled, who hobbled over from four houses down, he would say, "Are you dying?" He felt a special affinity for her affliction. "No—just losing my walking, like you," she would say with a smile, as she guided his weakened fingers to piece together a puzzle on the living room table. Sally, thirteen, from across the street, brought him candy, hoping it would somehow heal him. Sammy, twelve, who had no brother of his own, made Jeffrey his brother. So it was with all the other neighbors sitting beside Jeffrey, whose tiny hands stroked, on his lap, Toby, his calico cat.

Jeffrey had a special friend, Beth Carey. The day he met her, he called her Rachel, though she and Marti told him her name was Beth. "I know you, Rachel. You are the friend of the Teacher." The friend? The Teacher? Marti asked. But he smiled, and then slept, and when he awoke he called her Beth. Pondering the moment, Marti and Beth decided he meant she was Greta's friend—Greta had been a Unitarian minister—

hence "teacher." The "Rachel" was a mystery to them, though Beth did point out that her grandmother had been named Rachel. Jeffrey, of course, had never met Beth's deceased grandmother.

Marti asked for Beth's help with her son when she learned that Beth was not only a nurse, but also a woman who had been, like Jeffrey, a gifted child. Beth insisted her gifts were dry, yet Marti saw the smile of a hidden life in the large woman's eyes.

"Come over and meet the Romers," Greta had said one day to Beth. "Their son is so special." Beth, who lived across town, sometimes spent weekends with Greta, whom she regarded as her second mother. They had met at the Unitarian church years before, at a workshop put on by Matthew Fox and a Huichol medicine woman whose workshops in the United States Greta had helped organize. The two women had gradually become close friends, with Greta pushing Beth into spiritual excitements that she, quite often, resisted.

Beth deeply admired Greta, who, now in her seventies, had been an anthropologist before becoming a Unitarian minister. Beth had laughed the first time she heard the old woman call herself a "mutt," but she didn't like it when her boyfriend, Nathan, had joked in private, "and she looks like one." Greta was indeed an odd combination of bones, flesh, and history—part Slovenian, English, Scottish, German, and whatever else; she let her hair hang almost like a dog's long hairy ears, and with her long nose and seemingly unblinking dark brown eyes, yes, she looked a little like an old dog. A lover can provide questions, Beth often thought, but old women provide answers.

Beth had never felt she quite fit in. A salesman's daughter, brown-skinned from her father's Cherokee blood, blue-eyed from her mother's Norwegian side, she was overweight from age ten. Beth hid in books and disbelieved Catholic rigidities. She helped raise her two brothers when her mother died of lung cancer. Beth was proud of having lived a difficult, tenuous childhood—her father a drinker, her mother an emotional recluse—and never to have been broken. At twenty-nine, she was a large woman, at least seventy-five pounds overweight and short, five two, so that the weight showed more than it might otherwise. She did not fit social conventions for dressing well. When not at the hospital, she wore old jeans and white V-necked flannel shirts, and cared little for makeup. Beth was one of those people who do not get much love as children but somehow, as if raised by angels, bond naturally and wholly with the vulnerable around her. Jeffrey, she saw, was beloved by all, and she became his special friend. She baby-sat him often, reading *The Chronicles of Narnia* aloud and telling him stories, as she had done with her own younger siblings. She listened to Jeffrey and watched him and wondered if she would one day have a child like him. He shared with her his dreams and visions.

"I saw a tube of light, as long as the valley," he reported one evening, when Marti and Landry went out to a movie. "It was like God's long finger."

On another occasion he said, "I talk with spirits, you know. They're very nice."

Beth confessed, "When I was really young, about seven or eight, I saw my dead grandmother standing right beside me as if she were alive. I talked to her."

"I know." Jeffrey smiled, as a child will do when he does know.

Near Christmas, Jeffrey told Beth and his mother that there was a bad man by the river who only liked to talk to dead children. This man came to Jeffrey in nightmares that scared him far more than his own cancer. Everyone had heard about the two children who had disappeared, and the man who wrote letters to the newspaper claiming to have killed them. Landry had often spoken of this sad case at the dinner table—everyone at the precinct worried over it, but when Jeffrey's nightmares began, Landry promised not to talk anymore about these occurrences in front of his son. One night, when Beth was over for dinner, Jeffrey said, "Daddy and Beth and I are going to stop the bad man, you know." Already, Beth thought, the little boy is planning to become a hero. Her own brothers had been that way, from very young: plotting their future victories.

Beth once told her boyfriend that Jeffrey had taught her how to love children again. A part of her heart had been closed to children since finishing raising "the brats"—her father's name for her brothers. Beth told herself that she had become a pediatric nurse out of the habit of child care, but she knew that she wanted the chance to love children again. Over the years, her chosen profession had healed a part of her, but Jeffrey softened her heart more than anyone could.

If this were to be all he did for Beth, or for any of those in the neighborhood who loved him, they would have considered it enough. But it was not all, not by far.

Around four in the afternoon of July 5, 1992, a 1989 Toyota Camry turned off Driscoll Boulevard and headed west, toward the river, on Fairview Road. It picked up speed and began weaving left to right, right to left, like a race car in trouble, veering off Fairview onto Lower Riverview Drive, righting its course, then picking up speed again, turning, as if on impulse, onto Henderson Road, the ingress to Lucia Court. Harry Svoboda, in his backyard watering plants, remembered hearing tires squeal just east of him. He remembered hearing the harsh rev of an engine. He remembered hearing Greta cry out from her front yard, then the squeal of brakes, then impact.

Sally McDonald, thirteen, sitting at her desk in her second-story bedroom, heard the crash and froze, a book by Judy Blume open in front of her. She knew in that frozen second that someone was dead. She ran out of her room and saw her brother, seventeen, wearing a headset, listening to music—later she was to learn that he had on U2, and heard nothing outside the stream of the rhythmic noise. Her parents were not home. She ran out to see Sammy Range, from across the street, running out of his home.

Sammy, twelve, glanced at the sun for a second as he left his front door then, momentarily blinded by a golden orb in his vision, staggered more than ran toward the other adults at the carnage. Amid cries and calls, he stopped some feet away from the toppled car, mesmerized by what he saw.

Greta Sarbaugh had been weeding her planters on her front porch when the maroon Camry sped through their street. She turned and watched the car crash through the peace of the evening, weave, jump the curb, and smash into Jeffrey, who sat in his wheelchair up on the lawn, watching, Greta said later, "with wide-eyed fascination."

Alex Bass, sixteen, who was on the phone with his best friend, Brent, also sixteen, heard the crash and looked out his second-story window. Dropping the phone—"Jesus!"—he ran down the stairs and out the door and toward the wreck, recalling later that the right front tire of the uprooted Camry spun and spun like a roulette wheel. He stopped for a second near Sammy Range, who was trembling.

Annie Trudeau, twenty-eight, who lived with her brother at the house nearest the subdevelopment ingress, sat drinking an iced tea beside her 1986 Honda Civic. Her back problems had gotten so bad that it had taken her nearly all day today just to wash her car. Exhausted, but filled with the hope of a job attempted and completed, she watched the whole locomotion of the Camry as it sped into the neighborhood then jumped the curb. For a second, she thought it appeared as if it had targeted Jeffrey Romer long before it entered the court.

Inside Greta and Trudy Sarbaugh's house, Beth and Nathan, over for the weekend from his duties as a resident at First Memorial Hospital in Seattle, lay resting on the bed in the guest room. From Beth's home across town, they had called Greta earlier and asked if they could use her house as a base for a two-day camp-out down at the river. They had both woken up that morning around 3:00 A.M. with a jolt, each of them having dreamt about the river. Beth had dreamt of a small boat moving toward the Spokane Falls, a boat that toppled over then became a bird of some kind. Nathan had dreamt that he was a boy again, fishing with his parents by a river like the one behind Greta's house. Both Beth and Nathan lay awake talking, feeling called to the river, calling Greta.

Now the sound of the crash, Beth shouted and Nathan jumped up and ran out. Beth followed him, seeing Sally, Sammy Range, Annie from down the street, Harry and Laura Svoboda from next door, and Greta all converging on the wreck. Landry and Marti Romer had run out of their own house toward their son. Marti was screaming.

Nathan took charge. Beth and Greta ran to hold Marti, and Landry grabbed for his cellular phone. Beth did not know how many of the loving neighbors saw that Jeffrey could not be saved, but she knew from Nathan's grim face, and the feeling in her own stomach as she gasped with adrenaline and tears, that Jeffrey Romer would soon die—his head covered in blood, right arm and leg awry and broken, mouth dripping blood. Landry, just back from his shift, his shirt open and shoes off, yelled his address into the phone. Estimating that six or seven ribs had broken and sliced into Jeffrey's lungs, Nathan provided Landry with information for EMS, which Landry passed on breathlessly, his voice choked, face stiff and pale, his hand trembling. Marti wept beside her son's head, her body also trembling, the edges of her short brown hair already matting with moisture of tears and blood.

Beth dropped down next to Marti and helped her boyfriend gently right the broken left leg. Tears flowed from her eyes, but Beth focused as she knew she needed to for life to be nursed, even if only for a few more moments. Sammy and Sally stood back, both of them swaying with the terrible reality of a body broken nearly to pieces. Annie, signaling young Sally to help her, hobbled on her cane to the woman in the Camry, calling out that she was unconscious. Nathan yelled not to touch her as he rose and ran over. The cry of the fire engine cut through the air, station #61 only a mile upriver. Nathan saw that the woman had broken her neck, confirmed that she was dead, then rushed back to Jeffrey, whom Beth so often spoke of, and cared for like a mother.

In the far distance, if anyone could have seen it, they would have noticed Donnell Wight, eighty-one, from across the river, holding his binoculars on the scene, mesmerized. Above the river a hawk shrilled its song, flying above Jeffrey Romer, whose eyes were closed, his wheelchair thrown up against the house, his delicate body lying like a rag of flesh on the blood-red grass.

When Jeffrey tried to say something, the boy's dimming eyes moved to Beth and he murmured, "Don't be afraid. The Teacher is coming," and again, "Don't . . . afraid . . . Beth . . ." then his eyes closed and Beth, confused, weeping, looked at the others around her as if singled out.

"Oh, don't die," Marti cried, and Beth held the boy's mother in her big arms.

A golden light began from within the Camry, then moved just above it. It began just after the sound of the fire engine came from the west. It went unnoticed at first, until Jeffrey's murmur, and his own attempt to look toward the Camry.

"What is that?" Alex cried, pointing at the light rising above the spinning tire. It seemed to be a tube of light, rising from within the grass, pushing through the base of the car, up through the wheel, up through the woman so awkward in death, up through the car roof and up toward a point about twenty feet into the sky. Alex and Sammy bent heads upward to watch it (it was close to them, not twenty feet away), and Sally and Sammy and the elder Svobodas saw it hovering above the Camry. Wordlessly, Sammy pointed and everyone stared.

"What is it?" Laura Svoboda whispered, and Sally said, "It's an angel." The sound of the fire truck came closer, louder.

"Look! There!" Annie cried. Now the light appeared above Jeffrey and his mother and Greta and Beth and Nathan. It was a kind of three-dimensional tube of light as tall as a house. It reappeared now as a light reappears after a doorway reopens. This was the first thing Beth thought of, that a door had opened and closed and opened as the light burned bright, then flickered, then disappeared, then burned bright again. It was white-gold, like both moonlight and sun reflected off glass, so that nearly imperceptible lines of rainbow showed. It pulsed in its tall form, then seemed to reach gradually toward the river valley, forming a three-dimensional, rounded wall that spread from above Jeffrey toward the cottonwoods in the Svobodas' yard, then past them toward the tamarack and ponderosa pines and the river, then across the river to Donnell Wight's large red wood house.

It was not a flashing image—it was a wall of light as tall as a house and stretching at least a quarter mile, from a fallen boy to a house on a cliff. It brought a hypnotic calm to the scene of injury before it. No one said anything, except Nathan, who seemed to be talking to himself about what it could be. Everyone would later report feeling calmed, and hearing a sound like pure wind. Greta stood up from Jeffrey to reach toward the light and to touch it, but she held back her hand, wondering if it would disappear. Beth recalled having the presence to look around at everyone and see if they saw what she saw. Everyone was mesmerized. Everyone saw it. Only blind Trudy, standing alone across the street, did not see it with her eyes.

No one could tell exactly how long the light lasted, and none of them knew that there was a tall man in a hooded sweatshirt watching this scene from about fifty feet away, concealed at the edge of the river gorge, between a white pine and a tall cedar, mesmerized by the light and the violent death of the very boy he had come to see.

Nor did any of them know that Donnell Wight, across the

river, knew exactly the time of the occurrence, 4:47 P.M. Donnell saw it with binoculars that gave the distance of the focused object as well as the date and time. The wall of light reaching the high Wight house did not show through the binoculars, only the light as a distant rectangle across the river, above the dying boy. Donnell did not realize that the light reached across the river toward him. He only saw it emerge, saw the people mesmerized, then saw it disappear at 4:50 P.M., as the people came out of their trances and the fire truck roared down Henderson Lane. Had Donnell moved his binoculars to the left, he might have seen the hooded man in the trees.

When commotion of rescue and procedure and talk became loud, the man in the hooded sweatshirt stole away, his throat constricted with sadness, drifting back into the river gorge, in a way he would later describe in his journal. "I moved silent as Light itself."

The three firefighters, dressed in their yellow robelike coats, jumped from the truck, one moving to the Camry and two to the boy on the grass. Whatever strange serenity had existed for a moment—whatever complete sense within each person of their own mortality and weakness and strength—disappeared as the bustle of saving life began.

As Nathan and Landry briefed the firefighters, Beth stood back and away, noticing above the river a strange, hallucinatory flow of images. It was as if her mind was opening to a new modality, yet had not opened all the way. She felt a need to move toward the river, and yet frustration that her vision did not clarify. She saw children floating in the air. They appeared pale, like the dead. Greta came over to her, noting the immense concentration and focus on her young friend's face. She asked Beth what was happening.

"What was that?" was all Beth could say. "What was that?"

In very little time the miracle of light was washed away by the exigency of motion. Later, all present, young and old, would say that it seemed not as if the light disappeared, nor as if the door closed, but as if the light exploded into a million pieces, flying over toward the river, and fading into a filmy, imperceptible shroud. The noise of a saw in the Camry ground not only metal, but the ears of everyone nearby. The quick clang of gurney legs opening and the silty sound of bodies being lifted; the whimpers of adults in the face of a child's pain that return their large bodies to childhood itself; the indecency of blood and broken bones, irreparable, that call for silent words spoken by the pure needs of the hidden human soul; and the busy energy of crisis and terror and the sheer joy of not being the one smashed to pieces by fate—these coalesced to move time forward, and bring out the best in everyone present. Each helped in whatever way needed.

Not until later did the witnesses speak about the miracle of light.

The ambulances were gone, the fire engines too. The tow truck driver, a dark-haired young man drinking a closed cup of Starbucks coffee, worked to latch the Camry to the winch. Landry and Marti had gone with their son in the ambulance, refusing offers of companionship from Annie and Greta and the Svobodas. Across the street, watching the Camry lift from Greta's yard, the neighbors sat together, the sun beginning to fall to the west. The adolescent children were each still crying in their own way, Sally with tears, Sammy with his head downturned, and Alex with eyes glazed in anger and grief. Sally's mother and father had returned from work and joined Sally and her brother at Greta's. Alex's mother had also come home, standing in shock now with her son amidst the crowd, listening to what had happened and voicing silent prayers for Jeffrey Romer. Even amidst the talk there were, for moments, different tones of silence. Children and adults stood firm in the desire to become quiet, each in their own way, before the events of destruction and light were fully discussed. None knew of discussions going on in the mind of the watcher from the trees.

Trudy, nearly eighty, dressed in her nightgown, sat without embarrassment, as the blind often do, sipping iced tea in the middle of the small crowd. Both Harry and Laura were spotted with blood, yet had not gone next door into their home to change clothes. They drank mineral water, their hands, like all the hands, still trembling with adrenaline and the need of each other.

Annie, less than half their age at twenty-eight, sat back-straight on a foamy futon Greta often used for herself. Everyone knew that Annie would be in a wheelchair very soon, and probably forever forward. But now, with her blond hair pulled back from her aquiline face, she looked younger and stronger than usual, as if the adrenaline had flushed her not only with energy, but with a new brightness in her eyes and cheeks. She sat next to Trudy, staring with the blind woman at the Romer yard, the mangled wheelchair up against the house, the stains of blood on the grass, and the wrecker, who was hoisting the car with the slowness of a man and a machine that cannot work any faster than mechanism allows.

Beth and Nathan, like Greta, had gone inside to change clothes. Beth now wore her backup pair of blue jeans and a white T-shirt that outlined her large breasts. She helped Greta serve the lawn of guests who had gathered in sudden community. Never before, Beth suspected, had absolutely everyone on the block been together this way—everyone except the Romers, of course. Greta, with gray hair past her shoulder blades, a gray moustache and thin beard, carried a tray of ice-sweating glasses. Greta's hair stood out in the lowered sunlight, so that Harry Svoboda, a silver-haired man himself, thought, "We are old. It should have been us." He clasped Laura's fingers, a public act of affection rare for him.

Nathan, gray-blond, muscular, with close-cut hair, a one-day blond stubble-beard, a quarter-sized rose-red birthmark on his left cheek and neck, his face always frowning in a look of concentration, was dressed in his backup jeans and a blue button-down shirt. His yellow button-down shirt had been drenched with blood, blood under his finger nails too; he had gone into the bathroom to clean up, stooping at Greta's bathroom mirror, mounted low. Whenever Nathan accompanied Beth on trips to the house by the river, he felt too tall for it, like a giant whose head is always just above the clouds.

He had wanted to cry heavy tears in the bathroom, and now, here, in the middle of the lawn. His throat was still tight with emotion and adrenaline. One year from taking his boards in neurology, he recalled, his eyes closing now, how he had gone instinctively toward the head of little Jeffrey, sensing even before he saw proof that there would be no saving the boy. Nathan stood now, listening to Annie saying something to him about how good it was he had been here, then Greta, standing beside the Svobodas, pointed upward at the rising moon, a near full white orb. "Was it the moon or the sun we all saw?" she asked rhetorically. "Is there anyone who thinks the moon or sun is all that we saw?"

No one did.

"Will you please tell me what it was like," Trudy asked, "that light?" She had gathered snippets over the last minutes as children had explained it to parents, and adults to each other.

"It was huge—a whitish and yellow light," Annie recalled.

"It was like a long high wall," Beth said. "It stretched from Jeffrey to across the river, toward that house up there."

"Donnell Wight's house?" Trudy asked.

"Yes, Donnell's," Greta confirmed. Of all the people on this side of the river, Greta was the only one who had actually met Donnell Wight, a retired physician, world traveler, now more than eighty and dying, like Jeffrey, of cancer.

"I heard some kind of music coming from the light," Nathan added.

"Music?" Beth turned to him. "Or just a sound?"

"At least a sound, like wind, but maybe music in it."

"Maybe I heard it too." Laura Svoboda nodded. "I didn't think of it till you said it, but yes, maybe that's what I heard. It was like a beautiful tone."

Nathan agreed. "It was mainly one tone."

"There was a warmth to that long stretching light." Beth closed her eyes, seeing it, feeling it, again. Her arms reached out in front of her. "It was warm. Real. Alive."

"Alive?" Nathan asked. "What does that mean, when we talk about . . . light?" He shook his head. He didn't know what he was asking. "And Jeffrey spoke to you, Beth—he spoke right to *you*."

"I know." Embarrassed, she pushed her black-rimmed glasses up her moistened nose. "Poor Jeffrey," she said, biting back tears. Laura repeated the words aloud and tears came to her eyes.

As Beth saw the path of light again in her mind, she knew,

deep in a place that rarely spoke, a place beyond grief, that this light was not done here. It had not gone away. The miracle—for it had been a flash of miracle—was not dead. She felt it was just being born.

As if reading her mind, Greta said, "Whatever it is, the light is going to change us all. This was some kind of group religious experience. These things don't just explode then disappear. This is like the flashing sun in Yugoslavia, or the magical light in North Japan that the villagers see. This is like the light on the Aegean Coast of Turkey. This is something to take account of."

Alex Bass, standing with his mother, asked Greta, "What do you mean? Things like this happened in Yugoslavia?"

At sixteen, Alex was regarded by everyone in the neighborhood as one of those adolescent boys who can be trusted, not feared. He was a straight-A student, a quiet young man who often honored his elderly neighbors by asking them questions. He and Harry Svoboda had spent time in Harry's garage working on a 1957 Chrysler.

"In Mahjurredke in Yugoslavia," Greta told him, "100,000 people a year go as pilgrims to see the sun flash and pulsate as it does nowhere else. And people have visions there like they have nowhere else. Same near Kyoto, and near Bodrum in Turkey. In India there are a number of visionary places people go. Is what happened here like that?" she asked rhetorically. "It must be.

"Are we going to talk about this to others?" she asked.

Three or four voices at once said, "No," but there was no unanimity. Most of the neighborhood did not speak. Beth saw Sally's mother and father holding their daughter closely.

Nathan said, "We should do nothing about it until a day or two from now when we see if anything else . . . along the same lines should occur. How about that?"

Now more voices were heard, most in agreement. Mrs. Range, Sammy's mother, said, "Jeffrey was so kind. Maybe he'll live." She began to cry, a woman who had buried her own husband years before.

Nathan did not have the heart to speak the truth. In an hour he would call his colleagues at the hospital; he knew what their news would be.

Harry Svoboda came to Nathan and shook his hand, thanking him for his help. Nathan found himself in a number of conversations as people asked, without really asking, what would happen now with Jeffrey. Nathan found himself answering without really answering. He could see that everyone already knew that Jeffrey was gone.

Almost an hour later, the crowd began to disperse. Each person seemed lit a little to Beth, everyone walking in twos and threes together toward their own houses. When the two elderly sisters, Trudy and Greta, and their two young friends, Beth and Nathan, were left there in the yard, Beth and Greta cleaned up the glasses and Nathan moved the trays and the extra chairs. These tasks took them only a few minutes, then they were all four back on the porch again, talking a little, subdued, as they sat watching the moon rise, waiting to see if again the light would appear where Jeffrey had lain, or Jeffrey would reappear, as he was, smiling at the world from his wheelchair.

It was dusk when Nathan and Beth finished their packing, struggling through the inertia of emotional exhaustion to continue their trip down the slope behind Greta's house and to the river where they would set up a camp. They had agreed they would still go down to the river, though Greta and Trudy asked them to stay in the house.

"The open air will be better," Beth said, thanking her friends anyway. "I want to just cry by the river."

Nathan called his colleague at the hospital and Greta had called Landry on his cellular phone. Landry did not expect to return home till morning. Jeffrey had died. He would be immediately cremated. "Marti wants to go to her mother's for tonight," Landry said, holding back tears. "Will you watch the house, Greta? We'll be back in the morning." Of course, Greta agreed, crying as she gave her love. Landry asked if Marti could speak to Beth. Marti thanked Beth for being such a special friend to her son, then hung up, choking on tears. Beth and Greta wept, swollen with the helplessness that a dead child brings to the world. Nathan, sitting with them in the living room, remembered sitting at a place called Ann's Beach, on the Florida Keys near Islamorada, a few years before. He had been so filled with grief at the loss of a girlfriend that he sat as the tide lapped up nearly to his chest, pressing him and finally uprooting him so that he floated and had to return to the position of a standing human or be carried into the water.

After the phone calls, Beth, Nathan, and Greta walked across the street to the spot where Jeffrey had been. Looking at the bloodied area, Nathan asked whether he should hose the red-brown residue into the grass.

"No," Greta cautioned. "I think Landry will want to do it." Then she began to cry and Nathan and Beth held her.

"You should go get your camp set up," Greta told them, fighting her tears. "I'll go back to Trudy."

"You sure you'll be okay for tonight?" Beth asked her old friend.

"I will. You get going."

Beth and Nathan accompanied Greta back across the street then said their brief good-byes to the elderly sisters. Packs on their backs, they walked silently down to the river. They found the area they wanted for a camp at the river's edge—a tiny meadow with its back to the east gorge wall, surrounded by forest, beside the river's flow. The two experienced campers worked with efficiency, setting up the pup tent, starting a small fire, and preparing for the night. Beth let Nathan, so much more used to giving orders, organize the evening. When the setup work was completed, she sat with her journal in the firelight, trying to write out not only her heartache at the boy's destruction, but also the strange occurrence of the light.

Nathan, who had informed parents on more than one occasion that their child would die, felt different today than any time before. He sat alone at the river's edge recalling his own troubled parents—his father, who was generally depressed and withdrawn, and his brutal, enraged mother. Jeffrey, though he'd been physically sick for so long, had seemed to enjoy a loving childhood. Jeffrey would probably miss Marti and Landry. Nathan had never missed childhood at all and knew this was true of Beth as well. "Nathan and I are together," he once heard her explain to a friend, "because who else would understand us as well as we understand each other? Sometimes it feels like we went through the same childhood together."

Beth stopped writing in the fire's light and laid her head on Nathan's lap. Nathan thought, "What would Mom and Dad have thought of Beth?"

Suddenly, Beth's head bolted up. "Nathan!" she exclaimed. "I can see Jeffrey at the hospital."

She sat up very straight. "I see him with one of the doctors. I see him perfectly. How can I be seeing him?"

"You're seeing him right now?" Nathan asked. "Like some kind of remote viewing?"

"Yes! I see Landry, Marti, the doctor, a nurse, Jeffrey."

"Wait!" Beth put her hand up. "I see a man now. I don't see the hospital. I see a man. He's got a hood over his head. He's sitting at a table."

"Where?" Nathan asked.

"I don't know. Now he's gone. The hospital's gone."

"Gone?" Nathan repeated. "Is it like a flash or something?"

"It's just like a scene. I'm exactly right there. Then it's gone. It's like when I was a little girl. I saw things."

What had Nathan called it? Remote viewing? Beth thought the words described it: watching something else from a different—"remote"—location. But the words were so mechanical.

"I'm going to write this down. The exact scene. What if I could describe it to Landry and Marti later, when they're up to it? I could see if it's my imagination or it really happened."

"You should, yes," Nathan encouraged. Beth bent down again to her writing. The act of writing seemed very important now, as if Beth needed to record her internal experiences in order to make them real. She began to write words she had not completely realized as thoughts, words that must be coming in response to Jeffrey's dying. But why was suicide in them? She just wrote, until they were written down.

"There is nothing to fear about death. It is an ally to anyone who has made the life journey with an open mind. Among the million possible deaths, one of the finest is the death that we choose for ourselves. By this I do not mean suicide borne of despair; I mean the death chosen after a long breathing in of the Light itself.

"Often we hear, 'Is there a right time to die?' Of course there is: when one has been invited back home. The Light will invite you. The Doorway will open. You will look outward at the world and experience a sense of peace that only the opened Doorway and the Light can provide.

"If you have fulfilled your destiny in this lifetime, and have experienced the invitation, know that there is no moral boundary worthy of keeping you from the next step in your spiritual journey."

"Nathan!" she whispered, as the words finished in her. "Read this."

Nathan read, concentrating in the firelight.

As he raised his head she said, "I don't know why I thought those things, or who I'm writing them to. It's so weird! Jeffrey didn't commit suicide."

"Wow," Nathan said, rereading words that sounded a little like Beth, but somehow not altogether her. "He did die. The light is part of it somehow. This is interesting writing, Beth."

"It's like someone is speaking through me," Beth said. Suddenly, she saw a flash of image: a child carried by a hooded man toward a grave.

"Nathan! Jesus. I just saw a child. Not Jeffrey. A girl. Maybe nine or ten. Her head's limp. Her neck's broken. A man. That man. He's burying her. His face is covered in darkness. I'm having hallucinations, Nathan. What is going on?" Beth groaned, holding her head in her hands. Nathan sidled next to her in the dirt and reached his arms around her. She was trembling.

"That light we saw," Nathan said, puzzled. "It's affecting you somehow. You're having some kind of lasting neural impact?"

"Maybe Greta and the others, some of them are having these things too?"

Nathan had brought his on-call cellular phone with him, more out of habit than need. He hadn't planned on using it, but while holding Beth with one hand, he reached back for it behind him with the other. He dialed Greta, described Beth's hallucinations. "Has anyone else called you with similar experiences?" he asked. Beth could see Nathan's head shaking, "No."

"Okay," he said. He thanked her and apologized for the late call, then hung up. "I don't know what to think," he said. "Greta says she'll ask the others, and she'll keep in touch with everyone."

Beth was very tired. She saw tiredness in Nathan's eyes too. "Let me just write a little while longer," she said. "See if anything else happens." Nathan lay back as Beth returned to her journal. God how she loved that journal.

Nathan formed a picture in his mind of what might be happening in Beth's neocortex and limbic system. Her optic nerves had been stimulated by the light near Jeffrey. Its signal flooded through the occipital lobe, then spread through the limbic system into the hippocampus, the thalamus, then broke apart and flooded the right hemisphere, then shot into the left, creating both the disconnection and immersion of split brain and memory functions that hallucinations are. Yet in her brain might more be happening? What if these were not mere hallucinations? Was there a difference between how "visions" and hallucinations worked in the brain? There had been no class on this in med school. Nor had he learned anything about how a group could see the same light, that same optical stimulant.

Beth laid her head back down on Nathan's lap. She finished writing, no more visions or strange words coming to her—just a description of this long life-swollen day. As she closed her eyes on Nathan's lap, she listened to him describe the path of light her "visions-slash-hallucinations" must be taking in her brain. She had always enjoyed his descriptions of the neural mysteries. In her exhaustion tonight, they were like a bedtime story that took her toward sleep. She thought of Jeffrey. She willed his life force to find its comfort. She tried to see the hooded man, the little girl. She tried to do the "remote viewing" again. Nothing came except sounds—crickets, water flowing over rocks, a coyote far off, and then, the silence of the night.

Part I

These Deaths So Quick

1

The House of Light

DONNELL HAD NOT slept much that night. After watching the swift drama of the wreck he had wept quietly; wept for Jeffrey, for all the pain of life, and for his own eighty-one years. It was a catharsis of weeping, there on his back deck overlooking the river. It was the river of tears that had remained at a distance since he'd learned, almost a year ago, that he was terminal. And now the brutality of life emerged again with a little boy, dying of cancer, who dies from a car wreck instead. Donnell had not cried that hard since his wife died.

The sky was a bright blue this morning, a few stray high clouds off to the east. This was a blue like Donnell had seen so often in the turquoise water of the Indian Ocean, the blue just before it splashes toward white. Donnell's mind was clearer this morning, and he knew that Jeffrey's death was also his own. He was an old man dying of colon cancer who would die, like Jeffrey, before the cancer took him, today. Watching death's bloody bath, Donnell realized that during his nine months of very painful decay, the cancer eating him alive, he had forgotten the brutality of life—brutality he had known in two wars, and as a doctor, and as a man. He had observed his own decay so closely—his constant pain, his emaciation from lack of appetite, his bald, liver-splotched head, his hairless arms and legs, tiny as sticks, his trembling hands, his deliriums—that he had forgotten the real and quick randomness of life. Watching Jeffrey and the many people around the boy, then seeing that beautiful light, Donnell sensed suddenly that he had reawakened to life itself, like a dying soldier gets a last passionate vision before death.

Donnell Wight, now a widower for a decade, had been married fifty-two years. He and Mary Ann had two children, six grandchildren, and now three great-grandchildren. With his white hair and long white beard, living as he did on his huge house on the cliff above the river, isolating himself with no trespassing signs and few invitations, Donnell had long ago, even before his terminal illness, passed beyond communal murmurs about his character or state of mind. He had, in old age, become what he had yearned to be in his boyhood—a part of the land, not a tree but not a talisman either, a human portion of Earth, attentive and stewardly.

His father and mother had bought this land after World War I. Donnell wasn't even ten, but he had felt the land enter him like an invisible breath. For three decades he'd been away in college, medical school, then private practice in Napa Valley; but thirty years ago when his father died and his mother moved into a condominium care facility, Donnell had moved back with Mary Ann; received from his grown son, Sandy, invaluable help in building a new place; lived with Mary Ann here; and felt the land grasp him again.

Donnell had always known that he would die here. For the last few months he'd known that he would die on his own initiative. When a grandchild would say, "Popper, you should be in a hospital," he would think, "Yes, I should," and then he would remember the hospital world in which he had done so much of his work. He always held a special feeling for the hospital. He knew spirits there others did not. But still, it was not where he wished to die. He wanted to die in the world of foals, moths, osprey, bats, and herons, and in the margin of the small neighborhood of people across the river who had become, through his telescope, a second family.

Donnell recalled all the arrivals to Lucia Court a few years before. He had resented them at first. Though he lived far across river, the noise and the smell of diesel fuel from the bulldozers, were like an invasion. He recalled being thankful that Mary Ann, an even more private person than he, had already died. Yet, invasion aside, the development was after all quite far away, and he lived peacefully in bereaved loneliness. Gradually, he came to enjoy his vision of the subdevelopment from far up on the plateau in his huge home, which to the new interlopers must have seemed eternal. He had even come to feel a personal resonance with each of the families across the way, as if his own life, pieces of it long forgotten, was now being reviewed in the lives of young families. Sometimes he found himself talking to them aloud from his back deck, carrying on conversations with Jeffrey's parents about what to do for their sick boy; with Greta Sarbaugh, whom he had met once, an elderly woman who, like himself, had seen much of the world; with Harry Svoboda, nearly Donnell's contemporary, so inflexible in his posture; with the younger teenagers, Sammy and Sally, encouraging them to become friends in an old man's voice that perhaps the children heard like a whisper on the wind.

Over the last few months, Donnell had spoken to them all about his cancer. He told them about preparations he had made—his living will; a long letter to his nurse, a young man of thirty or so who had befriended him and his land; letters to each of his children; his memoirs. He told them he would take death into his own hands if need be, and probably soon. He told them he had been preparing his son, Sandy, to help him. Sandy, he knew, often walked in the door thinking this day was the day he would help his father die. Today, he would learn that it was.

"Dad," he had said a few weeks before, "you know I'll help, but I'll never feel completely right. I don't think a son can."

Donnell thought his son one of the most courageous men in the world, for Donnell himself could not imagine having to assist his own father die. Yet Sandy would help because he, like his father, believed in assisted suicide, and would always put love and truth above fear and guilt. Donnell told the young people across the river about his son and daughter and his own long life, his time in the second world war, the long marches in the snow. He told them about Mary Ann and what it had been like to watch her die. "And soon I, too, will rejoin the Universal," he had murmured across the river. He told them about his life with Mary Ann and the children, years ago, in New Delhi, and his more recent travels, as an old man, back to the teeming country of India.

"I have lived my life always hoping to justify my existence," he told his yogi, Muti Barunanda, a dark Punjabi half his age, at the ashram in Rajasthan on his last visit to India, at seventy-nine years old. "I have always worked to be acceptable to society and to God. Now I see that I no longer need to justify my existence on the Earth. I'm an old man, much closer to death than you. I have finished the fight that life is. I wonder what my purpose is now?" The yogi, an immensely gifted sensitive, and generous beyond the bounds of his youth, told the wealthy old American to watch out for a young American saint in India who would give him the answer to his questions before this life was done. "He is our little Krishna," the Yogi said. Soon Donnell went to the ashram near the seashore south of Madras and found Ben Brickman, thirty-two, his blond hair long and curly, his eyes a deep brown and eternal, a young man boyish in his enthusiasm for his elderly guest. "Yes, yes, I know you!" the saint cried. "You live in America in a house high up over a river. I see it very clearly. Let me describe it." He described it perfectly, down to the wood roof.

"My God!" Donnell thought. Even after all the years in India, all the squalor, all the people who were not saints, he was always shocked by the visionary gifts of some of these mystics.

"I see the day you will rejoin the Universal there," Brickman told him. "On that day, there will be a light that shivers through your world. I see a river dam far to your left. There is a wilderness all before you, a special place for animal life and animal spirits. I see a cemetery to your right. Your city has been surprised by the deaths of children, children of great promise. On the day you die will be another significant death, a boy, and the animals will speak; then there will be a significant spiritual birth, a woman. Your death, combined with the death of the boy and the woman's new visionary life, will be very special, my friend, more special that I understand. Good and evil will merge. Everything will be encased in death, and therefore awakened to hope. And a teacher will come."

"A teacher?"

"The woman of that day will know. Though yours will be a valley of pain and disease, she will become fearless. Many mysteries will become clear. This is what you live for now, sir. For that day. You will complete your life on that day."

"I will die?"

"I think so. Yes."

"When will this be? How many years from now?" Donnell asked.

"I don't know. But you will be very sick."

"How can you be sure?"

"I don't know."

The young guru smiled the eternal smile of the mystic, and became silent. Donnell stayed at the ashram another week, but "the young American saint" had no more visions for him, only questions about how things were going back home in the U.S.

Brickman's description, those years ago in India—of the river valley, the houses, Donnell's land, the little boy, who must be Jeffrey—so accurate. And Donnell had read in the news, as had everyone else in Spokane, about the killer who captured and killed several children over on the south side of town. Brickman had even seen those deaths, his eyes stretching through time. Donnell almost thought Brickman could be reading this morning's newspaper, in which the disappearance of a young child on the south side of town, transpiring a few weeks ago, was still a constant source of front-page news. For a few weeks, watching the terrible news unfold, Sandy talking about it, so many people worried, Donnell fantasized himself catching the killer—a fantasy perhaps everyone able-bodied might be having now.

Looking over the river valley as the sun heated his cold face and hands, Donnell was not sure what Ben had meant by the woman, but as Ben predicted, animal spirits had spoken to Donnell today—the great blue heron, the deer, the osprey, coming around to his house in the last few hours. Even the insects had come around in hordes—moths everywhere, butterflies, horseflies—coming around to say goodbye? At dawn, a beautiful doe and fawn had come to his back door. Though Donnell owned the hundred-acre wildlife refuge surrounding his house, no deer had come right to his door in fifteen years. And never a fawn. He tried to speak to the deer; he asked them what they needed. They stared, then walked off. With a sense of joy, he watched them go. A few hours later, a great blue heron startled into the air; instead of remaining away from the human, as it usually would do once in flight, it circled back and alighted on a branch twenty feet up and only a tree away. It looked directly into the human's eyes. Then, for ten minutes, the heron stared at the river without moving or, Donnell was sure, even blinking, as if clear in its vision, and heaven sent, sharing its life with an old man. And as Donnell ate a piece of soft bread on the deck just an hour ago, a flock of some fifty moths came to the deck's edge, fluttered there, flew off. Donnell found himself on his knees, in terrible pain, repeating a mantra to the Universal by which to focus himself toward his final hour.

In no time, Sandy would be here. Everything was in order. Donnell bowed and prayed and then sat back on the deck chair, near his telescope. He was in no hurry to be anywhere but here, in this place of refuge, afraid of the end of his life, and yet longing for it to unfold. He pushed his newspaper aside and continued writing the letter he'd begun to Sandy.

"Often we hear, 'Is there a right time to die?' Of course there is: when one has been invited back home. When the Universal is waiting. The Light will invite you. The Doorway will open. You will know this with either your senses or your intuition or both. You will look outward at the world and experience a sense of peace that only the opened Doorway and the Light can provide.

"If you have fulfilled your destiny in this lifetime, and have experienced the invitation, know that there is no moral boundary worthy of keeping you from the next step in your spiritual journey."

Donnell woke up with a painful jolt. He looked at his watch. It was 10:05. He'd taken a twenty-minute catnap. He pushed up, using the lounge chair and deck table as ballast to get him to the back door of his house. Entering the kitchen hallway, he used the walls to hold himself, padding in his socks, food-stained sweat pants, and gray V-neck T-shirt to the kitchen cabinet. Downing a Darvon on top of the morphine, he looked out the kitchen window for a moment, leaning there, then felt weak again, and moved to the wheelchair that sat by the back door. For a second, he felt the momentum of a body swan-diving off the cliff into the river.

As he leaned on the wheelchair, he was startled to hear knocking at the back deck door. No one ever came up the cliff-ridge to the back. Donnell was not expecting anyone until Sandy anyway. But there was someone. Donnell pushed the wheelchair into the hallway and saw a disheveled-looking man and woman, both in their late twenties or so. The young man had piercing eyes that twinkled in the light. His hair was blond-gray. He had a cherry-red birthmark along his neck and up under his hair, and a camper's early beard. He was dressed in jeans and a brown shirt. The young woman was short, large-breasted, overweight. Her brown hair was greasy and matted, her olive skin pockmarked. The man wore no glasses, but hers were thick, black-rimmed. Donnell recognized them. He'd seen them through the binoculars. They had ministered to Jeffrey last evening.

They smiled and peered in through the windows. Only the screen door was closed, so once they saw him pushing the chair, the man called out, "Hello, sir, we were walking down at the river and, well, we felt we had to come up here. It's very strange. You may kick us out. But we have a story to tell you."

Donnell got to the door and looked into the very serious eyes of young people who live for the mission of life. The woman chimed in, "It's hard to get up here. It was a heck of a climb." Indeed, the knees of their jeans, their hands, their cheeks, their forearms all looked silted in the red rock that comprised much of the cliff below Donnell's house. Donnell murmured—"human visitors too, from the river, along with all the rest?"

"Excuse me?" the young man asked politely, hearing but not hearing. Donnell pushed at the screen door as the young man opened it for him and helped him cross the threshold. The young woman, too, let him lean on her corpulent body as they moved to the back table and chairs.

"I'm afraid I'm rather occupied right now," he said a little breathlessly, unused to strange company. "But let's sit a minute and you can tell me why you would risk that perilous climb." In thirty years very few people had climbed up the tiny trail along the cliff mainly because one section of it—about thirty feet—was nearly straight up.

"I'm Beth," the woman said, going for his blanket on the wheelchair and offering it to his lap.

"I'm Nathan," the man said. Once the old man was stationed, they sat too.

"Donnell Wight. I own this place. Generally I don't like trespassers. You must have seen the signs." He had enjoyed sounding grumpy for about ten years now, but knew his face showed welcome.

"We saw your signs," Nathan continued evenly, "But . . . have you noticed there's been a kind of light pulsating near your house?"

"Has there?" Donnell asked, his heart beating like a drum. Then he had not been the only one to notice it. Just as he was about to say that, he realized they did not mean just the light last evening; they meant this morning as well. "You've seen a light recently? Up here?"

"Yes. Even just minutes ago." Beth spread her arms. "We thought it was some illusion from the sunlight, but even as we moved closer it was there. Like it was on every animal and every tree. It didn't matter where we stood. But just now, as we started up the cliffside and came over the rim, the light was gone. So I don't get it." She looked at Nathan. "We don't get it. And yesterday . . . I don't know if you heard about the boy killed yesterday?"

"Jeffrey Romer?"

"Yes." She and Nathan had decided they could mention the miracle at Jeffrey's accident to this Donnell Wight, even despite Greta's admonitions. His house, after all, was somehow part of it.

Beth explained, "Well, there was a kind of light . . . a light that rose and spread over toward your house, then kind of shattered away. Then it was up here again today. It was so strong for all the time we were walking here, like for the last hour. Then when we got to the bottom of the ridge, it disappeared."

It was this woman, not the man, who seemed an open-hearted soul to Donnell. She seemed radiant—like when he had first met his guru and felt a mysterious radiance. It was she whom he found himself looking at, feeling comfortable with. The man, Nathan, seemed a little remote, as if in a faraway world, but Beth leaned in when she talked, and even touched his hand. He found himself thinking he had known her a long time.

"A light," he mused aloud, as they fell silent, waiting for him. "A light." He wanted to close his eyes, to enjoy this warm woman's presence. The couple stared at him.

Donnell shook himself. "Do you want something to drink? You must be thirsty." They confessed they were. Nathan rose, insisting that he would go inside and get something. Donnell told Nathan where the bottle of cranberry juice would be, and the glasses.

While Nathan went inside, Beth told him how she and Nathan were camping out by the river, and how the morning felt—filled with new experiences but sad too, confusing. She said she was finding herself embarrassingly "opened wide" today and last night, and hoped he wouldn't think her strange.

"No, I don't," he said, smiling.

"I feel like I'm awakening, or being born."

Donnell thought for a moment that he'd stopped breathing. "Who are you?" he asked silently, looking into the young woman's eyes. This must be the woman the young American guru in India had spoken of.

She told him about strange little things that had been happening—visions, premonitions, insights.

Donnell yearned to tell her about Ben Brickman's prophetic words. Would she believe him? She probably would.

Nathan returned with the juice, Beth saying, "We're not on drugs, really. We have to follow that light, like we followed it up here to your house. Something's happening. We don't understand, but we know it's real somehow. Real like I've never seen things be real."

Donnell thanked Nathan for the juice, and raised it to his lips. For a moment there was nature's silence between them, then Donnell decided to open a little to this woman. It must be part of what he was meant to do.

"I too have been affected. I have felt Reality, as it is." He told the young people about the heron's visit, the moths, the deer. He did not mention that he had seen the light last evening through his binoculars, nor had seen them. He wanted to keep at least some dignity; not confess to being a kind of voyeur over Lucia Court. Thankfully, neither of the young people had said anything about the telescope and binoculars sitting just fifteen feet away. Instead, Donnell saw on their faces looks of relief, perhaps, that he shared their experience, and also, on Beth's, some other look—as if her face were not wholly her own, but servant of some other image. A shiver went through Donnell, a voice speaking at his ear, and a breath chilling down his neck.

"Something happened two years ago," Donnell said, kneading his painful left abdomen with his hand. He explained about the American guru, falling short of saying, "He told me I would meet you, talk to you, then be free." To speak the last part was too much revelation to these strangers who were not strangers, and yet they were. Nathan and Beth waited for more.

"The light you saw," Donnell continued. "Mystics would probably call it an electromagnetic phenomenon, one that needs certain kinds of optical faculties in certain people at certain times if it is to be seen. What has allowed you and others to see it last evening? You may never know."

"It's like the light is always around us," Beth said. "Near us, within us, but we just can't always see it. Only at certain times."

"This field surrounds us," Donnell agreed. "At least, that's what the Hindus say. We're immersed in it. At various times in human history, the Field in which we all live, a field we have come to call 'God,' becomes manifest to human sensory reality, usually as light. In Yugoslavia, pilgrims go by the thousands to see the eerily pulsing sun."

"You're talking about at Mahjudderke, right?" Nathan confirmed. "We were thinking about it last night."

"Yes. I have not been there, but I have talked to others who have seen the light there, like a color of cream, undulating against the eye. In Mecca, late in the seventeenth century, this same kind of phenomenon was reported over a three-day period. In ancient Greece, the light from the mountain known as Olympus pulsed so heavily that the Hellenic people saw gods there. What they were seeing was the electromagnetic field made visible for some reason, unknown. Moses saw the Light Field in the burning bush.

"Just a few years ago, a light coursed through a small town in northern Japan so completely that residents were unable to account for five minutes of a Saturday."

"Yes." Nathan nodded.

"The saints in India have been saying for centuries that people are evolving with each generation—more and more people—who can see this Light. Humans are just now evolving into populations that can actually *see* things like this, actually *experience* them, as ordinary people, over and over. One of my gurus in India taught me that 'a new human' is emerging in the new millennium. One of these millennial mystics taught me that we are evolving as a race from *Homo sapiens* to an unlimited human he calls *Homo infiniens*. He told me to live until I shared that knowledge. Have you been to India before?" he asked Beth.

The big head and camp-dirty black hair and black horn-rimmed glasses moved side to side, gesturing "no."

"You've made me happy by pushing your way up here. Because of you and your eyes, I see not only the animals that came, but that there is a light all around me right now. Thank you for that."

"There is definitely light around you," Beth assured him. Donnell found himself silenced by emotion, his eyes tearing up and his chin creasing. Beth's eyes became teary with empathy.

"Freedom and free will," Donnell coughed, "these are to be beloved no matter the form they take, especially in circumstances such as mine. Nathan, I think you are a doctor of some kind, is that right?"

The young man nodded. "Resident. Neurology."

"I was a urologist. Let me ask you: Would you want to

die in a hospital? You have gathered by now that I am terminal."

"Yes," Nathan admitted. "I'm sorry." He thought a moment and said, "Not if I could avoid it."

"And you won't die in a hospital, will you, Mr. Wight?" Beth said.

"Who is to say?" Donnell temporized, again avoiding her eyes. But Beth put her hand out across the patio table. She clasped his small hand, her hand warm with life. She was speaking into his eyes, clasping him with such sudden affection that he felt flushed. She filled him with something passionate and loving. It was almost as if he saw through her translucent spirit to the interior world where Mary Ann was. Mary Ann was on her face, in her eyes, on her flesh, like a shroud. Donnell held her hand and drank her gaze deeply. He experienced a rare clarity. He felt as if the young woman were healing him somehow—not his flesh, but the soul behind the mask.

Then, suddenly, it was too much. He pulled out of Beth's hand. "My son is coming soon, and I must ask you to go," he said to Nathan, avoiding Beth's eyes but knowing she would go too, and missing her already.

"I think I have seen the new human. I'm sure you both will participate in stripping away some of the veils of consciousness."

As Donnell began to stand, the young people pushed up immediately. Nathan asked if he could help. No, no, Donnell assured him. It was time for them to go.

Beth's eyes were moist. "May we hug?" she asked Donnell.

They hugged tightly, and he felt her beautiful soul's warmth on his skin. Again, unbidden, Donnell felt Mary Ann's presence. She was suddenly here, close, perched on

Beth, effacing all else that was real. Had she had come for her beloved? Could this be? Was this the morphine? What was this—it was like a jolt of energy from Beth, like a shock. He did not want to let go of her.

"Are you sure we should go?" she asked, holding him hands to shoulders now, peering into him.

He said nothing for a moment, wondering if Mary Ann would go too. But he knew she would not. She had come to take him.

"Who are you, really?" he wanted to ask Beth, yet he wanted to be free of strangers.

He said, "Good luck to you both." Nathan gave him a crisp hug, and then a look touched with longing. Donnell saw Nathan as himself years ago. "You, like me, will have to search long and hard to regain your innocence," he thought silently into the young man's eyes.

"Please take care of yourself," Beth said. "Will you?"

"I will." Donnell smiled. "Go now. You must both enjoy the light while you can. And you, Beth, don't be afraid. You are like my Mary Ann. She shouldn't ever have been afraid. Neither should you."

"Thank you," she sighed, a tear dropping off her left eyelid. "You're the second person in twenty-four hours to tell me that, Mr. Wight, thank you."

Donnell breathed deeply as he watched the young people walk toward the cliff's edge and the small, barely passable trail. Beth turned, as if to speak or come back, but she kept on. Soon the two heads disappeared over the ridge and Donnell turned back, looking upward, at the tops of pine trees. Only sunlight shown on them now. He saw a blue jay, a sparrow, then a squirrel.

Donnell found himself trembling, and found his wheelchair. A sudden, immense fear of the reality of death swooped over him, like a dark shadow. He tried to divert it. It was almost as if they had never come, the muscular man and the big woman. But Mary Ann was definitely here. That feeling, so strange, distracted him from the trembling shadow of what he was now going to do. But then he trembled again, as if he were sitting beside a train track and a train rushed by. Donnell felt himself resisting the vibrations, then gave over to them. He opened his eyes and heart to the shadow, the great and terrible fear of losing even his broken, battered, diseased body. Donnell Wight swooned with the darkness and the vibrations of the locomotive death and looked for a light of some kind in the center. He did not see any light of a spiritual kind, now at this moment; but he felt something, something very warm, like the warm wake after the locomotive passes. "I'm afraid to die," he mumbled. "I'm afraid to die." He found his eyes tearing up, his body, though unmoving in its chair, nonetheless falling toward a deep hole. "But Mary Ann . . . you're here now." As he peered into the hole, he thought he saw Jeffrey now, that little boy, with Mary Ann, both bathed in light, reaching upward toward him. A swamp of tiredness overran him, and he drifted into the hidden world again, murmuring to his wife, who had, it seemed, never really left him.

Donnell was already in bed when Sandy arrived—jolly, red-haired Sandy, a balding, smiling son of fifty-two, coming as he did nearly every day—to find that his father had decided that today it was time to die. Donnell told him about the visitors, and that Mother was here.

For months, his emaciated father had talked about the end

of life, absorbing Sandy in debates on the morality of suicide for the terminally ill. Sandy, an ear-nose-and-throat surgeon, took the con position, but knew that in his father's shoes he would not have chosen even to live this long. Then today his father talked about does, fawns, moths—and after quixotic explanations, including his mother's presence, he said he would end his life today, using two thousand milligrams of Darvon, which he took in his son's presence now. He asked that his son give the gift of his assistance. Donnell confessed to being afraid, but confessed also to hope in the form of a large woman who had visited, and been predicted in India. Sandy had heard so many things from his father since the morphine began that he did not try anymore to sort them out. And he had been girding for this day since the previous Christmas, seven months before, when he realized his father would ultimately ask for his help in opening death's door.

"Dad, you could have called me at least, prepared me," Sandy said. "I have a cellular phone. You know the number." Sandy had decided months ago that when the moment came, he would assist his father, for the pain his father succumbed to, all day and night, was like a terrible disease all its own—but now that the moment was here, Sandy was scared and sad and angry.

Yet the course had been set. Sandy knew this clearly. "I love you, Dad," Sandy said, hugging him. "I'll keep good memories alive. I'll take good care of your home. You'll never be far from our hearts. You're very brave."

I think I do know that, Donnell thought. Are you still here, Mary Ann? "I could not have a better son," Donnell said plainly to his oldest child. Sandy knew he meant it, and for this reason did not respond.

Donnell lay propped up on the bed, Sandy beside him now, facing him. Donnell reached for his son's left cheek—he ran his finger along the old chainsaw wound that cut Sandy's face even now, the initial cut filled with that hard, wounded scar tissue that give spirits a place on which to perch.

"I remember the day it happened," Donnell said, remembering the roof work fifteen years ago, the buzz saw Sandy held, its blade hitting a wood-knot, then bounding into Sandy's flesh and cutting with a dull skin-tight roar down to his son's jawbone.

"You know, son"—Donnell closed his eyes—"you can't change the past. The cat gets its tail wet. It just happens."

What do we talk about now? Sandy wondered. He said nothing, maintaining a silence in which voices spoke that were more important than his. Should he also have given his father two Seconal, he wondered, which would have put him to sleep before termination from Darvon actually came. No, he would want to be awake to the last moment.

"I don't want our lives to run out of words," he said to his father, holding the bony hand. He busied himself checking his father's pulse.

"I know," Donnell murmured. "Your mother always admonished me for not *saying* how much I loved you kids. I love you, son. I love you all."

"I know. Jennifer . . . we all know. Have a safe journey, Dad," Sandy whispered, trying to hold on to his own confusing feelings. "You always were way ahead of all the rest of us." Donnell recalled a time when Sandy thought he was the worst father—but that had passed long ago.

"A bunch of wildlife came to see me," Donnell whispered, forgetting he had said this already. "We're not alone," he whispered. "The movies make spirits out to be scary, angry ghosts. No. They aren't usually scary." Then Donnell thought he saw Jeffrey where his son was sitting. Jeffrey was bathed in light, saying something. And there was Mary Ann.

"That Coeur d'Alene Indian who used to come up here, forty years ago. Sandy, do you remember?"

Sandy remembered someone vaguely. "Sure, Dad."

"His people used to live up here. Had 'home spirits' here. Dead people he needed to talk to. I understand now."

"Yes." Donnell's eyes were shut and his pale face seemed to his son to have lost its life already. Old, more fragile than a baby, he broke his son's heart.

"Okay, Dad," Sandy said, his voice cracking. "I'm with you, Dad." He thought his father was going now, but Donnell seemed to be sleeping, not dying. Then he woke again, looking into Sandy's eyes without saying anything.

"Dad?"

"A clean break. My clean break." His voice trailed off into imperceptible words.

For a few seconds, his father's breath stopped.

"This is it," Sandy thought. He checked the pulse again, touched along the skin of the arm, and he melted into tears, holding his father's hand.

Donnell Wight did not speak again. He died in his own bed, in his own home, surrounded by the light of the river valley, and all the invisible encounters held there. His son could not see all the worlds of light right then, as they are seen by the dying; he simply experienced Donnell breathing, stertorous, his hand bony and limp, getting colder. The heat that comes with light was diminishing in the body, like rain drying. The son saw significance in the father's life, and powerlessness too.

So suddenly it had all happened, and yet it was right—it was okay. His father, shaped for many months by the indignities of dying, had found dignity again. Had Sandy known it, he would have thanked Jeffrey, Beth, his mother, and all the spirits who were at play today in his father's life; but Sandy Wight just held the old man's hand.

2

Beth Carey

THE LIGHT HAD formed above the red cedar house just after dawn. It seemed a kind of umbrella of light up there, white-gold and spreading out at least forty square feet. The sky above and around it spread cloudless and blue, the glow of light near the house on the plateau like a huge stand against the blue, or a shadow across a stretch of ocean. Beth was first to see it. She had awakened before dawn, moments before Nathan. Both were stiff from hard ground and the adrenaline drop and the sadness following Jeffrey's death. Beth's night especially had been filled with dreams and flashes of images, many of them nightmarish.

"It is so beautiful." Beth pointed at the glow up on the cliff. At first, both she and Nathan had looked silently. Then Nathan said it must be some kind of electric field shocking their neurons. He felt a twinge of longing for PET scan equipment, an MRI, and everything else from the medical lab. "We won't be able to keep this light a secret," he told Beth. "Some other people have got to be seeing this."

She nodded, taking her black horn-rimmed glasses off, then putting them on again, testing whether the vision was just some sort of occlusion.

A hawk cried out, flying up toward the light; if no other humans saw the few minutes of glow there, certainly the wildlife did. A blur, like a horde of flies or bees, ascended from the river valley toward the high plateau and the house there.

"We've got to get up there," Beth said. Nathan knew she was right.

Now, after meeting the old, dying man in that house of light, Beth thought he was one of those old people who look you in the eye and wish you were container enough to hold everything they know. She saw with certainty that he had planned his death, and she shuddered as she remembered the sentences coming to her last night about suicide, as if this were a kind of premonition regarding Donnell Wight.

She also thought, now, as she walked away from his home, that he himself had seemed surprised by something revolving around *her.*

"You mustn't kill yourself," her human mind wanted to cry, but she had said nothing. Could she be sure of what she was seeing? Should she invade his privacy? She and Nathan had joined Washington State's failed fight for the assisted suicide bill. Was not Donnell's right to die the very cause she believed in? Her human mind groaned to save his life, but felt true in letting him be.

He had to have been scared of dying, but he didn't appear overwhelmingly so. She had told Nathan as they walked away from his house that his skin seemed watery to her. His long delicate fingers seemed like little rivers and his skin like a glassy lake at dawn.

As she and Nathan finally got back down the steep hill and cliff, and as they both lifted their little day packs again onto their backs, Beth looked back upward. The light was long gone, but now she received another of the flash visions she had been having since that light appeared at Jeffrey's accident. She saw Mr. Wight lying in his bed with another man nearby. The man was younger, maybe in his fifties, with a family resemblance in his nose and chin. His hair was red. This must be the son, Sandy, whom Mr. Wight had mentioned. She saw Donnell holding his son's hand as he died. The vision was as clear as the tree in front of her. She must be seeing the immediate future. "My God," she murmured to herself. These flashes just keep happening, visions that had appeared earlier in her life, these psychic experiences, but never like this.

People often wanted to tell Beth Carey that she was a big woman. And she knew she was. "You're big as the Earth," one therapist in Vancouver told her when she was just out of nursing school. "You *are* the Earth," the therapist said, complimenting Beth in a New Age way. A year later at a Body, Mind, Spirit Expo Beth paid twenty-five dollars to see a psychic. Though Beth came from a family of "witches," she had never paid to go to a psychic before. In fact, she had left all that behind for hospitals and doctors and the daily politics of healing.

"I know you," the expo psychic said, quite a large woman herself. "You're the round woman surrounded by light. You're a cosmic star." The planetary metaphors, coming two years in a row, were too much for Beth. She got up to leave. The psychic held out a puffy hand. It looked to Beth like a baby's hand. Staring at it, shaking it, she heard the woman's gravelly voice say, "You are afraid of who you truly are. Don't go forward into spiritual pursuit until you have experienced the revelation that there is nothing to fear."

That was five years ago. Now Beth walked at the edges of the Spokane River with Nathan, and the two were feeling something so strange, so frightening, so beautiful. Beth felt like when she was a child and read *The Chronicles of Narnia.* Aslan, the holy lion, by his very presence, made people feel both afraid and at peace. Beth felt the way she had felt when she had, for about a year, become a born-again Christian in her early twenties. Everything made utter sense. Yet there was a difference between that experience and this one; this wasn't like an ecstacy someone could take away, but like a maturity few others would ever be able to grasp.

They walked down the trail toward the suspension bridge that crossed the river. Nathan was talking. "What happened when Jeffrey got hit? The light—it's some sort of field. It must be. Is there a local, geographical source? A special longitude/latitude intersection? Is there some kind of power surge from an electrical plant nearby? I mean, yes, it's spiritual, okay, but what's the physics of it right here, right now? And we have to wonder—why us? Why did our little group see it?"

Beth had no answers to these questions but told Nathan she had just had another one of those flashes. "His son, older than us—I saw him with Donnell. He has red hair."

A short man, shirtless, in black shorts, with a round, hairy stomach, came up the trail, stopping Beth's thoughts. He held a towel, a man on a summer day moving toward the river to swim or sunbathe. Nodding a hello, he dropped his eyes. Beth knew she and Nathan must look strange—disheveled from spending the night under the stars—overdressed in jeans and shirts in the hot sun.

She stopped, turned. "Sir, have you been seeing anything strange out here, weird lights or anything?"

The man halted and scrutinized her. "I haven't. No," he said simply. "Is something going on?"

"I guess not."

The man turned back and away.

"Thank you," Beth said, walking with Nathan onto the suspension bridge, which the man had just crossed.

The rushing water beneath them gave off a loud roar. The wooden bridge still shuddered, as wooden suspension bridges will do, vibrating beyond the presence of seeming cause and effect. Beth leaned against the rail, staring into the flowing water beneath her. She saw something, just under the river's rushing surface. Jesus! What was that?

"Nathan!" she cried. "Look."

It was a girl dressed in sweatpants and a sweatshirt.

"What? Where?" Nathan saw nothing except water.

She pointed downward so Nathan would look harder, but now it wasn't there. "It was like the same girl I saw in a vision last night," she said. But this wasn't the same girl—just a girl in a similar, terrible situation. And this imaging seemed different—a different inner texture than the flashes of vision she felt sure were real clairvoyance, like the sight of Donnell Wight's son at his side, or the remote viewing of Jeffrey in the ambulance. This wasn't like those. It was quicker, more transparent. This had to be imagination. She looked hard at the water. She saw only small curls of waves.

"I guess I didn't see anything," Beth said. She started walking, hers and then Nathan's soft tennis shoes squeaking on the smooth wood.

She felt frustrated. She interrupted Nathan, who had opened his mouth to query something. "Do you think we have a responsibility to save Donnell Wight?"

Nathan closed his mouth, pondered, then said, "What does he have to live for? We believe it is his right to die. But it's hard," he admitted. "Hopefully he'll live a little while longer."

Nathan clearly had not fully understood. Beth put her arm on his and told him she knew Donnell Wight would die very soon, and with his son's help.

"Jesus, Beth! You saw all that? You didn't tell me *that.*"

"I know. Do you believe that I saw it, that I know it? Could it really be? Is it imagination?" How could her experience make sense, even to Nathan, who knew her so well, and believed in her?

Nathan stopped walking, looked into her eyes. She stared at his rose-red birthmark, stretched and mottled on his neck and cheek.

"I believe you saw it," he said, nodding. "You're being affected today."

"Should we call an ambulance or the police?" Beth asked. "He's going to end his life. But if not for my clairvoyance we wouldn't know that. We don't even know that my clairvoyance is true. So what are our responsibilities?"

"Jesus," Nathan sighed. "Everything's changed, the whole human intercourse could be changed by what you're seeing, experiencing. And yet we don't know if it's real."

Nathan leaned against a tamarack, looking upward into the mesh of tree branches, toward the blue sky. A piece of bark lodged into his gray-blond hair. "I don't know what to do," he said. "I don't know. If we assume you're right about his auto-euthanization, we have to say he has a right to his death. He's not going to make it past another few weeks, maybe a month or two. He'd be a hospice patient soon. He can't stay in that house."

Nathan closed his eyes. Beth stood with him in silence, listening to the river. She watched as his eyes moved like tiny animals under his closed eyelids.

"And we don't really know anything about his intentions," Nathan reminded her, though she could see he didn't believe this.

Beth felt like a child in the face of an adult dilemma. She turned off her intellect and just let images come. She saw Donnell on his deathbed, lying happily, his watery face becoming air, then his airy face becoming ether. She saw spirits circling to welcome him into whatever is the invisible world. She did not know if this was imagination, but she saw herself nowhere in this drama. She did not see her rights or Nathan's rights or the purported rights of a death-frightened humanity. She felt her whole human society pushing her to do something to keep the man alive in the human community, but she didn't see herself involved with Donnell Wight in that way. She felt far away from human society, and an electrical current of recognition moved through her. She had always felt slightly wrong in the world, as if she lived in another time, or with too much difference of mind to ever belong—and yet she had been a cooperator, a conformer, since infancy. If she did nothing at all to keep Donnell alive, she was making a statement of opposition.

"It's his choice," Nathan said crisply, pushing hair back

from his forehead, opening his eyes. "The cancer is in the bone marrow. All he has is pain and death."

"But maybe we should just talk to him again." Beth said it as habit, and yet began walking forward, not back toward Donnell's cliffs. Nathan followed her, then as the path expanded they joined hands, moving on the earth, the trees whispering around them and the wind conducting the whispers. The underside of a cottonwood's leaves went white from an updraft of breeze, like a dress lifting.

Suddenly Beth recalled her grandmother, Rachel. Flashing images flooded her mind, forcing her to stop again on the path. "Jesus," she cried. "Flashes come. They're like electrical current shocking me."

"Tell me," Nathan said firmly, guiding her by arm and elbow to lean against a white fir tree. The trunk felt warm to Beth. As her spine touched it she saw a flash of an image from Native American times, a village of some kind, and a girl in a tree above water. The flash was replaced again by her grandmother: a prescient woman who had dreamt the death of Grandpa three days before it happened, a woman who used the ouija board to help her make decisions throughout her life. Beth remembered Gram, and then her own mother, showing her the Tarot cards and teaching her dream analysis and calling her to watch the movements on the ouija board and doing her astrological charts. Beth remembered how at first, the mysteries made her tremulous, but soon the company of women itself gave her safety, and the mysteries seemed normal.

Beth remembered being ten years old. She remembered a ghost in their house, and watching her mother nearly die as she tried to help the ghost find a calm passage into the next world. Gram was dead by then, and an old neighbor brought an Indian shaman to help with the ceremony of passage. Beth and her family had to hide the "strangeness" from their friends, but she sensed even then that the world was vast and unlimited and not to be confused with the restrained world of societies as they were thus far laid out for a young woman.

They returned to their camp and looked back up at Donnell Wight's house, both of them cupping their hands over their eyes against the sun, as if they were saluting. From this distance, Beth couldn't see much of Donnell's house except outlines of window and wood. As she dropped her backpack beside Nathan's camp pack, Beth saw some kind of motion in her peripheral vision—two dots of light about twenty feet away. What was that?

"Look at the lights, Nathan; do you see them?" Beth saw two living dots of light moving in a circular motion. They were the same white-gold color as the light yesterday near Jeffrey and this morning on the plateau.

"I see it," Nathan whispered, as if the lights would be bothered by noise. "Remember how the light last night seemed to shatter, like into tiny pieces? This might be it—pieces of the light."

Beth took his hand and squeezed it. She didn't know what to do.

"There are more lights coming," Nathan whispered, and Beth saw them, so glad Nathan saw these too. She had a witness. This wasn't just a trick of sun in the leaves and trees. It couldn't be.

New lights emitted as if from the line between a huge boulder and the earth. Thirty or forty of them seemed to shimmer up, coalesce, separate, commingle again. More and more of them rose. They hovered and the humans waited. Then the thin line between boulder and earth, like a line of light between door and floor, started closing up again. All the lights sucked inward there into the earth and were gone.

"Jesus Christ," Nathan hissed. "What the hell was that? It was like a proton-electron flash of some sort, then gravity suddenly grabbed it."

"I don't know," Beth said. As Beth spoke, her gram's name, Rachel, formed in her mind, and she felt an impulse to move, and her mind filled with the Native scene.

Beth waved her hands in front of her, as if against the vision, to erase it.

"I just saw something. A village. Can you see it?"

"Nothing."

She pressed her eyes closed, seeing better. "There's a village here, a village of Native Americans. White people coming in—two men, one a priest and one a soldier. There's a girl, about ten years old, looking down from up a tree—a tamarack—beside the river. I smell the tamarack. She's looking down. I'm looking through *her* eyes. This is like a dream. They were right here a century ago or more, is that it? I think so. But the girl looks like the girl I saw in sweatpants, in the river. Nathan, listen."

She tried to explain. A man was carrying a girl's lifeless body, a girl dressed in blue sweatpants and sweatshirt; the same girl in the river, who looked exactly like this girl, now, from the village.

"This is bizarre," Nathan said, not helpful, except that he grinned his uselessness, making her laugh. "How else may I help you, Beth?" He grinned. She laughed and hugged him.

"We *must* write this stuff down." Beth squeezed his hand. "We're going through something. We have to write down what

Mr. Wight said. The lights. The girl. Our impressions. These visions. We *must* have a record. We're in trouble if we don't have a record. No one will believe us."

"*Will* anyone believe us?" Nathan asked.

She pulled her journal, maroon with a gold-laced binding, out of her own pack. Nathan had given it to her for her last birthday.

Nathan frowned. "These visions you're having. They're incredible. I saw those lights, the light, but not like what's happening to you. Your neural web is so alive!"

"I don't know why," she said, turning to a blank page in her journal, dating it. She knew Nathan's sometimes fragile ego, hoping it would not rise, hoping he would manage it well, as he usually did—for she was caught up in something at this moment and didn't know how to do anything but write everything she could. She couldn't worry about him feeling inferior.

As she started to write, Beth felt a vibration on the ground under her. It was sudden, instantaneous, then gone. She looked to Nathan, who had felt nothing, his eyes gazing across the river at a small meadow there, a woodpecker flying across. Beth felt warmth in her left hand, feeling as if something formed in her hand, something material, like a piece of cloth. She waited for it, saw the girl in the sweatpants again, holding a cloth out to her, like a piece of lace that might sit on a grandmother's end table beside a window seat. The girl, about ten years old, was blond with brown eyes, wearing gray sweatpants and a sweatshirt that carried the emblem of Washington State University.

Beth tried to grasp the cloth, holding out her right hand, leaving her left holding the pen at the open page face of the journal.

"Thank you," she said to the girl.

Nathan said, "What's up?"

The sound of his voice ended the vision. Beth noticed her arm held out, realized she had spoken. She shivered, the shiver of gooseflesh that sometimes happens in hot sun.

"I'm going crazy!" She grinned at Nathan. "I am simply going nuts!"

"Another vision?" Nathan asked seriously.

"I have to write it down. My God." She returned to the blank page.

Nathan said nothing more, just watched her. When Beth concentrated, as she did now, her eyes, her large, flat nose and boxy forehead crinkled and her lips diminished to thin lines—her face framed by her brown hair and her shoulders bunched in a half-shrug, as if to say, "Don't pay too close attention to me"—her demeanor had the hungry humility of an innocent, and yet her blue eyes focused like a sharpshooter's. She knew that Nathan liked her in these moments, was attracted to her focus. She knew herself to be generally unattractive, and she and Nathan did not have sex a great deal. She did not push at him for it, nor feared very much the truth of her physical unattractiveness. She and Nathan had talked often about the love they had, one that would not last forever because it was not meant to.

As Beth began to write, starting first, as if by compulsion, with the visions of the ten-year-old girl, she was aware of herself in Nathan's eyes. Within minutes, she lost herself in the act of writing. "I think writing the truth down might be the most wonderful feeling I've ever had in life," she once said to Greta. At moments like this, it felt just so.

"Did you hear that?" Nathan cocked his head. It was a gunshot, just downriver. Farther upriver sat a shooting range from which Beth and Nathan had heard, during the morning, distant cracks of sound. But this shot was quite close, and to the south.

"There's not supposed to be shooting there," he said. "It's too close."

He was right. She felt something terribly hard, cold, painful—a quiver of a soul touching her skin. The gooseflesh came again.

"Let's be careful," Nathan said.

The image of a dead bird filled Beth's mind. Near it she saw a bloody man. Shocked out of revery, Beth dropped her journal beside her, pushed upward, fists into earth.

"No one's trying to hurt *us,*" she said, sure of it. "But someone's going to get hurt."

Nathan did not question her. He helped pull her up and put his fingers to his lips. He grabbed a stick, a makeshift weapon, held it to his side, and with her behind him, moved on rapid feet along the river trails, toward the south.

The watcher moved along the cliff's edge. The man and woman had crossed the suspension bridge and could still be seen. Soon they'd be lost in the thick trees. The two of them seemed important somehow. They had been there with Jeffrey. The watcher knew they didn't live in Lucia Court. He had studied every resident carefully. Lucia Court was one of two neighborhoods he had cased for his work with children.

The watcher moved further north toward a walking trail down behind the ridge. He fondled a black stone in his jacket pocket. Jeffrey Romer's death yesterday had been a profound disappointment. But he could shift focus quickly. He had studied different children's lives so that he could be immediately adaptable.

He looked at the sunlit blue sky. As it had for many years, light seemed almost dark—like a shroud. When he saw a sunny sky, he knew intellectually that it was sunny and light, but with his peculiar optical nerve he saw darkness above and around him. The effect came not merely from sunglasses, but from another place that he had access to since birth, and even further, through training. People thought there were two states—darkness and light. They didn't notice the amber-gray that existed all the time. They didn't see the whole palate before them.

The watcher did. The first child in his experiments, who looked a lot like Jeffrey, had been so scared he just nodded when asked what he saw.

"Stare into this—now what do you see?"

The boy was stoic, even while he took beatings. He would not cooperate. The watcher had selected more malleable children since then.

The watcher stopped moving. Above him a woodpecker had hit a tree—flew right to it, talon-clasped the bark, and started its pecking. Energy was growing in him, energy of darkened light—the other side of the truth. Since last night, since watching Jeffrey Romer die, he'd felt it—the building. First the shock, but then the rightness of it all. The Light had now selected for him. He would extract the other child, the girl. It was safer, anyway. It was better to stay on the north side of town. The Light had not wanted him to risk anything here, so close to his laboratory.

He needed to keep himself occupied till evening. He needed to stay focused. He fingered the stone. He had brought it along as an object of concentration, and then relinquishment. He would do as needed for the next few hours. He would stay focused. He walked deeper into the forest, toward the river. He had a few hours now to play, like a child, with the light and darkness.

3

God's Wounded Hand

Even in the ambulance, there had been no doubt that six-year-old Jeffrey would die within hours. And then, in Jeffrey's hospital room, Landry Romer sat in shock, rage, grief, and pain, a bomb of feelings exploding in him to match the outward savagery done to his son's torn bones and flesh. Then Jeffrey died—just stopped breathing while Marti laid her head on her son's tiny hand and Landry touched his cold forehead. Landry wept and moved away from the child, letting the doctor back in to the body. For two and a half years Jeffrey had been dying. Now, suddenly, he had died, his body a punching bag.

Long before the accident, coming about the time of the cancer, Jeffrey seemed very much a magical child, the dreamy kind of boy you want great things from one day. When he was almost three he asked Landry, "Where are we, Dad?" eyes half in another world. Thinking his son meant, "Where do we live?" Landry told him their address, the city, the state; but Jeffrey frowned as if he had meant something else.

Now, with Jeffrey dead more than twelve hours and already cremated, Landry was back near home, wandering toward the river. His son's dreamy words, which had returned to his memory last night, represented somehow all that he could not understand about his son or do for him, all the journeys he could not make with him, all his helplessness, all of it a gaping wound in him as he sat with the boy in the hospital room like a monk in the realm of death. Landry knew what it was to hate himself, to hate the impotence that sometimes was manhood.

Now, in the river gorge, he stepped over a fallen branch, holding a ceramic urn in his left hand, his gun holstered under his jacket, his underarms and forehead sweating under the hot, noontime sun. As the path unfolded to him easily, he touched the urn tenderly with his free hand. He tried to meld himself with it and with the stillness of the wilderness. His son had been reduced to ash, yet the ash still felt like an essence, and Landry felt he would protect it with his life. At this thought, tears came up from behind the wall of his eyes, waited there for permission, and receiving none, fell back.

Landry instinctively wiped his dry eyelid with his sleeve and moved to a fallen log next to the river's edge. He placed the urn carefully down at his feet and sat, about ten feet back from the river, slanted toward the south.

"Jeffrey," he whispered, as if his son could still talk.

The river near him was nearly still and received the whisper without hesitation, but without encouragement either. A bird flew above Landry among the pines. If not for a distant twitter, he would not have heard its presence. He peered upward, looking to locate it, aware that within himself as he searched for the animal were both the eyes of an admirer and of a predator.

During Landry's walk to the edge of the canyon up by the house yesterday morning—Jeffrey still alive, then, that eon ago—a great blue heron had sat on a high tree, letting him come not twenty feet from it. Stolid, the heron moved only its eyes. Landry stood with it and stared at the river water. Landry stared until the chatter of his mind died away and he could only feel stillness. In the stillness, he imagined a huge, disembodied, and bloody hand out of which sprang children, already sickly, deformed, dying and so only half-born. He hated that hand, God's wounded hand, the crippled other hand people didn't talk about. The hand his son had touched.

"Daddy," Jeffrey had cried so often over the years, vomiting and heaving. "Daddy, my head hurts." Landry and Marti knew during those days and nights that their only child would die. Landry, brought up Catholic, had often dreamt about the divine and bloody hand. He had seen his son in it, cupped in its huge palm. He had seen his son take flight out of the hand and as he flew a door opened in the hand. He had told Marti about the dream, and she, a more "positive" person, said she thought there was something beautiful in the dream, something mysterious, something that might be okay.

Landry saw only death.

Looking upward now at the bird, Landry saw a woodpecker in the high tamarack. The woodpecker alighted, dropped in a glide, and restuck on another tamarack, this one to the left of him. The bird's twin red breasts parted for a speckled brown chest. Its long beak searched like a divining rod for the already nurtured ingress then, finding a dimple, began pecking the bark, its beak a black twig against a wall of brown wood. The woodpecker's industry, the tree's emission of silky sawdust, the drum-tap-tap all distracted Landry for a moment from the immense endurance of life; then a hatred of some kind, hatred seeking an object, built up in him. Later he would describe the feeling as a vise clamping him tightly, from both without and within, a bizarre black mood worse than grief, worse than pain, as if all the darkness of the universe, once kept secret or only imaginable, now became real. In the sheer persistent useless pecking and silting, in the harsh echoing of the woodpecker's loudness, like Jeffrey twisting the volume knob too loud on the television, Landry felt tears of rage rise. He felt himself split in two for a second, then felt the two split into four, then four into eight, then lost count. His hand moved to the holster of the .38, moved like the gradual drop of a branch in the wind, unclipped the gun, pulled it out, tweaked the safety. An inward voice murmured, "You were planning all morning to hurt something; why else would you have brought your gun?" All happened in a fluid motion, the work of a man in a trance. He gripped the gun in front of him, dropped to a knee squat, sighted the bird, hesitated, asking the air, the bird, the tree, the Almighty to intervene, and in the absence of intervention gave the trigger the inward tap it called for. The world exploded, the bird careening thirty feet into the distance, stopping only because another tamarack trunk arrested its final, maimed flight.

When the bird hit the brown-barked trunk, Landry smelled gun-burn and saw a silt of feathers like the silt of sawdust, the dross left always from any explosion, the silt of Jeffrey's bones. Landry stared at the bird on the ground; it lay as if welcomed between a rock and a root mound at a tree's base. Landry let the explosive sound wane from his ears gradually, dropping his gun arm and automatically clicking the safety back on. The .38 had been a part of him for twelve years. He remembered other shots, then closed his eyes against the site of all of them, and of Jeffrey, wondering in a flash whether he thought he himself was responsible for Jeffrey's death, regretting as he wondered it that he had such trouble touching the deepest parts of his own experience, even when they seemed to be reaching up to touch him.

"Help me." he murmured aloud, trying to startle the internal chaos with insight. "His life was a gift. Why must I be so dark?" Tears would heal him, he knew, but the best he could do was stop the rage from flowing again, the gun from rising. He breathed very deep. "My God," he murmured, "help me."

He heard no answer. Rising from his squat position, teetering then balancing on a cramped leg, he moved to the dead bird. Action was required, and he pushed himself to it, the river flow like a murmur and the wind like the sound of a brush on canvas. His tennis shoes stepped loudly beneath him. Somewhere he heard birds complaining and a squirrel clacking. In a bush to his right, a bird or chipmunk rustled. He turned to it, avoiding the dead woodpecker for a moment with his eyes, but his feet still moving to it like a hunter's.

He heard himself breathe with the wind and the river, and he knew that the blackness, the hatred, was gone. It was as if someone had opened a window, or dropped a veil, then closed the window, the veil lifted. In the place of the darkness was a strange sense of illumination, of lightedness, yet not something he could see in front of him.

Landry stopped walking. He could see something. He was

confronted with internal images that filled the space of the light. His mother was in them, thin and gaunt-faced and gray-haired, a woman who had been abandoned by her husband and lost two children, one to stillbirth, one to pneumonia, and had only her son, Landry, and her own mental illness. Landry saw her so clearly, opened his eyes, returned to his forward motion. The journey to the dead bird was like a journey into his mother's heart, his mother's life. He had seen her at Eastern State Mental Hospital just a few weeks ago. She looked as she so often did, as if she had awakened inside a huge empty castle, a queen wanting to be in control of the world, and able to control nothing. God's wounded hand had created her, and her children, and her grandchildren.

"What just happened?" Landry asked the air aloud. "Why did you let me hate so much so fast and then stop me so that now all I feel is shame?" Even his mother would never do what he had just done, kill an innocent bird. She was not capable of hatred. "Help me," Landry whispered. "Be clear, please be clear!" He knew he must look so bizarre to anyone else, pleading with an invisible God, or no God at all, yearning to be brought into the light and either taken away, or cured of all that was bad in life.

Landry bent onto his knees before the bird he had shot. Its head was missing, only a residue of neck remaining with the body, tendrils of brown-red blood curling over the edge of the truncated torso. One wing lay against the body in perfect fit, the red square on the breast unruffled. The other wing had remained splayed by trauma and lay crushed at the bird's side.

Landry picked up the woodpecker, first in both hands then holding its warmth on his left palm. Blood trickled onto his index finger as he stared. He saw the divine hand bleeding and his son in it.

"I'm not myself," he heard himself say. "I'm not myself." He watched himself but could not stop himself from bringing the bird to his face, from rubbing its blood and feathers along his cheek, from caressing his eyelids with the broken wing. Opening his eyes, he bent forward to smell against the tree bark the death of the bird where it hit. The smell of bird and bark were musty, sweet, not rancid or grotesque—sweet as the smell of death would be if one were the earth itself, accustomed to the palimpsest of the seasons. Knowing that he was in a kind of madness, Landry breathed in deeply the sweetness of the death and felt a strange opening for himself, as if the bird's gaping little body were a doorway, a mad, resplendent doorway. His mother held his hand at the doorway, impish and loving as she had once been. She led him into the doorway where Jeffrey waited with smiling eyes. His mother led him with a kind of certainty she once had, whispering, "It's time, son, it's time."

He knew it was time. He felt more than human in the ordinary way humans are. He felt himself sensitive to some spirit around him, the spirit of his son, yes; one with that spirit, ready to do as it wished. There had been a split in heaven and earth, and he had caused it by killing the bird and by all his sins and both evil and good spirits had come out, and now they were compelling him to meld with the dead bird and meld with death itself.

Landry leaned against the tree, staring at brush and trees and river. He saw the brown-black urn at the base of the trunk. He took a deep breath. Stop this madness! See reality. He tried to automate himself. I'm by the river. Marti is coming to spread the ash with me. He catalogued his work, his car, his house, his friends, himself. He saw everything at that moment that a man ever knows—the naked truth of his life as it is lived—and it was not enough. The trance, the killing, his mother, his son, the bird against his skin—they were he and he they. "It's time," his mother said. Then his insane mother became the beatific Virgin Mary. It was as if she transformed in a flash of light. How had this happened? The flash of light encompassed everything, blinding Landry for a second. Then the Virgin Mary started to fade away.

"Don't go, Mary," Landry called. "We need you, Blessed Virgin, be with us in our time of need."

"If I can't cry," he murmured, "I deserve to die." He couldn't even bring tears to his eyes now. He saw himself clearly—bird in his left hand, his gun in his right, and the rhyming words "If I can't cry, I deserve to die" controlling his mind. He put the bird down, seeking a twig by which to carve out "I deserve to die" in the dirt. Mad and wild with the notion that only the woodpecker's beak should be used for the carving he searched for it. He found it nowhere, finding instead a pine twig, carving, "If I can't cry . . ." then dropping the twig and picking the bird up again and moving to the water's edge, entranced by his own death and ready for it, his blood pumping in his eyes and the gun rising to his mouth.

Beth knew what Landry was going to do before she saw it with her eyes. She saw him surrounded by darkness, his gun rising to his face. She and Nathan were running, then walking, then running. Tree branches stung their arms and cheeks. When they found a deer trail, they came to the river's edge, but saw no one. Then Beth saw in her mind's eye the figure of a man somewhere among trees and birds just away from them. The image faded into her vision, stopping her steps short, forcing her to close her eyes. She asked Nathan to stop as well, which he did. In her mind's eye, she saw the man turn, and saw that it was Landry, standing in a kind of glow of darkness, like a shroud, but a glowing presence of light near him too. And he had his gun up, in his face.

"My God!" Beth cried. "Landry. No!"

Her voice shattered the valley's silence.

Nathan touched her arm. "Beth, what is it?"

She resisted opening her eyes. "He's across the river somewhere—down that way. We have to stop him."

"From what?"

"Come on!" She had to open her eyes to run. Though to save Landry she must open her eyes, there was some part of her that didn't want the vision to end: some strange, even shameful part of her that wanted to see forever, eyes closed, never moving, in this strange way of seeing.

She led the running but neither she nor Nathan saw Landry anywhere. Could her vision be wrong? Was she mixed up, worried about Mr. Wight killing himself and so imagining Landry killing himself? No, she wasn't wrong. She just knew she wasn't! But her sense of his location was.

"He's across the river. I saw him, then we ran . . . that way . . . damn it." She closed her eyes, begging the vision to return—to show her where Landry was. How can this be? So much death today. "We have to save Landry."

"You can see him? The remote viewing?"

"Yes! But where?"

"What's happening?"

Now she saw again—Landry. The gun. A glow hovering

near him, near the shroud. She did not know why—nor was she merely Beth, separate—she was able to touch the glow of light, as if connected to it, and even at a distance, able to communicate with it. It reached toward Landry. It was like the light yesterday, and the light over Donnell Wight's, and the shooting dots of light by the rock. She was being carried by purpose and mission. She was guiding Landry to see through the shroud toward the glow of light, speaking to him without words. Look at the light, Landry. There's darkness around you, but look at the light.

"What's happening?" Nathan challenged. "Where is he?"

She couldn't answer Nathan. Had to tune him out. Stay focused. Help Landry. The light and she were healing him somehow. Together. She had power—or was a part of power itself. How could this be? Was she just seeing her own projections of light and darkness? Was she imagining her appointment in all this? Was she really not seeing him at all?

He turned his head, just slightly, to the light. Wasn't this real? Her clairvoyance seemed so real. He turned his body, the gun still like a face or a mirror held in front of him, but everything turning. Beth felt an intense heat, and tears filled her eyes. Landry turned more to the light now, more, more; now he saw it! Yes! He actually saw the glow near him. He saw light and stopped the flow of his own dark purpose.

The gun drifted downward.

He began to cry.

Suddenly, Beth saw his location. She recognized the fallen tree trunk near him. The scene faded out of her vision but she knew now where he was.

"He's going to be all right," she exhaled in a whisper, opening her eyes and wiping them with her sleeve. "Nathan—I know where Landry is. The shot echoed and sent us the wrong way. He's there, *down*river. I'm sure of it."

"You can see him?"

"Yes! I don't know how. Come on. Let's make sure he's all right."

"What happened? You've got to tell me."

"It was incredible," she said, as they moved south now. "Nathan, it was incredible. I think I was part of it. Oh, Nathan, I don't know how. And there was a shroud around him." She tried to explain as they jogged, Beth feeling sure that Landry was okay, yet aware of her human uncertainty, and pushing Nathan to run.

The watcher had been concentrating on the black stone. Seated in a coppice of cedar trees, his back against an ancient trunk, his legs out open in front of him, he had placed the stone between his knees, focusing his eyes on it. He had tried to hold it in his vision without blinking. This concentration brought a hint of dryness to his eyes. He let himself blink, but lost none of the concentration that always brought him a sense of warmth and safety. In that concentration he now saw an image of the Virgin Mary. It came to him as a picture, one that hung during his boyhood on his mother's bedroom wall.

His mother had been the first to show him the power of the Light. All his life, he had experimented with it—with waves, with particles, with quanta. Because of her.

The stone he would soon relinquish to the river valley, this black stone of images, was quartzite from the Ivory Coast. His mother had collected it in their travels from post to post. He had used it to manage the experimental blood of the children he'd taken thus far. With Jeffrey's death last night, he had decided to let this stone go, though he was finding the task difficult right now.

What were the sounds to the south? Gun? People? Running? How far off? Breezes made distance of sounds quite deceptive in the river valley. Something was happening—the two campers? Was it them? The watcher resented their presence in his valley.

Pulling his legs up, using the tree as ballast for his ascending back, he rose. He stretched and straightened then bent over, retrieved the stone. He squeezed it a second, feeling it, *reading* it. Everything carried electrical energy. Everything carried a signal that could be read. The flashes of clairvoyance came if he just concentrated. The children had helped so much.

No flash came right now—no image to help him see what was happening downriver—but he thought he heard sounds closer to him. At all costs, he had to avoid discovery, especially if he was to succeed in this evening's work.

He listened carefully, a hunter, moving carefully away from the sounds of these people.

Marti had heard a shot echo through the river valley, but did not know where it came from. She never suspected her husband's gun. To the north was a rifle club and shooting range. She assumed the shot was nothing more extraordinary than a man shooting a decoy.

The sun hurt Marti's eyes as she walked down the gorge incline toward the river. The blinding sun reminded her for a moment of the light last night, but then her thoughts returned to where they had been all morning. She had thought six months ago that she would divorce Landry. She felt certain now about her timing. They would throw Jeffrey's ashes to the wind, and then she would turn to Landry and say, "I can't love you." Landry, numb and like a void for the last two years now, would set her free. He would move out and go wherever separated men went, and she would be alone to fully grieve. She thought she might even love Landry still—but she couldn't carry the burden for them both anymore. He wouldn't understand, of course. He would just tell her to be strong, or he would go quiet for days, hiding behind his teary but silent eyes all the hauntings he had been taught to protect from women.

Marti stepped off the incline deer trail and onto the river's level. As she did so she was greeted by the rich purling sound of the water. The river this year had risen to the tops of ground shrubs, which peeked out above the green flow, like a mesh. Marti stopped for a moment, in no rush to go further down-river and find her husband; she stared at a near-drowning shrub, remembering a time in October when the river was quite low and the shrub land-bound and she walked with Jeffrey, who had just come off two days of chemo. He wanted "to go hear the song of the river," he said, repeating from a children's book:

> *"The song of the river is loud*
> *The song of the river is quiet*
> *God listens like a happy cloud*
> *The sky is filled with light."*

"I've talked to God at the river," he often said to Marti and his father. "Everything is going to be really good."

Tears came to Marti's eyes as she remembered. She saw herself and Jeffrey, his voice gaunt and raspy.

Marti turned away from the shrub and the memory, letting her eyes dry themselves of tears. A woodpecker, brown speckled, with two red squares on its chest, flew past her, perhaps two feet away! Then it alighted on a pine tree. She had heard, even felt, the breeze of its wings on her face, so close to her had it flown by. How bizarre—this was the second woodpecker to fly so close to her, or perhaps the same one. Just as she stepped out of her house on Lucia, a woodpecker flew by, not three feet from her, on its way toward the river gorge. Marti thought it was not the same one she saw now, though she didn't know the source of this intuition. She thought both woodpeckers were trying to talk to her, and didn't know why she thought this either. Jeffrey had insisted he could talk to the birds. Marti thought, in sentimental "parental" moments she was never crazy enough to share with anyone, that he did indeed know the language of the birds.

"Woodpeckers," she wondered now. "What do they mean?" She imagined, for a moment, that one of them carried Jeffrey's soul on its back. She was one-sixteenth Coeur d'Alene Indian. She had spent no time in her native tradition but often remembered fondly her grandfather, who believed that every animal had a unique spirit or "energy." He consulted his medicine cards constantly. Jeffrey had been born a year after Grandfather died.

Everywhere was death and memories of death. The pain, relentless and without compassion, came at her from without and within. She yearned to get free of it, and yet she yearned to have her loyalty and endurance tested by endless pain. Jeffrey was dead, and she could not forgive herself and knew that to do so would be an act of disloyalty akin to abandoning her Catholic faith or killing someone. "It's not your fault," the paramedic had said in the ambulance.

Wiping her tears with a Kleenex, she replaced the minipack of tissues in the right-hand pocket of her light cardigan. She thought she would hold on to the soiled tissue rather than shove it with the other in her left. Tears would come again, in seconds.

Where was Landry? Wasn't she getting near the spot he had told her would be their meeting place? She saw the branch he liked to sit on, next to it the large granite boulder, about four cubic feet and flat. She walked toward both and thought she smelled a burning or smoky scent. She looked for a fire, saw none, and looked around bewildered. A sick thought flew though her—that this was the smell of ashes strewn out; that Landry had spread them without her. No—he wouldn't do that! And ashes didn't smell except up close.

She saw the urn now, on the other side of the tree. My God, where was Landry? She lifted the urn as if lifting a delicate flower. She opened it and saw the ash still in it and closed it again, breathing like an asthmatic, her heart pounding.

"Oh baby," she murmured, tears coming again. "Oh Jeffrey." She reminded herself that his soul had flown on, free to be with the Virgin Mary, and Jesus, and Almighty God. But she wept, cradling the urn as she had cradled Jeffrey a hundred times and her husband, Landry, only once in twelve years, cradling his huge weeping head the day Jeffrey was born, never since Jeffrey had gotten sick.

Through her tears, Marti saw movement some fifty feet away. She held the urn in her left hand, feeling its weight and using her hip for part of it, like holding a baby there.

She wiped her eyes with the tissue in her right hand. The movement downriver was big, human. She walked toward it and saw the white short sleeve shirt and blue shorts her husband wore. The shoulders were broad on the bent figure and the hair brown and full on his head. He bent, back to her, over the river's edge. As she came closer, she saw he was retching. She saw his gun by his right hand. He was bent over on all fours like an animal, his hands knuckle-fisted on the pebbles.

Marti ran toward him, calling. He tried to turn, but retched again, a yellow bile dripping. She saw now a puddle of peach-colored sauce and lumps and lemon yellow next to his right side. To his left she saw a bird with its head blown off, its tiny pink talons shoved up into the air just near her husband's wrist and leather watchband.

"Landry, my God!" she cried. "What happened?" Now he did look at her and she saw his blue eyes covered in tears, tears staining very dirty cheeks. Marti saw his face in pain and felt her heart open. She felt almost afraid of his tears.

"I have to find the head!" he whispered like a hiss, a tear dropping onto his right cheek. His lips and chin quivered and curled with weeping.

"What did you do?" Marti cried. She bent down and set the urn on flat dirt and put her left arm around her husband's back. He retched again, his whole body convulsing. It reminded her, strangely, of labor contractions. He moaned. She had never felt *this* vulnerable, not at Jeffrey's birth, not even in sex. She held him.

"It's okay," she said. "It's okay. Did you kill the bird?" She saw the death-mottled woodpecker and felt a chill. Was this the one she'd seen by the house? The gun shot occurred a few minutes later, as she entered the wilderness; it must have been Landry, killing this innocent bird. She felt ire rise and then heard him say, "Marti, I was going to kill myself." The words seemed absurd for a second, like quick words you hear on a radio station, fleeting as fingers flick the dial. No one was less likely than Landry to show weakness.

"I had the gun in my mouth, I don't know why," he said. "Marti, I pushed it too deep and I pushed. Then, I can't explain, just as I was going to pull the trigger . . . the Virgin Mary . . . I swear . . . beautiful . . . light . . . I was so . . . I don't know . . . I saw it before and didn't believe it, then I saw it again, I saw her, maybe . . . I don't know . . . but I did see her, Mary, there was an angel with her, Marti. They saved me, didn't they?"

He was so like a little boy. He convulsed, turned away to puke again but nothing came this time. She held him and understood now. He had shot the bird, then put the gun in his mouth to shoot himself. He sat with the urn, then saw the bird, shot it, went to it, leaving the urn, then brought the bird to the water's edge and pulled the gun out and shoved it in his mouth, its tip smoky, hot, shoving it deep in and retching, and he saw the Virgin Mary?

For a second, like a commentator of the events, she heard a voice-over: "If only he had succeeded." It was the worst thing she had ever thought in her life. Tears filled her eyes, and then a kind of weeping began in her, starting in her feet and fingers, like when she had felt marijuana affect her years ago, the same marijuana that she suspected, a decade and a half later, had invaded her reproductive organs and produced a sick child. This grief and shame now tingled through her, shimmering through her body. She held on to Landry, who now rose up on his knees like a bear to hold on to her. She wept and grasped him and felt and heard him weeping convulsively with her, by her, of her. His sobs were an explosion of wails—he was an animal long trapped and now loud, louder than he ever was in sex. She felt God's hand clasp her and clasp Landry and clasp them together. She had avoided holding her son too tight, for fear she'd break his already breaking body. But now, swirling in her husband's madness, she felt free to hold fast to life itself. What had Landry meant by seeing the Virgin Mary? Like an angel? Was it like that light last night, around Jeffrey?

Marti had no idea how long she and her husband held each other, two people on their knees by the river. She thought she heard rustles in the trees across the river, even the whispers of other people. Yet she saw no one.

"I'm sorry," she heard herself say. "I'm so sorry."

"I'm so sorry too," he whispered, not letting her go, though both felt pain directly in their kneecaps. "God knew I couldn't love a son yet, so he took my boy away."

"Oh no," Marti cried. "No, no."

"I shot the bird, and I thought I could shoot God's wounded hand and get rid of it, but I couldn't."

"What are you saying?" He rarely talked about God.

"I don't know myself or you or anything. I never have. I'm going to be reborn. That's what the angel said." What amazing words coming from his mouth, words of spirit and soul like she would expect Jeffrey to speak.

"All I do these days," she said, parting his hair with her fingers, "is wait to die. I've been dead inside for a long time." What was she saying? She hadn't talked to Landry this way in years. Her eyes left his and found the truncated bird and she saw the urn just the other side of herself and she knew the world was a place of immense mystery, where walls crumbled and nothing was as it seemed.

"I love you, Marti," her husband whispered, touching her arm tenderly.

Her chin quivered and she said through brimming-again tears, "I want to love you, Landry, but I don't know how anymore."

He said nothing, just looked into her eyes, accepting her words and, as he always did, accepting her. She lowered her eyes and grasped the urn, standing. They both stood. For the first time in a long time Marti saw Landry's immense strength and admired it. For some strange reason she thought of his mother, his crazy crazy mother. Of course he would be strong, she thought, to survive her. And she thought of the gun in his mouth. Can I live with that? she wondered. She did not know. As she rose with him to reenter the world of standing humans, she felt she did still love him, and she did not recoil.

"We have to give our son away," Marti said, talking as much to the urn as to her husband. "Are you all right now, Landry?"

"I'm all right." He nodded. He wasn't sure what "all right" should feel like. He felt like he had survived his own death. The madness had left him, replaced by love. He did not understand what had happened and felt especially confused that his weeping had cleansed him, left him feeling not ashamed but in wonder.

As Marti rose, so did he, arms tingling from embrace. Marti held the urn in one hand and with the other moved instinctively to brush her knees off, as if someone would come upon the scene and see dirt there. When she had finished cleaning the knees of her jeans, she felt almost as if a set of humilities had been lost. Perhaps God would have wanted them to carry evidence that they had been kneeling. The gentle penance and spiritual flavor of the thought warmed her, for she had not loved God in a long time. As she stood separate from Landry, she remembered that she had wanted to leave him and fell back into the world of that resolution for a moment, staring at the water and Landry's six-six bulk beside her, waiting patiently for her. She pictured the gun in his mouth and pushed the picture out. We need help, she said inwardly to the river, we need so much help. Biting her lip, she began to open the urn.

From across the river, Beth and Nathan saw a man and a woman sprinkling gray snow on the river, on the pebbles, the shrubs and trees. Beth felt tears in her eyes as she saw the tears. Nathan's eyes were tearing too as from behind a stand of trees, both she and Nathan leaned to listen to the words murmured across the river. Beth heard no single word, but felt a sense of the miracle of life in the air the grieving couple breathed. She shivered with the events of the last hour, yearning to write everything down.

Hearing a kind of barking chirp, like a sergeant giving orders, Beth looked upward into the trees above the couple and saw a woodpecker picking at the trunks of a pine tree. Landry and Marti must have just been speaking about the headless woodpecker; must have decided, finally, each to hold a wing and throw the bird into the water. Beth watched them bend to the dead bird. Marti took the good wing, Landry the broken one.

"Look!" Nathan whispered. "It's so sad, but it's so beautiful."

Beth held Nathan around the waist, watching with him as Landry and Marti, in tandem, threw the savaged bird into the river of water, which absorbed it as a bobbing then floating thing, moving it downstream as it would move any other spirit, or loud cry, or piece of debris.

Part II

Between the Light and the Darkness

4

Greta

Greta Sarbaugh sat on her back lawn wondering over the sound of gunshots and the location of her friends down in the river valley, the sweet young couple who had become like daughter and son-in-law to her; she had stood to peer over her ridge into the valley, seen nothing but trees, river, sunlight, and shadows. She had returned to a file of newspaper clippings, thinking to herself that while a walking trip with her cane down the dirt paths was difficult, she might have to make the trip, should Nathan and Beth not return this morning for a visit. Reading through prescription sunglasses, she sought in the words she'd read many times before some new insight, given what had happened last night.

SPOKANE KILLER CLAIMS MURDER OF SECOND VICTIM

SPOKESMAN-REVIEW, SPOKANE, WASHINGTON

March 18, 1992

The self-titled murderer, "the Light Killer," has claimed in a letter sent to the Spokesman-Review that he has murdered a second child. The letter was received at the newspaper on Tuesday—six days after the child was reported missing.

The killer said in a letter that he has destroyed the body of a young girl. The child's name has been withheld pending the notification of next of kin. The killer also claims to have killed a young boy. Neither body has been found.

Spokane Police Chief Todd Harrington said, "The girl, whom the killer names in the letter, has been missing for six days. We are working our hardest to find her and the other child, a boy." In regard to whether the children might still be alive, Harrington said, "We would never tell anyone to give up hope."

In response to the murder reports, Harrington has formed a task force, in consultation with local FBI officials, to investigate the reported crimes.

The lengthy, untraceable letters began arriving at the Spokesman-Review city desk on November 18, 1991, threatening the disappearance and death of local children. A nine-year-old boy disappeared on January 26 of this year. A letter from the self-proclaimed abductor arrived at the Spokesman-Review two days later.

The most recent letter arrived six days after the second of the children, a ten-year-old girl, disappeared. Both children disappeared from their neighborhoods in North Spokane. The task force is focusing its efforts in that area. But, Harrington said, "We will follow any leads anywhere."

An anonymous source within the task force provided an alternative reason for the abductions. The source said the children may be part of slave trade in Asia.

However, Harrington countered the idea. He said, "That is a minority view on our task force." The chief said the police department has asked federal authorities to check out the lead.

Adelle Tourtellotte, a Spokane psychologist and a consultant with the task force, treated serial murderer Bo Sievertsen in 1988, after he was arrested for raping and killing six women. Tourtellotte believes the Light Killer's claims are true. "The Light Killer is murdering children. I'm certain of it," she said. "I don't think it's slave trade, and I'm sorry to say I don't believe the children will be found alive."

The two children are of different sex and race. Tourtellotte concurs that this does not necessarily follow a serial killer's "typical" pattern. "Serial killers usually pick one type, either male or female, either blond hair or brown—but not always," she said. "But since there is no other evidence of slave trade, nor of the first child having returned, I think we have to face the idea of murder in the cases of both children."

The FBI profiler assigned to the Task Force did not return phone calls today from the Spokesman-Review. However, last week the FBI profiler released a statement that concurs with Tourtellotte's view. The profiler said, "Serial killers generally hope that their work will be admired and scrutinized. However, in this case, without bodies to include in forensic analysis, the so-called Light Killer may be even harder than normal to apprehend."

The "Light Killer" signed his letters with this name, and,

it has been used by police and media to identify the suspect. To date, five letters have been mailed by the Light Killer to the media. In the first letter, the so-called Light Killer wrote an explanation of his name:

"I see Light and then I see the children inside the Light. They come to me that way, as complete images of real children. There is a Dark place on each of them, or in each of their Brains. I see that also inside the Light. I drive around schools until I see them, or find other ways of identifying the kids. Once I identify them, I plot a way to get at them, I kidnap them, I try to help them, to remove the darkness, to Heal them."

Until the letter received today, it had been two months since the self-proclaimed Light Killer has written to claim an abduction of a Spokane child.

Greta had not slept much the night before, filled with the pain of Jeffrey's death, the wonder of the light, and maternal concern for Beth and Nathan. She had arisen in her bed while a pale white light of the moon shone through the window. This light, like new white paint reflecting in on her desk, dark wall, and floor, seemed to suggest a memory.

Just a week ago, a few days after the newspaper article had appeared, another child had been abducted. This brought the count to three. Greta, who rarely read the newspaper, had been following and clipping articles about the Light Killer because of the killer's obvious religious confusion. While she did not live in the neighborhood where the children had disappeared, it was difficult to neglect neighborly conversation about the poor abducted children and the insane man who wrote with capital letters and of light as if he were in a medieval world.

Then last night the light near Jeffrey. Light. The Light Killer. She had awoken in the middle of the night: What about the light she and the others had seen? Could there be a connection? She got up, took out the envelope in which she had built a file of saved clippings, and reread the articles. Adelle Tourtellotte, whom she'd met over the years, was often mentioned.

The clippings sat with Greta now as she lay back on a lounge chair on her grass, looking out over the river. Her reading had been interrupted before by a gunshot—not one from the shooting range up north. She felt queasy in her stomach for Beth and Nathan—a paranoia that they were in some trouble, that some criminal was down there shooting at them. Eerily, the gunshot and the articles about the killings mixed in her mind as if they were related, which she knew, if she remained rational, they could not be.

Be rational, she coached herself. The shot in the valley could have been anything. Sometimes young boys shot off guns down in the gorge. And now that it had been a while with no more gunshots, Greta could more easily quiet her fears. Shielding her eyes with an open palm, she looked toward Donnell Wight's house. Breathing deeply, she talked herself into feeling the warmth of the late morning sun, a warmth like being shrouded in swaddling clothes when she was a tiny baby in the village. What a nice feeling—much better than reading those terrible letters. Thoughts of girlhood sent her mind to a friend of her middle age, from Sarajevo, Simone Suk Admir, a woman of Muslim origin Greta had met in Starr King Seminary when she returned, at forty-five, to graduate school to become a minister.

Simone, tall, well-dressed, quiet, speaking always with a

low voice, her throat gravelly from years of smoking, had come over to Greta's apartment one night after class. Greta had mentioned during their "Religious Experiences" class that as a child she saw lights she thought were angels. Simone, over tea, talked about being a survivor of Auschwitz where she, too, had seen strange lights. There was a physician at Auschwitz, she recalled, who talked about "light" as if it were a living thing. He talked about children of light, children of promise who were coming in the future. Coming to Auschwitz? Simone had asked him. No, he smiled, but coming from it, into the world. Humanity, he had told her, would always be seen now through the lens of darkness and light of the destruction of the world's children. Simone described this physician as strangely empathic, for a Nazi.

On this day when the rites of summer were hot and golden, it must be that the gunshot, and Jeffrey's death, and the newspaper clipping all conspired to spur her memory toward Simone and the doctor in Auschwitz. Greta closed her eyes behind her sunglasses and let the sun's heat penetrate her body. Greta thought of the child-abductor and his Light. There must be some relationship with Jeffrey. But what?

Her own daughter, Natalie, flew into Greta's mind. As a girl, Natalie liked to put her fingers on the surface of the water where the river was calm. She liked to touch the water and leave no fingerprint, just send out ripples. At seven years old, she said she saw light in the water as she saw herself reflected. She said she wanted to leave her fingerprint on the light.

"Mama, I can't make a fingerprint on the light, or even water." She frowned with all seriousness.

"But the ripples are your fingerprint." Greta had smiled,

joining her daughter at the water's edge, touching it with her fingers too, rippling the sunlit river water.

Calmed by recollection, Greta knew that she was sitting in her yard up from the river, yet she knew she somehow knew right now, at the river itself, standing with her family, touching the water, trying to leave a fingerprint with her Natalie and the boys and Francis before he died, and before everyone moved to other cities and jobs, becoming the wonderful, independent but faraway children she and Francis had worked so hard to raise.

Greta's memories were interrupted by the sound of a plane overhead, one of the B-52s from Fairchild Air Force base. She usually thought of their sonic booms as a sad disturbance; now she looked at the plane as if it were a tiny, blessed bird.

"You're right here with us, Jeffrey," she murmured. "I can't see you, but I feel you. You're still here, taking care of things. You were so magical." Poor Landry. Poor Marti. Greta closed her eyes in prayer for her friends.

Greta opened her eyes to sounds from down the river incline, sounds of footsteps, emerging as the airplane's groan faded. The sounds became Beth, whose head peeked up over the top; her big body, then loping gait started toward Greta across the sun-shined carpet of grass.

"It's just me!" Beth called out. "Came for a visit." She dropped down into the folding chair next to her old friend.

Greta hugged her. "I heard a gunshot before. I worried. I was thinking I should try to get down there."

Beth breathed hard. "Something happened with Landry. I have to tell you. I don't think he'd want us to tell anyone but . . . well, you'll see. You can help me, Greta—help me to understand."

What an incredible story Beth told. Listening, Greta felt a warmth for this daughter of the soul, who talked so like a swarm of bees, as if she'd been pent up in experience.

Beth began to tear up, wondering over Donnell, over the rightness of what she and Nathan had done, then deciding again that they must let him live his own life.

"Did Donnell look," Greta asked, "like he was ready to go?"

"Oh yes." Beth smiled. "He looked like he was half in the other world. Even his skin was already more white than it was fleshy and alive."

Greta said, "Jeffrey dies of a car wreck, not cancer. Donnell dies from suicide, not his cancer. Light emerges into our valley, touching each of us. . . ." Greta trailed off, taking her sunglasses off and dropping them onto the news clippings.

Beth leaned over and put her arms around her friend. "I never knew I could feel so much grief and so much joy at the same time, like I'm feeling today. And with so much going on. Oh God, I have to tell you something else. I saw a man in a . . . I don't know . . . like a coat with a hood. He was carrying a girl's body. I couldn't see the man's face, but I saw the girl—she's blond, about ten years old, and she's wearing a WSU sweatshirt, navy blue. I saw her with the man—that was last night. Then I saw her in the river today. She was trying to hand me something, like a lace cloth. It was white . . . it was like I was sharing a mind with him, or something. Or could it be I'm sharing my mind with the poor girl? How weird to say this 'sharing my mind,' I don't know, Greta, it's just . . ."

When Beth trailed off, unsure of her experience, Greta said, "Beth, have you been following the news? The Light Killer?"

"The Light Killer," Beth repeated, immediately recognizing the words. "Up on the North Side."

"There have been two girls and one boy abducted. I woke up last night remembering. I've kept the clippings." Greta lifted her glasses off the loose file. Beth, in turn, lifted the papers.

"I think this killer is deeply invested in religious life," Greta said. "Maybe Satanism."

Beth took the clippings as if they were dangerous.

"I've been reading the articles since last night," Greta continued, "thinking about the light we saw, Beth. Think about a psychotic or schizophrenic man who sees light, a Light with a capital L. That light must be a palpable vision to him. He finds children in it. He takes the children. Then last night we saw a wall of light near a child—Jeffrey. There is a connection."

Greta did not quite know how to continue.

Beth opened the file of articles, peering at words, but not reading. She looked up. "Greta, as I was walking up here I was thinking, 'Where will the world go next?' I was thinking, 'Could I imagine what life would be like if everyone experienced the kinds of things like I'm experiencing?' I was sad for Landry and Marti and Donnell, but I felt such a joyful feeling too. My head is bursting my heart is bursting, I don't want to think I'm seeing something so terrible. What if I what I saw was this evil man holding one of these dead children? What if I'm touching his mind somehow? That would be too strange, Greta!"

"We don't know," Greta cautioned, thinking, What will Beth be like as an old woman? I hope she'll be happy. Then Greta felt certainty about picking up the phone and trying to get ahold of Adelle.

"I think I will call Adelle Tourtellotte," Greta said aloud. "I've met her a few times. Please read some of this. See if anything comes into your vision." Greta pushed up from her chair. "I'll be right back." Adelle Tourtellotte understood these kinds of things. Especially with this incredible possibility that Beth was seeing a psychopath in her mind, or at least clairvoyantly seeing the abducted child. Adelle would know details. The WSU sweatshirt hadn't been mentioned in articles. What if this was a detail that only those close to the investigation, like Adelle, could know?

As she walked across her grass toward the back screen door Greta recalled being the one who, just last night, hoped all present would talk to no one. But by the time she had her little brown and white address book in hand, she knew calling Adelle would not qualify. Adelle could advise her whether to call the police. Though what could Beth possibly tell them that they would believe?

Greta dialed Adelle's office, then home, getting an answering machine at both.

"Adelle," she said, "something has happened . . . an explosion of light . . . you have to call me as soon as possible." She described it all to her until the machine beeped, then she hung up.

Greta stood a moment in front of the phone. Then she lifted it and called Natalie in Hartford, speaking into her machine. "Hope the kids are okay. Had a terrible accident here. Little Jeffrey I told you about . . ." Without trusting the whole experience to the machine, she hung up, enjoying for a moment the air-conditioned cool of her house. She looked outside and saw Beth reading one of the clippings.

The phone rang. It was Mrs. McDonald, Sally's mother.

"Greta, it's Tess. I've been thinking about what Sally told me. She's so upset, but she keeps talking about the light she saw, like it's . . . so beautiful to her. I wonder if I should call our pastor."

"Let's give it a little more time, Tess," Greta requested. Would Tess call her pastor anyway? She and her husband were not immensely religious people, but they were loyal churchgoers—Presbyterians. How difficult it was to contain experiences like those last night, Greta thought, feeling hypocritical for calling Adelle, but saying, "I just think we should wait and see what happens before a lot of people get involved. Don't you?"

Tess just wanted to talk about it all, Greta realized with relief, as Tess asked questions about the light, wishing she had been home to witness it. "You're the glue that holds this neighborhood together," Tess said. "Thank you for keeping in touch with all the children and the parents."

When Greta finished her conversation with her neighbor, she saw Beth putting the file of clippings down onto the grass. Moving to the kitchen, Greta carried her cordless phone under her arm. She decided to give Beth a little time to absorb. Still watching her friend, Greta prepared a pitcher of iced tea. What would happen to this gifted young woman who was called to the world of dreams?

LIGHT KILLER REPORTEDLY MURDERS 11-YEAR-OLD BOY

SPOKESMAN-REVIEW

April 15, 1992

The Light Killer identified an eleven-year-old boy, who has been missing since Friday, as his third murder victim. The boy's name has been withheld at the request of the family.

The suspect, who refers to himself as the "Light Killer,"

began to claim in January that he murdered young children in Spokane. Each of the children he has allegedly killed remain missing persons, according to police sources. To date, the Light Killer has claimed two boys and one girl as victims. Each of the three children suffers a disability or illness.

Police Chief Todd Harrington said at a news conference today, "We must assume now that all the children are dead. This third victim is a tragic new development for the family, for the children and families of Spokane, and for all of us. The Light Killer Task Force is working around the clock. No child is forgotten—this includes the children who have been missing for months now. We are doing everything we can."

Police and FBI authorities repeatedly note the difficulty in pursuing a killer who does not leave behind a crime scene.

All elementary and middle schools in North Spokane and the surrounding area have also hired extra personnel and recruited community volunteers for after school patrols. Two of the children disappeared after school.

Local churches as well as the synagogue and mosque in North Spokane also have increased security. "It is as if we are under siege," said Rabbi David Rickerson of Temple Beth Israel. The synagogue hired private security to monitor all of its events after a ten-year-old girl disappeared near the synagogue's North side location.

Fifth Episcopal Church, of Hastings Road in North Spokane, formed a network of church volunteers after a nine-year-old boy disappeared. The victim and his family are members of the church.

"It's the same story everywhere," said Unity Church Minister, Rev. Deedee Swarthart. "Houses of God are not

> safe; nowhere is really safe. We pray, but we also band together to care for our children. Unity Church has formed a Safe Church Committee, which meets two times a week."
>
> The Light Killer Task Force is providing three police officers for community education in school, church and neighborhood safety. Block Watch directors in all North Side neighborhoods have been encouraged to take advantage of the community educators in uniform.
>
> Task force co-director FBI Special Agent Bernard Washington asked area citizens to be patient, to report anything out of the ordinary regarding their children, and to turn over any potential evidence or leads to authorities.

Above her in the sky, Beth saw a long spiked cloud that looked like a dinosaur spine. Putting the article down, chills running through her, Beth stared at the cloud long enough to watch it breaking, with glacial slowness, apart.

Beth shifted her glance toward the river gorge and saw an earth-bound rainbow arched over a stretch of pine trees. Pine and maple trees stood alert all around, their branches caught in breezes just as they tried to relax. Everything was so lined with death today. Would any of the other articles mention the WSU sweatshirt? She wanted to read all the articles but feared them, as if they were alive.

"Here's some tea," Greta said, coming up behind her. Beth rose immediately to help, but Greta set the tray on the ground between them easily, and both sat again.

Beth asked, "What if pain and suffering, especially when they're really concentrated, are a magnet. For what, I don't know. But Auschwitz—it was like a magnet."

Beth wasn't sure what she meant but Greta always knew

how to speak of such things. Greta knew about the world of spirits like no one else.

"I remember when I was working as an anthropologist," Greta said. "I came back to the States from Mexico because my father was dying. I sat with my father alone there in his hospital room one hot afternoon, and I remember feeling like other friends and ancestors sat with me, as if they were attracted—or magnetized, as you say—by the dying. Later that day I asked my old favorite auntie Hurta about it and she told me that when there is a terrible sadness in a person or family, many of the ancestors come around to help. Years later, when my Francis died and I was grieving, I felt him coming to help me from the world of the dead. Sometimes I still do."

Will I make it to Greta's age? Beth thought, sipping the iced tea. "A lot of what's important in life is hidden," she nodded. Beth was glad she had come back up to be with Greta.

Greta seemed to read her mind. "It was kind of Nathan to let us ladies have some privacy."

"Nathan's meditating down by the water," Beth said, feeling she must bring up the articles, and feeling how carefully Greta was waiting for her to do so.

"Perhaps," Greta mused, "perhaps he's trying to see if he can leave a fingerprint on the water."

"What a beautiful, impossible thought." Beth grinned. "But if anyone would try it, Nathan would. Nathan and me—mainly me, I guess—we've experienced today so many of the things you've talked about for years. Those lights rising from a seam between a huge boulder and the earth—they were lights, spots of light in the air, like seeing stars when your head's been hit. But they weren't circling stars, they were shooting, diving, laughing lights. Nathan saw them too. These little lights, like dots, fireflies . . . it was like I felt they were the ancestors, the spirits, coming to help us. That was the feeling I got. They were almost real to me. They could have been light through the leaves, but I knew them as more."

"Some might say they were angels who came to help the Romers today."

"Do you think so?"

"Well, angels are energy, after all; we only anthropomorphize them into cherubs and old pudgy men in James Stewart movies. I mean, really, why couldn't they be palpable energy that you could see, in this altered state you are in?"

Beth closed her eyes. "Teach me, Greta. I'm so vulnerable." Beth felt the glow of the hot sun and felt herself glowing with the world, as if she were a body but also pure soul. She didn't like sunglasses and never wore them, but now her closed eyelids worked like glasses, tempering the sun. She sat back and for a second all life's confusion was gone, and her own aliveness did not frighten her.

"Today it's like I'm part of some alien experiment, Greta, and my mind's been altered. Like *The X-Files!*"

Suddenly a loud sound exploded from the right.

"It's all right," Greta said, realizing what it was in a second. "It's Harold Svoboda getting ready to mow his lawn for the second time this week. You leapt, Beth!" Beth had not realized it, but at the sound of the mower trying to start she had jumped in her chair.

Now Beth turned her head to see Harold, Greta's neighbor, the tall white-haired man dressed in red flannel shirt and overalls. He shut the mower off, bent to a gas can, then poured gasoline into his mower.

Beth felt an urge to get closer to Harold—to get up from

her chair and become physically closer. If he had acknowledged the two women across the lawns, it must have been a wave or a look while they were preoccupied, for now he concentrated only on his work.

"Greta," she said, "these visions, these experiences I'm having. Am I going to be all right?"

"You're going to be all right," Greta said, hoping it was true. She followed Beth's eyes back to the Svoboda yard and Harold's work.

Beth felt an immense urge to go over there. This was strange. Why such a powerful urge?

Beth saw Laura, Harold's wife, through the window of the Svoboda house. Laura was tutoring a teenager at the dining room table. Beth felt a pull toward Laura, who was standing up now, walking with the girl away from the back window. Both Laura and Harold had always been so nice to Jeffrey.

The sudden thought of Jeffrey brought unbidden inner sight of yesterday's carnage. Beth began to tear up. She closed her eyes and the tears receded. She just felt so damn many emotions today!

Turning back to Greta, Beth asked, "Do you think Donnell is dead now?"

"I just don't know, Beth. I haven't seen any EMS vehicles over there yet."

"Why can't I 'see' if he's dead? I mean, I'm seeing amazing things today, the remote viewing, clairvoyance—whatever it is. But I can't see things I *want* to see. Like whether I'm really seeing children being killed. I sense that Donnell is dead. I sense grief over there. Whoever is with him is spreading grief out of that house now. I can't 'see' it, but I sense it, like I might hear a song on the radio in the background."

Greta formed words, knowing that it was her role to do so, and hoping she knew the truth this young woman needed. "I think you are in some sort of altered state. I think you are a soul and spirit enlivened by contact with other souls and spirits near you. You are in a very sensitive state. Your visions will take many intuitive forms. Do you sense anything else?"

"No. I'm still confused," Beth said, then added, "Thank you for being here, Greta. And for knowing things."

The older woman laughed. "My dear friend, I hardly know a thing."

Beth said nothing, letting the humble response pass. People like Greta, who had spent time in many places, were often the humblest people around.

"Did we do right, are we sure we did right, letting Donnell die?"

"As you ask the question, what is happening to your sensitivity, my dear?"

Beth closed her eyes and felt alone, her intuitions gone, her "sensing" gone.

"Let your intuition tell you if you did right . . ." Greta was saying. Now something else was happening. Beth listened to Greta's words, but found them vague compared to a fierce pull she felt toward Harry and Laura Svoboda's. She nodded at Greta pensively, in a gesture that might appear polite and distracted, turning her head to the neighbors' house and seeing two new people in the yard gazing at Harold. They were about his age and looked like him—they must be his parents, Beth thought. How could this be?

Beth stood up to go toward them, moving by force other than her own. The two "people" turned toward her and smiled, smiles that carried eternal gladness in them, pulling

Beth even further toward Harold. These people wanted to talk to Harold through Beth. It was suddenly obvious to Beth, so obvious she didn't think to find it crazy.

Beth turned to Greta and said, "I'll be right back. Something . . . I'll explain in a moment." Beth felt her bare feet on the lawn as if she were walking on cool fire. Voicelessly, she begged the two people not to leave. She walked slowly. She had the sense of too loudly rumbling the earth.

But they remained standing there, smiling at her, and smiling too at their son who, seemingly oblivious, pushed his lawn mower across his summer grass, his body languid with the routine motion on this hot, sleepy afternoon.

5

The Visitors

THE WEALTH OF sounds started for Laura with a train rumbling far off in the valley. When the wind was just right, Laura heard the Burlington Northern rattling its wheel cages. With the sound of the train came a hawk's shrill call, then an airplane's low roar on the hawk's edge, then two magpies shrieking, in the center of that loud mechanical brush stroke. Laura felt her ears—chock with hearing aid in the left and dust in the right—open like a child's ears to the carnival of pleasant noises. A sparrow in the eaves pushed its tiny chirp past the end of the plane; then an osprey, trilling and tweeting as it flew the river, passed the sparrow's sound.

Generous, the river gorge flicked its baton at a squirrel who dropped a pine cone on the tin deck roof, startling Laura's tutorial. Sixteen-year-old Meredith jumped, her chair scraping slightly, then exhaled a barely discernable whistle as she ruffled through her social studies book for a page of questions. Laura listened, mesmerized, as the girl's whistle became the edge of a drip of water at the sink, then the wind chimes on the back porch, then a duck quacking.

Laura felt as if her ears had left her body. They lay like young girls out in the meadow, swimming and listening, the sound of water coupling with a pine cone, then a *bang,* a gunshot in the valley, and then another, then the sound of her husband, Harold, readying the lawn mower, then a sudden memory of her son, Chris, calling into the cabin up at Priest Lake all those years ago, "I got one, Mom! My first rabbit!"

Meredith considered her tutor. "You look like you just remembered something."

Laura laughed. "I . . . heard something fly by." Like a sweet spirit paying a visit, she thought. She giggled her old-woman giggle, which her tutorials all loved.

Meredith giggled too then said, quite practically, "All I hear is my dad saying, 'You got a D. You're grounded.' " She imitated her father's low tone, burying her chin in her neck. Just outside, a sparrow chirped its delight. "Layne . . . you know? My boyfriend? He says he thinks my father's okay."

Meredith wore her blond hair very short. She had pale blue eyes, clear skin. She wore a good deal of makeup, a push-up bra, and a thin blue blouse. She was a popular girl, Laura knew that—insecure too. Meredith asked many questions about boys, men, the world. Sitting over her Contemporary Social Studies book she did not look tall, but she was five eleven, a center on Mead High School girls' basketball team. Her height could be a burden in the world of boys and dating. Laura remembered. She herself had been five ten, though in her day there had been no basketball for girls to play.

At sixty-nine, Laura's once-blond hair was gray and thin.

"Wispy," Meredith once called it. Laura was a thin woman who wore jeans and white blouses and short hair and tried to keep a positive outlook on life. Especially after what had happened to Jeffrey, Laura knew she lived for a second chance today, Meredith a sweet distraction while she waited for the phone call from her son. She was listening to Meredith talking about a boy now, here on the edge of something else that had just happened, or was still happening perhaps, something she wished she could grab hold of. It had something to do with a confluence of sounds, and all the animals of the river, coming to visit. She heard Harold's lawn mower, moving toward the backyard, invasive. He would be distracting himself in his own way, overwhelmed by Jeffrey's accident and the wait for a phone call from Chris about the imminent birth of their first grandchild—perfecting his immaculate lawn against the backdrop of the wild river.

Laura tried to focus on Meredith's narrative as she heard the word "Jeffrey."

"Last night, Layne and me? We were talking, like, about little Jeffrey, right? About him dying yesterday? I can't believe it happened just right out there. Anyway, I cried, and Layne kissed me and touched me, but then he got scared again! Boys are so scared! He didn't even try! I think boys grow up too slow. It's like what you told me—they mature late. It's frustrating. I tried to talk to Mom about it. She's, like, in the mode of"—again the chin-buried imitation of the grueling parent—" 'With AIDS and teen pregnancy, why go looking for trouble? Let the boys be immature.' It's like she thinks I'm taking drugs or something! I love Layne. He loves me! Mom doesn't get it. God, Mrs. Svoboda, if I didn't have *you* to talk to . . . you know what I mean? Are you sad about Jeffrey?"

"He died, and I saw an amazing light," Laura wanted to say, "and since then have heard little events of sound . . . and I'm so sorry for Landry and Marti . . . and I dreamt about Jeffrey last night . . ." Laura wanted to say many things, but knew she must say nothing for a while. She saw her own hand on the table next to Meredith's, old bone beside young flesh, one gold wedding band beside three garish rings. She looked at Meredith's blue-gray eyes, wishing she had wisdom for the girl. She wanted *not* to sound like "Mom." She remembered many years back with her own daughter and felt a nostalgic yearning that mixed, at the edges, with regret.

"When I was your age," Laura said, touching Meredith's blond hair, "it was 1941. Harold had left engineering school for the war. I didn't know him well yet. I had my woman's body, but I knew nothing about being a woman. I had never even masturbated."

Meredith giggled and Laura smiled, staring out the window at the high pines of the lake gorge that peeked over the top into her backyard. She saw Harold cross with the lawn mower, and over him she saw Donnell Wight's house on the ridge. "I have to put a little sex in a story every once in a while, don't I?"—she winked—"just to keep you young people interested?"

"You're too much!"

"Anyway, there I was, sixteen, and totally innocent—we lived in Northern California—Sebastopol. There was a young man who lost his leg in the war. He lived down the block—oh a year, year and a half older than me, I guess. I felt so sorry for him. I'll bet he was a bit of your Layne, and a bit of little Jeffrey. There are patterns to things and people, even across the generations."

"Jeffrey!" Meredith sighed, her chin crinkling with emotion. "It's horrible!"

"You go ahead and have a good cry if you want." These children were so full of emotions, always on the edge of some expressiveness. Laura didn't have to think too long to remember her own mother—cool, aloof, not unkind, but a self-proclaimed Puritan. Laura was a more passionate woman, more like her father. Her passion had nearly destroyed her marriage and family. Christopher found out about her affair and said he would not speak to her again. For almost a decade, relations had been nearly nonexistent between mother and children. Who can ever describe the pain of a mother's regret? Just after he learned of her infidelity, Harold had carried on an affair to punish her. But then, after nearly divorcing, she and Harold made peace. They found a new kind of love. At seventy-two, he needed her and, in his way, loved her. Her children had their own lives. Neither kept marriages for long, Chris now, forty-two, Jenny, forty-one. No kids—until now. After another bout of silence, Chris had written a postcard, "My girlfriend's nine months pregnant. I'll call when the baby comes." Reading the card, over and over, Laura had welled up with tears. "Please give me another chance," she murmured at the postcard. "You're not the only ones who have lived in loneliness these last few years." Harold had seen the note and a wave of tears came to the back door of his eyes like the whole lake wanting, yearning, to push through. Laura had cried for them both, and he held her. The phone call was all she needed now, all she could hope for. That her first grandchild would be born and would reunite her family. All night she saw and heard the carnage of Jeffrey and thought she would lose her grandchild in the womb.

"I'm not going to cry, not anymore," Meredith sighed. "I've cried and cried. Everyone liked little Jeffrey so much. Finish telling me about the injured guy in the war, Mrs. Svoboda."

Laura touched Meredith's shoulder, staving off an urge to squeeze her in embrace. "Well, yes, all right. My point had to do with . . . oh, I don't know what. I'm a little spaced today."

"You seem kind of, like, preoccupied."

"I am, Meredith." Laura leaned back, trying to find a beautiful meadow to lean into. She closed her eyes. Why not just come out and say it? "I'm scared, Meredith, I guess that's it."

"Scared? You? Of what?"

"I'm scared my grandchild will die, or that I'll never meet him, or her . . . oh, I'm . . . just scared. I'm waiting for a phone call, waiting, that's all, like a girl waiting for her first date, I suppose, or like my mother waiting to hear if my brother was killed in the Pacific. We all worried over phone calls in those days, or telegrams. The waiting, even at my age, is hard."

"You know, Mrs. Svoboda. I hope I turn out just like you when I'm old . . . old*er*, I mean. You know? You're so honest."

Laura just breathed deeply. "Let me give you a piece of advice. Don't trust honesty. It can be faked." Laura thought of that amazing light she had seen above Jeffrey's body, and the strange feeling of peace it had given her, a feeling that everything would be okay. "Live for passion, but don't let it control *you*. Be joyful. Sex, love, work, art, kids, honesty, politics—none of it is the truth unless you live it passionately. But none of it will mean much to you if you become irresponsible. No matter what all the TV shows seem to tell you: being irresponsible is not the same as being free."

"You just sounded like a mom," Meredith chided her.

Laura grinned. "Well, I'm going to take that as a compliment!"

Meredith grinned too, then said, "Hmmm." She frowned. "I have to think about what you said, I guess, Mrs. Svoboda." Maybe, Laura thought, the young couldn't understand—they who lived passion so unconsciously. To understand it consciously they would need to create circumstances that needed redemption. They didn't really need redemption yet. What sins could little Jeffrey have had that needed redeeming? None, surely. Sick from the age of two on, dying, and then dead, yet still seeming so lit from within.

Laura heard the lawn mower go off. She leaned forward over the dining room table and the open books and peered out to see that the back lawn wasn't done. Harold peered at the little engine, wanting more gasoline? Now he came back toward the house. Laura heard the door open in the back of the kitchen.

"Should we continue with your questions, Meredith?" she asked, turning back to the social studies book. Harold clinked ice in an iced tea glass in the kitchen. "At your age I wanted good grades, and that's it. I wanted to be a teacher." She looked at the page from Meredith's book right in front of them. The Civil Rights Act. 1967. She remembered that year: just starting to think about going back to work, just feeling a renewed passion to teach, now that the kids were in school. She was filled with passions she could never get Harold to understand.

Meredith studied again the list of questions her teacher had given her to answer. Laura heard birds chirping, then Harold move out the back door, then a squirrel running across the grass, then the sound of the lawn mower starting up again.

"Nineteen sixty-seven." Laura smiled, nodding her head in

memory. "It was like the beginning of a new era. Harold and I—we actually got into antiwar activities pretty heavily—well, me. It was my passion."

"Cool." Meredith sat back.

Laura paused for breath. "My son, Christopher, went on a march with us when he was six—he pointed to the American flag and said he saw angels on it. I remember Harold said, 'Son, those are stars.' 'No, they aren't, Dad,' he insisted. 'Those are angels.' How funny the memories a person can have."

Now it happened again, just as Harold and the lawn mower crossed the window frame. Though the noise of the mower cut off all present sounds, Laura fell into a meadow of old sounds from the antiwar march—the calling over megaphones, the strings of a guitar playing within the sound of a song, voices low and familiar, the sound of footsteps, the buildings of San Francisco looming up and around them, the feeling of her children's hands in hers. Now a ringing sound?

Laura rose to answer the phone. She picked it up but there was only a dial tone.

"Didn't the phone just ring?" she asked Meredith.

Meredith looked at her blankly. "No, Mrs. Svoboda. It didn't ring."

Laura smiled sheepishly. "It's this hearing aid. Come on, Meredith, let's get back to work. Enough of my nonsense. Do you know the definition of a Puritan, Meredith?"

"Like with the Mayflower?"

"No no, this is a joke." Laura laughed even before telling it. "A Puritan is someone who's afraid somebody, somewhere is having fun."

"That's my parents!"

"That's everyone's parents, I suppose. Come on now, let's

get back to work. Nothing so special is going to happen right now that we can't do what we're here to do."

Now the phone did ring. "There's the phone," Meredith said. "You had a premonition."

Laura answered it. Yes! A premonition.

"Mrs. Svoboda?" It was the voice of Meredith's mother.

"Hello, Gail."

"Is Meredith still there? I need her to come home. One of the cars broke down and I need her to help look after Billy at soccer. Paul's at work. . . ."

Laura turned the phone over to her young protégée and stood back, watching Harold from the window. Gail's fluster reminded her of her own previous busy times with little children, and how fast the world could run. Fast, of course, except when you yourself were waiting for a grandchild, and a role again. We could use an angel now, Laura thought. Was that light last night an angel that came to take Jeffrey away? She found herself, only a mildly religious person, suddenly, inwardly, talking to the light: "If you are an angel, our first grandchild could really use an angel at his shoulder now."

"I have to go," Meredith sighed, hanging the phone up. "Can I come back tomorrow?"

"Of course. Same time." Meredith packed up her books and Laura looked out the window at her husband, tall, gaunt, determined Harold, pushing his green Yardman lawn mower.

It was what he did when he waited for angels—he worked on that lawn. As Laura said goodbye to Meredith the wealth of sounds she had heard was reduced now to just the roar of the lawn mower, but she listened to that carefully, near the phone.

★ ★ ★

Harold Svoboda, who had the best garden on the block, had just turned seventy-two. He and Laura bought into Lucia Court years ago, before any construction, when it was supposed to be a retirement village. Greta and Trudy had bought also and, though Harold didn't know it, so had the Romers, who had been told something else—that it would be family oriented. The developer, everyone finally learned, was in the process of going belly-up, and the development got "rethought" by new partners. It ended up a hodgepodge of concepts, the younger people moving in—nice folk, all of them, but not quite the plan. Because Harry and Laura liked the river access, they chose not to take the new contractor's offer to sell their land share at a profit. They got their house built and stayed.

Now, there were only themselves and Greta and Trudy, for "elderly" folk; the rest were young people—Sammy Range and his mom, Sally McDonald and her mom and dad, Annie and John, the Romers and that sweet boy Jeffrey. It was a little like old neighborhoods used to be, where young and old lived around each other. Harry thought of Jeffrey's broken body, then shook his head at Fate's insanity, bending to pull the cord on the mower.

The mower awoke on the first pull, and Harry began his contemplative ritual of cutting grass, pushing the mower across in diagonals, as he liked to do, and watching each row of grass soften. He had long thought cutting the grass to be one of the only absolute successes a man could have in life: each row an accomplishment. And nothing quite made a place look nice like cut grass.

Jeffrey, he murmured to himself, it's all a circus anyway, you know. Sure you do, you know it better than me. He pictured a circus as he moved to the hum of the mower. The flaps of a circus tent opened up every few years in a neighborhood, and a person could see, really *see*, what a colorful chaos life is. But only for a moment. Always the flap closed quickly. That light last night. Was that the opening of the circus flap? Had that light even appeared at all? Everyone saw it: it must have happened. No one really wanted to talk about it. But word would get out.

Thirsty, Harry stopped his mower and walked toward the house. He recalled his glass of iced tea on the counter. As he walked across the half-cut grass, he felt a strange chill, then a warmth. He stopped, peering about, noticing Greta out in her yard with Beth. He waved, though the two women were facing outward, toward the river, and did not see him. He turned back toward the house, entering the back door, finding the sweating glass of tea on the counter. Draining it, wiping sweat off his forehead, he refilled the glass with ice and liquid, choosing not to disturb Laura and young Meredith.

Stepping quietly back outside, he set the now-colder glass on the edge of his wood deck. The screen door paused, like a pause for breath, then shut behind him.

Harry went back out to the mower and started it up again. He felt the sun's warmth from an almost cloudless blue sky, but he also felt a strange warmth coming from near him, near the flowers to his left. Looking there, his glance again went to Greta and Beth, who were talking; he was aware that his face must appear stern, his posture too. Behind his old gray eyes accustomed to work, he knew himself to be one of those men who were what they appeared to be: small nosed, lips without emotion, eyes looking straight at the world, posture erect, a man ready to help. He had lost fifteen pounds since his retirement, which worried Laura. He wondered how it would be to be as large as Beth who sat there with Greta. Beth had a shyness in her that Harry wanted to see beyond. She was like Jenny had been—an observer, like her father.

Harry bent to the mower and turned it on again, aware of being watched. He turned to the women, but they were not watching him. Shaking his head, confused by the feeling, he turned the diagonal, starting north, thinking he must be very bored to imagine being watched. He had been experiencing a lot of boredom lately. The bloom of retirement was over. He felt too old to travel much, so he just walked, slept, watched TV, did some fly-fishing, played a little golf, went grocery shopping, talked a little talk with Laura, and stared at the river gorge. He admitted it to no one, but he was lonely. When he had rushed to the wreck yesterday, alerted by the terrible cry of metal hitting metal, his body had suddenly, if momentarily, remembered what it meant to be completely alive. Last night he lay in his bedroom listening to Laura tossing in hers. He wanted to talk to her, ask her what she thought of the strange light, of poor Jeffrey, of her life, of her husband. He couldn't ask her the question that frightened him the most—is our grandchild going to die too, so young? Will we be allowed to see him?

Harry had learned somewhere decades ago that a man could choose who to be in the face of life's basic insecurity—he could choose to regret his deficiencies, his own oversternness, his preoccupation with neatness, his lack of social skill, his sins, his feelings toward his children, which they took for being "not-loving-enough"—or he could choose to treat his deficiencies with a friendly distance, as one treats an old relative, or a pet. Harry had made this kind of peace with himself;

it was a peace he held on to as he let his automatic lawn mower pull him gently along. Laura wanted something from the phone call, wanted it desperately. Harry wanted it too but he feared it. The circus door might open again, two days in a row—first with Jeffrey, then next with a grandchild. The circus flap might open, and his grandchild might be killed before it lived. No reason to get too attached to the idea of a grandchild.

Harry felt himself getting agitated and didn't like it. He focused only on the rows of grass being cut under him until he had finished the lawn. A bead of sweat dropped off his right eyelid onto the lens of his glasses. He did not stop to clean them until he had finished the grass and could turn off the mower. He pushed the mower back to the deck and pulled his handkerchief out again, cleaned his glasses, then walked his mower to his garage.

The smell of fresh-cut grass was everywhere, like perfume in an elevator. Harry put the mower in its corner, bending to brush some blades of green off the engine. Then he walked the few steps toward his outdoor broom, held it firmly in his palsied hands, swept the grass out the garage door. He replaced the broom, confirmed that his job was done, and started back out of the garage to the deck, where he found his sweating iced-tea glass.

Beth was walking over toward him from Greta's. She was such a large woman, her skin color a darker than average pigment, though she wasn't black, perhaps a little Hispanic in her, or Indian. She wore thick glasses over her blue eyes and walked with a lope, a little strange for a short, squat woman. She wore a dirty white T-shirt under which her big breasts moved up and down like waves. She wore blue jeans almost as dirty as the shirt. Her hair was matted, greasy brown. She had the look of someone who'd been camping at the river.

"Mr. Svoboda," she said, seeming a little nervous, her right hand rising as if to be shaken. He wiped his wet hand on his pants leg, switching the iced-tea glass first to his left. She shook his hand firmly, then moved her arm right, pointing toward the rhododendron just behind them. What was she pointing at? The flowers?

"I'm not sure how to tell you this, Mr. Svoboda," she said. "But right over there. Right beside the rhododendron. Well, sir, I'll just say it."

"What is it, Beth?"

"Well. The thing is. You have visitors."

Laura had just finished a glass of iced tea when she saw Beth with her husband through the back window. Seeing some kind of irritation, even incredulity, on her husband's face, Laura put her glass down on the kitchen counter and walked to the back door to join them. As she came out, Laura heard Beth say, "You are glowing, many colors, rising off of you, as am I. Hello, Laura."

"Hello, Beth." Laura smiled. "It's good to see you. You're back up from your camping?"

"I came back up for a minute, to visit with Greta."

"I haven't been able to get Jeffrey and . . . last evening out of my mind." Beth carried a weariness from the world of the woods and the water, but her eyes twinkled with extra energy. She was fidgety nervous too, pointing to a spot by the rhododendron. "How are you doing with it all, Beth? You were so close to Jeffrey."

"I'm . . . well . . . fine," Beth faltered. "I was just trying to tell Mr. Svoboda . . . Harold. I don't know how to say this to you, but there are two people . . . two spirits . . . here . . . right here . . . who want to talk to you. I sense they want me to help. They say they are Harold's mother and father."

"What?" Laura found herself grimacing and stepping back a little against Harold. Harold frowned, looking about, not for a sight of the spirits, but to see if this insane woman had brought friends with her.

"I know it sounds weird," Beth said, "but it's true. They've been standing here awhile. They know you are about to get a phone call and want to talk to you about it." Beth seemed to say this without knowing she was about to say it, as if her own knowledge surprised her. She seemed to cock her ear up to the left as if preparing to hear something.

Harold cleared his throat. "I don't know how you knew about the phone call, but yes, we are waiting for one. As to these . . . spirits . . . well, are you taking any drugs?"

"I'm not," Beth said, standing up a little straighter. She did not seem hurt by his comment. In fact, it seemed to give her time to listen to something. "Your mother wants me to tell you that you turned seventy-two ten days ago; you were born in Rochester, New York; she called you 'Goopy' when you were a baby because it was the first thing you said after 'Dada,' and you said it while you were looking in a mirror on your hands and knees. She says she can see everything, and everything is going to be fine. You shouldn't worry."

Laura's breath caught. In his shock, Harold put his arm around his wife.

Before Harold could respond, Laura knew something was happening here that he might have more trouble with than she.

"Beth," she jumped in, "it's possible that you could know about his age and birthplace, but how on earth did you know his mother called him Goopy?"

Harold was frowning. "And the mirror? She's right, Laura. What is going on? What are you up to, young woman? Have you been talking to Laura—Laura, did you tell her?"

He pulled at the sleeve of his yellow golf shirt nervously.

"Harold, I didn't tell her anything. Beth, tell us what's going on."

"Laura," Beth said to her, pointing again to the spot beside the flowers, "Harold's parents have come to talk to him. It seems to be about a phone call you are about to get. I know it sounds strange, but I have been having a very strange day at the river. Since that light—last night—something is going on. Your mother and father know about a phone call you're going to get. You're going to get a phone call, right? I mean, am I just going nuts or is this really happening?"

Beth clearly had some sort of power and was an innocent in it. To Laura, she genuinely seemed confused, yet saw what she saw and heard what she heard, for there was no way she could have made this up about Goopy or know about the phone call, nor was there reason for her to do so.

"We are hoping to get a phone call today, yes," Laura said calmly, gripping her husband's arm.

Beth continued, "Harold's mother says to tell you her name is Victoria and her mother's name is Harriet—so you'll believe she's really here. Harold's father says he wishes Harold would cock his arm back better when he throws the fly into the water, and he has to quicken his wrist, or the fly won't catch the water right. Harold's mother says she lost a baby just before Harold was born and another just after, and she knows he used to make up names for these children even though they never lived."

Harold was wide-eyed and speechless. Laura looked at Beth then at Harold who murmured, "How could you know . . ."

"Does any of this ring a bell?" Beth asked, though from Harold's response the answer was clear.

"She couldn't have known these things," Laura said to her husband, using the moment to get her own bearings. "This has been such a strange time. Jeffrey yesterday. Today so many sounds. The phone call. Is something happening to the world?"

"Are my parents really here?" Harold asked.

"They are here." Beth nodded. "Do you want to say something to them?"

"I . . . this is so . . . well, I mean . . . they died when I was young . . . are they all right now?"

Beth paused only an instant then spoke. Her eyes were a little glazed, yet she seemed very alert. "They are fine. They have remained available to shepherd another life that is coming into your family. Your mother is saying they had to finish something, and it's about the phone call, and it's going to be fine, and when it's done they'll feel they've finished their jobs here.

"You are both glowing, you know? It's not just the glow from your parents, it's your own."

"Glowing?" Laura murmured.

Beth nodded. "You're glowing, like the light from a sun." Beth bowed her head. "I don't know what's happening to me. I see things."

Laura came away from her husband and over to Beth,

touching her shoulder with her right hand. Beth seemed a little scared, and Laura did not want her "powers," or whatever they were, to end.

Beth looked up at Laura, smiled, then looked over at the two spirits. Laura thought it seemed as if Beth was hoping they were gone. But they were not.

Beth looked into Laura's eyes. "Harold's mother says that you knew when the baby was born, you sensed it earlier today in a . . . in signals and a weaving of sounds from the river . . . does this make sense?"

"Yes!" Laura cried. "There was an incredible moment of so many sounds . . . like visitations. That's what I meant when I said . . . Anyway, the baby was born *then?*"

"It seems so. Energy moves along strings or lines of some kind and moved to you, even though your son and . . . and . . . his friend, yes, not married, I see that—they live in California, is that right? The baby was born there?" Beth could tell it was right and didn't wait for an answer. "Harold, your father says that you should no longer worry over the cousin who died while you were both boys; it was not your fault. He died in no way in relation to what you did. Does this ring true?"

Laura looked at Harold and felt her heart open for his, pumping with his, as his eyes began to become teary. For so long he had carried the wound of responsibility for the death of an eight-year-old cousin.

Beth was talking quickly again. "He died without effect from you. And he was meant to die. He had finished his mission in the world. His spirit is related in some way to the baby girl that has just been born into your family."

"It's a girl?" Laura blurted out.

"Oh yes, it's a girl. You are going to get the call soon. These visitors have come to tell you that everything is going to be fine in your family. They say to tell you, Laura, that you have nothing to fear, and that both of you will be happily reunited in loving friendship with your children, and what is needed is for each of you to remember how it feels to be new parents, and forget everything else. You are not to worry anymore, and you are to remove something, some anguish some . . . betrayal among you and your children . . . you are to remove thoughts of it . . . and the coldness from your lives that is like an icy dew on the strings of energy you and your family weaves together. I'm sorry . . . I don't really understand this very well. It's like they are talking through me but my words are messing it up."

"No, no!" Laura cried, "it's okay. We can understand." Laura felt a wash of warmth through her, flushing her cheeks.

"Is our granddaughter going to live a long life?" Harold asked, his voice faint in the afternoon air.

"She is going to live to be an old woman," Beth said firmly.

"I want to believe you," Harold said. Laura squeezed his waist.

Beth cried, "My God, the colors around you, Laura, they're . . . it's like they're imploding and changing. It's like you have a cloak that's changing color. And you too, Harold, only a little less. What the hell is going on? I promise, I'm not doing any drugs."

"I know you're not, Beth," Laura said. "Something's been happening all day. Will you ask Harold's parents something for me?"

"Okay."

"No. Don't ask them anything. Just thank them for us."

Beth nodded, but as she did she frowned. "They're fading away. They are kind of composed of white light, and the light is just fading away, into the flowers. They seem to be happy with themselves.

"Look, here's Greta."

Laura had been so preoccupied she hadn't noticed her neighbor coming over. Greta, always in her wonderful long baggy sweaters, had a kind of limping, loping walk all her own. She used her cane to traverse the grass.

"Greta!" Beth cried. "Something has happened."

Laura felt for a moment the invasion of her neighbor, and then felt how old that feeling was, and then told Greta she had a granddaughter. Harold came over and touched his wife's shoulder, and Beth, who had been the center of the moment, stood a little frazzled and unsure, beside the scene of old people talking and embracing.

The phone startled everyone so fully that Laura cried out and ran into the house.

"Hey, Mom!" the voice exclaimed. "Hey, you sound out of breath."

"No no." She sniffled, covering her tears. "What . . . what has happened?"

"We've had a girl, Mom, a little girl."

"Oh, Chris, how wonderful!" Laura cried. "Oh, Chris! Congratulations!" Harold came in beside her and she saw Greta and Beth still outside, out the window, their eyes inquiring.

Laura nodded her head vigorously, a big "Yes!" and watched Harold go out the kitchen toward the living room and the other phone. Once he picked up the greetings started again, more clipped between son and father, but greetings for sure, and the news echoed again. Laura listened to her son giving her and Harold the brief version of the story. She loved the sound of his voice as she had loved it decades ago, when he was a boy. She heard a little of his coldness to her in it, but the love in it too that becoming a daddy enforced.

He had a million calls to make and hung up. Laura found herself weeping, and Harold came to her, and then Beth and Greta came in for a report, and they all held each other in the embrace of words, feeling joy at the promise of new life.

Laura cried, "It's a second chance. My God, Harold—a second chance."

Harold, the circus tent completely open, felt his eyes water.

When all words had been spoken—words of thanks and of hope—Beth and Greta said their good-byes, and Harold opened the door for them into his backyard. He closed it, returning to Laura, and for a moment, Beth and Greta stood by the rhododenron, silenced by Beth's new power.

Then, as if they had just lost something beautiful but knew it would not return to this place again now, they set out to look for it back in Greta's yard, walking across the Svobodas' freshly cut lawn.

6

The Return to Innocence

Part 3: The Light Killer Series
Spokesman-Review
May 2, 1992

As the city of Spokane comes to grips with one of the most violent and painful criminal episodes in its history, the Spokesman-Review has chosen to print the latest letter from the so-called Light Killer. The alleged murderer has claimed to have killed three children. The letter is not printed in full because of graphic violence not suitable for a family newspaper.

"Dear Citizens of the World,

"Do not think you can stop me. I have found my very beautiful place in the universe. There is nothing so beautiful as a Child healing in my arms. All the calamities of Life build up for days and weeks and I become a dark Soul em-

bittered by the world, and then the Light comes to me, burning images into my mind until I wake! I pay attention!

"Out of this light comes a hurt or sick Child walking, a little boy or girl, walking. I see the girl as if I have already met her. I know the boy is real and I know I will find him. I become a hunter, a hunter after the Sick Child I have seen.

"Then I find the my little Child of Promise. Sometimes it takes weeks, sometimes days. I have helpers. Their vision is sometimes better than mine. They serve me for no other purpose than to find the child who has come to me from the Light.

"Do you know the Light Maker? The Creator? The Creator makes Light out of Darkness. The Creator inhales darkness and exhales light. This is how I feel when I hold the child in my arms, that I can breathe again, breathe Light again. I can only breathe darkness out for so long, then I must again find the Light and inhale the grace of God."

The watcher walked away from the campsite. He had nearly stepped into the little meadow where the male camper sat meditating. The large short woman was gone. The watcher moved silently away from the man with the rose-red birthmark on his neck. The man's eyes remained shut, the watcher unseen. The watcher touched his hand to a boulder, felt warmth. How filled the valley was with warm spots, light spots, like this. "Here's a gift for you, red-marked man," he thought silently, dropping his mother's stone near the boulder.

Walking away, the watcher luxuriated in a feeling that started in his stomach—a surge of adrenaline, and of need. He saw in his mind the rail-thin girl with anorexia, Amanda, whom he would bring to him tonight. Closing his eyes, leaning against a tamarack, he pulled down his hood and lifted his face to the sun. The lust and luxury overwhelmed him with smells—the sap of the tamarack, the river's algae, fragrance of a nearby flower. Opening his eyes, he looked at a huge honeysuckle bush, spikes of white-flowered branch shooting out everywhere. He moved to it, burying his nose in the flowers. What a fragrance.

Closing his eyes, he swooned with grace. The Light was here again. It had been for two days. Tonight he would satisfy it. And he would smell honeysuckle. On the girl, he would smell honeysuckle. He was sure of it.

Inhaling deeply, the watcher raised his head from the flowers. Would he be able to cure the girl? Each time he took a patient, he came closer to the full successful power promised by the Light. Jeffrey would have been a very great challenge, greater than this second choice, this girl with an eating disorder. But the light had taken Jeffrey. Second choice became first choice—the easier patient to boost his confidence, perhaps. Oh, if only the world could see what he saw!

The watcher moved to the water's edge, squatting to wash his hands. He washed them many times a day, always thankful for the feel of water on his flesh. As he lifted his dripping hands he saw faces on the water, two very old people, gray-haired, a woman and a man. He often saw faces, heard many voices—these did not startle him. He wondered if the old people would speak. They seemed dressed as if from another time.

They disappeared as quickly as they came. "Nothing?" he murmured. "Nothing for me?" He listened to the wind, hearing the breath of Light. "There will be more voices soon, won't there?" he asked the wind. His stomach coiled with anticipation. A headache would come in about an hour, his head as if in a vise. Then it would go. Then the girl, chained and docile and ready to be healed. Would tonight be the night? He was so close to full power. So close.

Beth put the newspaper article down, smelling honeysuckles. She became almost breathless with the beautiful smell. There were none here, so why the smell? She sat in it till it disappeared.

Nothing happened as she read the article. No vision. Just a terrible sadness. Beth knew she shouldn't have read it, so quickly after the beauty in the Svobodas' yard. Yet the article had been irresistible. She and Greta had walked back from the Svobodas', but then Greta's daughter called, from somewhere on the East Coast. "Sit, dear," Greta had advised, cupping the receiver as she spoke. "Let the experiences settle in you." Beth had felt slightly dizzy. She'd lain back a moment in the plastic chair, basking in the sun, recalling Harold's parents, who were already as if in a dream.

Then, too soon, she had opened the envelope of articles jammed under a chair leg. "Maybe I might see something," she'd thought, "be stimulated in some helpful way, especially after seeing Harold's parents, and light around Laura and Harold." She was in such an intuitive state.

But now, even as a part of her couldn't resist reading more of the sick mind, the terrible tragedy—like a rubbernecker on a freeway after a wreck—she set the papers back down. "If I can help these children," she begged God silently. "Show me how."

"Here I am!" Greta called. Thank God Greta was back. Beth helped her old friend place iced-tea glasses and brownies between the two chairs.

"Is everything all right with your daughter?" she asked.

"Very well," Greta responded. "Now tell me what happened."

"The Svobodas' auras, Greta, I saw their auras. Do you realize? I've never seen auras before."

"Were there layered colors?" Greta asked, sipping her tea.

"Yes!" Beth sat back down. She could picture it clearly. "I saw an inside layer of whites, yellows, and pastels on Harold, then outside layers that were darker, like purples and navy blue. I saw less color-contrast on Laura's aura, but everything a little to the darker side—darker pastels. I saw the auras expand and contract. When Laura was talking to Harold's parents, her aura was very thin at first, but then it really began to expand. It expanded so much it seemed to include me and everything around us—the grass, the shrubs, the trees. When this happened I *felt* it, I mean I really did, as if it touched me. When it contracted again, you know, when our time together was finished, I felt sad, I missed its touch."

Beth looked for Greta's aura but couldn't see it. She felt a little disappointed, like a child who has just learned a secret but can't use it.

"Do you know what the soul is?" Greta asked. "What it is when we think of its actual physics and chemistry?"

"It's anything theological thinkers and the living want it to be, of course. But you mean, what is it if we actually thought of it as a physical thing?"

"Yes."

Beth had never thought of the soul as a physical object.

"Well, Beth, what if you've just seen it?" Greta smiled.

"The aura?"

"What we call the aura is probably the visible manifestation of the soul—the true color of Love."

"But the auras I saw were *outside* the body. The soul is *inside* the body. At least that's how we always think of it. The soul is . . . I don't know . . . it's the 'pilot' inside the body. Like Plato."

Beth felt a soft swift breeze. Greta must have felt it too, on her cheek, her right hand moving automatically to touch just below her eye. "Do you remember the movie *Peter Pan,* my dear?"

"Of course."

"Do you remember how the girl had to sew Peter's shadow back on him?"

"Yes, of course. He lost his shadow. That's why he came back to London, and that began the whole adventure."

"What if we picture the soul like his shadow?" Greta closed her eyes, speaking as if she were exhibiting a dream. "It is anchored, or attached, to the body at the toes, the feet, the legs, the genitals, the solar plexus, the throat, the crown, and so on. It is sewn on, and in. Peter Pan had a spirit, a body, and a soul. He lost his soul, remaining alive with spirit and body, but not whole. He returned to rediscover his soul, got assistance from the girl, angelic assistance, and had his soul reattached, returning him to a state of wholeness, self-protection, even adventure. And he opened other children's lives to their own souls—their own shadows, their own never-never land. Whenever we retrieve our souls, we are always inspired to serve others to retrieve theirs.

"You, Beth, were able to see people's souls today. You are lucky to actually be able to meet the soul as a visual phenomenon. Most people cannot. Most people have to rely only on imagination."

Beth embraced herself, crossing arms and rubbing at goose

bumps along her flesh. How wonderful to feel everything so profoundly ordered and encompassing.

"It's so much, so much to think about." Beth closed her eyes and recalled the two visitors in the Svobodas' yard. They had seemed somewhat alive, yet not alive. They had spoken, yet not spoken. It was as if they were there, by the flowers, but also inside Beth's head.

"When Harry's parents were there," she asked, opening her eyes and picking her words carefully, "when they talked to us, I called them spirits, that was what I felt I should call them, but were they? Were they the *souls* of those two dead people, or the *spirits?*" Suddenly, Beth resented the conundrum she was creating. "Never mind. I don't know."

But Greta answered. "Beth, the mind makes complicated what is really very simple. The mind is still undeveloped and afraid. Don't be afraid. What does your intuition tell you?"

"I think they were part me and part themselves. It was as if they lived in me, yet they had to be Harry's real parents because I myself couldn't have known what they told me about him."

"Is it not proof, my dear, that we are all absolutely One? When anyone ever doubts that all things are interconnected, you will know the sadness of their doubt. You will know that all is one, and you are one with all things, capable of being one with visitors from the past, long dead. Did you see today, near the rhododendron, a 'spirit' or a 'soul'? These are just words. The answer is both, for soul and spirit are never too far separate. The soul is always protecting the spirit. The visitors, the 'spirits,' as you called them, had not completed their mission while embodied, and so they waited, ever-patient, until they could finish, before they moved to their next mission. We should not think today was the first time they have helped their son, Harold, and his family. They have been nearby, helping all the time. Today, however, *you* were here, able to use more of your mind than most of us, able thus to see them, to speak for them."

"I feel like I've been touched . . . by God. I hope I'm not being arrogant." Beth knew she was in a kind of shock. She felt as if God had put a sumptuous kiss onto her forehead and awakened some center of her brain that had been dormant. She felt that God, the infinite energy of the universe, wanted her to run a race that never ended. She knew sometime in the next day or two she would collapse from exhaustion, but all she could do now was drink from an endless cup.

Beth had to stand up, had to change the position of her body. She went to the edge of Greta's land and looked out over the water, letting the wind touch her, pulling her focus out of her head and into the wind, the sound of water, the birds. She saw Donnell's soul expanding to touch the souls of the deer, birds, insects. She saw auras of light around each animal, insect, plant, and the human, expanding to meet each other, touching, feeling utter trust as they touched. She saw in their touching some immense effort of universal contraction and expansion, and recognized it as breathing. She saw life itself breathing, in and out, pushing energy to expand and contract like the rising and falling chest of a small child.

"God is breathing," she whispered. "Life is what happens as God breathes in and out."

Greta stood up to join her friend at the edge of the gorge.

"Look at those hawks!" Beth pointed. Flying over Donnell Wight's house and the cliffs over there, some ten or fifteen hawks were circling and gliding. The windy air seemed to touch each bird like a feather touching the upraised palm of a hand.

"They're trying to communicate something, I suspect," Greta said, leaning on her cane and peering out over the gorge.

Beth tried to focus on one of the hawks, the one highest up, then the next, then the next. She went back to the chairs for the binoculars and looked at the brown-winged, white-bellied, red-tailed hawks more closely; each was beautiful, soaring in its own way. Beth looked over at the Wight house, then onto the cliffs. She saw some people walking past the dam toward the cliffs, and someone walking away from the cliffs. She thought the big hairy man with the swim trunks was walking away from the cliffs. Past him she thought she could make out two teenage boys walking up the back of the cliff side.

Greta asked for the binoculars and looked at the hawks.

"They are so beautiful, and so many of them," Greta muttered aloud. "I haven't seen that many in a long time. Does it have something to do with Donnell? They're near his house."

"I wonder how Nathan's doing?" Beth asked, her attention to the hawks and the cliffs interrupted suddenly by a pull toward Nathan. There seemed a darkness near him. And honeysuckles again!

"He's fine, I'm sure," Greta said, touching Beth's arm. "Come, come have more tea. Sit a minute. I want to show you something."

Greta walked her three-legged walk into the house. Beth watched the hawks gliding and moving until the honeysuckle smell lifted again. She found her own breath gliding and moving in some motion just like the hawks'. She had the immense sense of harmony in a symphony when the whole orchestra breathed each part in perfect synchronicity.

"Beth?"

It was Nathan's voice.

"Nathan! I was just thinking about you!"

Nathan emerged from over the edge of the gorge, running across the backyard.

"Beth, I can't stay long, but I have to tell you something. Take this." His pack was not on his back. He only carried a stone, about an inch in diameter, round, mainly black with filaments of gray and white.

Beth took it into her hands and she felt a jolt of electricity shoot through her. She was back, suddenly, at the rock where all the lights had appeared earlier in the day.

"My God!" she cried, dropping the stone.

"It's amazing," Nathan exclaimed. "There's something on this rock. I felt it too, a little. I got it from right at the seam where the boulder hit the earth and we saw those lights."

"Wait," she said, suddenly seeing in her mind the two teenage boys across the gorge, just beneath the hawks. Their image overwhelmed her. Why was she pulled toward them? One of the boys was definitely Alex Bass, she saw, the black teenager with glasses—the other, Caucasian, his friend, Brent, whom Beth had met once or twice in the neighborhood. They were about sixteen. She saw that the hawks were trying to help the boys. Yes, that was it—the hawks were communicating.

"Is one of the boys going to fall?" she asked aloud.

"Who?" Nathan asked.

She told him and they both got up and went back to the edge of the yard, Nathan carrying the binoculars. "I see them," he said.

"No, they're not in danger," Beth saw suddenly. The two boys were going to be fine. The hawks had something for the boys that involved danger, but not immense pain. What exactly, she didn't know. There was light reflecting off the hawks now.

"Why, in the face of mystery, do we think of danger first?" she asked the air. "There's so much else."

"You want the binoculars?" Nathan offered.

She turned back into the yard, shaking her head. "We have to let their spirits breathe. Everything's going to be okay over there. I'm sure of it. There's a kind of dark presence near the boys, but the hawks have them under wing. What am I saying? I don't know what I'm saying. So much has happened here, Nathan. I'm going crazy!" She laughed, pulling at her hair like a mental patient. This brought a laugh from Nathan, and she sat back down.

"Tell me about this stone, Nathan," she said.

"I just found it there and felt something. Tell me what has happened up *here!* What do you mean, so much has happened?"

Beth collected her thoughts, trying to understand how to explain the visitors.

Nathan sat, holding her hand.

"I don't know where to begin," she said, but the words were a beginning, and she realized she had to start writing some things down again. Telling her story, she pointed to the rhododendron bush across the yard, feeling that urge she often got: to write. At moments, listening to her, Nathan sat incredulous. He asked lots of questions. Finally, she confessed she wanted to get the experiences down on paper. Nathan grinned, recognizing this state of mind in her. He watched her rummage in her daypack for her notebook.

"You should read some of those articles," Beth said, pointing as she pulled her notebook out. "Greta collected material on the Light Killer. You remember we read about him in the paper last month?"

"Yes," Nathan confirmed, "Spokane's serial killer."

"Let me get this down, then I'll tell you about that too. Greta has a theory. Greta thinks I might somehow be sensitive to this . . . evil stuff," Beth said, her pen moving.

"There could be a connection with the light we saw," Nathan agreed, skimming an article set on top of a pile of clippings. "God, this guy is sick." He read of a man trying to heal sick children then killing them. He sat up and moved back to the edge of the river gorge. The breeze greeted him there, and he let his body sway just slightly, like a quiet pine, towered and touched by air. Beth saw him there, delighted by him.

"Nathan," Beth said. "Read what I just wrote. Right here." Beth gave him her journal. "Some of the sentences I'm writing come from me, but it's like they're from some voice speaking through me. It's not really my style of writing, you know?"

Nathan read aloud words written in her neat cursive:

" *'Why do certain human beings feel they must believe that we already know all there is to know about the workings of the universe? To survive our human, ontological insecurity must we believe we can know no more about the spiritual physics around us than what we are told by traditions? Is it not possible that to understand even an iota of the spiritual physics we must listen to every possible voice and learn every possible language? Is it not true that God speaks not in one tongue but in every tongue?'* "

"This is *you* writing?" Nathan frowned.

"I don't know. I wrote some things earlier today that didn't seem like me. Now this too. This time it seems sort of . . . sad."

" *'Changes in perception are more frightening even than death. Changes in the way we will live and heal others and ourselves are frightening to complete.*

" *'What shall we define as a new perception or, better yet, a new "revelation"? Shall we say that a revelation is an experience of being told, by a loud bearded God, what to do next? Is the word "revelation" to be used only when one has been hallucinating? Is something a revelation when a thousand people, or even a billion, have accepted it as such, and relatively worthless, in comparison, when only* you *have experienced it, or felt it, or heard it?*

" *'Who will answer these questions? I will. I am.'* "

Nathan looked up at Beth. "This is not you."

"I know."

"What do you feel when you write it?"

"It just comes automatically," she said, moving her fingers to touch the clippings about the Light Killer.

"I am related to this evil stuff. I just know it," Beth whispered. "Greta's right. I just don't know how I'm related. Did you read the newspaper interview with the psychologist?"

Nathan shook his head.

"She talks about thinking the way a sick man thinks, and I wonder if that's why I think my writing is becoming like a man's and I wonder if I'm being affected, and what affects me, and how. Am I reading this . . . this killer's mind, his thinking? Is he writing or thinking the things I'm writing down? Would he say things like I just wrote down? That would be too weird, right?"

"It would be pretty weird."

Beth dropped her hands into her face. "I'm so sensitive. Everything is a vibration that can affect me, but I can't see what's really going on! If only I could see more, see into the dark more clearly. I'm between the light and the darkness. It's a crazy place to be."

Nathan closed the journal and watched as Beth touched the newspaper clippings. Her brow furrowed with concentration as she read, reading like someone trying desperately to see truth in tiny newsprint words. He came beside her, leaning against her, reading with her as an airplane crossed the sky overhead, and the sun, at its peak, heated the skin of their arms and face.

PSYCHOLOGIST PROVIDES THEORIES ABOUT LIGHT KILLER
SPOKESMAN-REVIEW
May 6, 1992

Dr. Adelle Tourtellotte, a local clinical psychologist who is a special consultant to the Light Killer Task Force, answered questions yesterday about the abduction and murder spree that has haunted Spokane for the last three months. An individual, signing "the Light Killer" on letters addressed to the Spokesman-Review, claims to have abducted and killed three children since January. The children are officially missing persons.

SR: Dr. Tourtellotte, we should let readers know you have been asked by the Spokane police, the FBI and the special task force to speak to the press.

AT: Yes. We are trying to get word out about what kind of man to look for. There is a $100,000 reward, as you know, for the successful capture of this man.

SR: You're sure it's a man.

AT: We are, yes. When you read the letters, you notice a lack of the kind of concreteness you would expect from a woman, and more of the abstraction you expect from an adult male writer.

SR: There is a certain way that men and women write letters of this kind that is different from each other?

AT: There are infinite ways we are different, yes, and this kind of letter writing is one way. This is not a woman.

SR: And can you guess the education level of this man?

AT: Yes. The perpetrator has at least a college degree and maybe has been to graduate school, probably in one of the sciences, and perhaps in religions.

He was brought up in a Christian religion but has experimented with other religions. Some of the profile consultants wonder about a satanic cult.

He is well read in esoteric literature, probably from the middle ages, and written by Christian Church writers: St. Augustine, St. Thomas, Martin Luther, and so on.

He appears to suffer a number of mental disorders, but manages them through esoteric practices, and through his hidden brutality, so people around him will not know him except as a gentle man who has a bit of a temper, at times, and seems remote.

He is probably no younger than thirty and no older than forty. He is probably not married.

He is Caucasian. He is probably just under six feet.

He is probably a very neat person. His house will be very clean. His shirts will be pressed.

On the task force, we have come up with a "top three" list of job possibilities. We think he is either a teacher, in science or math; a low to middle level business manager; a health professional.

SR: A doctor?

AT: No, we do not believe so.

SR: And even though he's very concerned with religious matters, you don't believe he's in the clergy, or a deacon, or a church employee. Why?

AT: I don't believe he is in a primary leadership role in a church. He may be in a lower role.

SR: Your conclusions are so specific. What do you base this kind of profiling on?

AT: We look for clues in language, grammar, hermeneutics in general. For instance, not only does he write a great deal about or in religious language, but with a certain vocabulary. In one of thc letters he used the word "noncorporeal." Along with other clues, this ties the perpetrator to Christianity that has been studied in some sort of scholarly way. The whole motif of light and darkness fits along the lines of ancient or medieval Christian poetics.

Also, the ease with which this perpetrator seems to write speaks to us of his education. I lean toward him being a teacher. The tie-in to math or the sciences is difficult to explain. It's an instinct some of us are having about him.

SR: Profiling is more an art than a science, isn't it? You could be wrong about these details.

AT: We are probably wrong about twenty percent of these details.

SR: Your profiling, and the work of many others, has led to countless phone calls and "tips" but none have turned out to be worthwhile yet. Isn't this true?

AT: Yes. Unfortunately, it is. There are 350,000 people in this city. This man may be very hard to find.

His arm around his lover, Nathan read what she read; he hugged her and suddenly felt goose bumps on her. He watched her face as her eyes squinted, holding her even as she let out a low exhalation, like a shrill whistling, then like a moan, both of pain and of recognition. She brought her hands up.

"God, my head!"

"What kind of pain?" Nathan asked.

She stood up. "Shooting pain."

"Are you okay?"

She breathed in quick breaths, holding herself.

"I'm okay, but my head suddenly hurts."

Nathan asked her more questions, but then she silenced him, just feeling the pain in her head. As it subsided, she looked out over the river gorge. "It's a dull pain now. Let me see the binoculars." It was as if she just had to look through them. Nathan got the binoculars off the ground for her, and she looked through them toward Alex and his friend.

"What, Beth? What is it?"

"Wait!" Beth hissed. "I'll know in a second."

"Was it like a sudden migraine?"

She swathed a visual path with the binoculars. She was definitely looking for something. Her eyes settled on some flying hawks for a second, but then descended into the forest on the other side of the river valley.

Nathan looked across with her, seeing hawks on air, then a beauty of pine trees tussled by breeze, quaking aspen, red rock and weedy rock roses on the sides of cliffs across the way.

"Is it there?" Beth cried. "Is that it?"

"What?"

"Wait. Now something else. What's that?" She closed her eyes, concentrating fully, her posture erect, not her usual slumped shoulders.

"What, Beth?"

Beth handed Nathan the binoculars. "Shhhh," she whispered, stepping two paces away from him. Her eyes still closed, she murmured, "Something is happening. The boys, the killer, the images from Bible . . . shhhh . . . the pain's gone . . . I have to follow. . . ."

Nathan searched the forest for something she had seen, seeing only pine trees enhanced in the lens. He felt an urge to get an answer from her, right this minute, to what was happening. He lowered the binoculars, turning to her. What about the Bible?

He said nothing. It was not his job to rush her in any way, he thought, his sudden retraction of impatience showing him, in an instant, how impatient he had always been in life. He sat back down on the grass, setting himself lotus style, breathing in and out, and concentrating on his breath. Beth remained standing, shivering in the sun.

Within moments, surprised by the immense peace he felt, Nathan moved into a state of meditation, entered it easily, more easily than he had at the river. His mind cleared of all content, even of waiting for Beth's voice; he was not himself for more than a moment, monklike, without inhibition or expression either, simply like an empty canvas, or a house not yet built, or as if a mind could be washed clean.

"I see it!" Beth exclaimed. "There's something there!"

Nathan rose out of his reverie and asked, again, "What?"

The watcher saw the hawks too. He did not see Beth and Nathan on the ridge, but he saw the boys. They were too old for his purposes. And they seemed in no way ill or injured. The watcher had been feeling, for moments, a presence of some kind, like a strange mind inside his. It was like being eavesdropped upon. This was a new and very weird feeling for him. Never before, as his healing energy built in his cells and moved him toward a child, had he felt this bizarre invasion of consciousness. An image of Cain and Abel had come into his mind. Why that image? Because there were two young men up there—that must be it. But the images came with the strange feeling. And the hawks were part of it. So many hawks near him. Why? No, not just near him, but flying over the two boys. Into his mind came an image of the boys jumping off the cliff into the water, first the black kid then the white one. There was no separation between himself and the boys. Future and present dissolved. The watcher saw it all so clearly, saw the boys, naked, hitting the water. The watcher felt immense power.

Was this some new phase of his abilities?

There were so many omens today. So much power. Oh, if they had him at Area 41, or in a government agency! If he shared his secret powers, where might the world go? Superman, Spiderman, the Incredible Hulk—these were fiction. These were made-up stories of people who have special power. He was fact.

Watching the hawks, the watcher waited for the strange feeling to come again. Did, perhaps, the hawks understand that he was the future—the future the world feared?

Part III

Of Gods and Children

7

Hurt Hawks

THE TWO BOYS were not men yet, not quite sixteen, at that age when they thought they would never be men, fearful even at urinals that their smallness would be noticed, yet full of themselves when the world was not looking too closely. Fitting their age, the world had opened to each of them in the last few months, an arcade that intimidated as it aroused. Though this new confusion was what they yearned most to talk about, neither had the words, or if the words, not the courage to speak. Theirs was the timidity of adolescent boys who are everyday faced with change.

They had known each another for thirteen years, since they were three, their mothers becoming friends in co-op, the boys playing together at preschool, then at playgrounds, then in each other's house. Brent, now tall, gangly, blond hair to his shoulders, ticketed by police once already for driving his father's car without a license, and threatened by his father with "never driving my car even when you're old enough," carried in his skinny body a wilder spirit than his friend, Alex, shorter, African-American, his family the owners of one of the newest houses in Lucia Court.

Brent liked to ride his flash-red Honda motorcycle the mile and a half between his house further north and Alex's by the river. He liked swimming in the calm lagoonlike pool just south of the cliffs above which stood the huge wooden house owned by the old doctor. He liked stripping down to nothing, flaunting himself in front of Alex, who was less developed, shyer, and easily embarrassed. Mad at him once for his flamboyance and "craziness," Alex had called Brent "an angry kid, always trying to show you're bad." Alex was right and his friend knew it. At school, Brent had been watching two Crips from a distance, wondering about gang life. Unlike Alex, he had tried crack once, sucking a pipe that scared him with its power. If not for that fear, he could really get into crack. If not for his need to keep things in control—even as he pretended to like craziness—he would quit school, run away, say fuck it to everybody. If not for his friendship with Alex, he thought he could really go haywire. Brent had never said it aloud, but he knew that if Alex died, the way little Jeffrey had, he could die too.

Alex had been on the phone with Brent when he heard the crash. He had hung up fast and rushed out; when he got back home an hour later, more upset than he could remember ever being in his life, he called Brent back. Before the hang-up, Brent had been on Alex about how "into" being a Muslim he was becoming. The two friends had been mildly arguing. When Brent heard Alex's voice on the callback, Alex was subdued. "Brent," he said soberly, fighting back tears, "Jeffrey's dead." He described the carnage. Then he said, "And something else happened . . ." Alex had begun to say more, then stopped himself. "What?" Brent said into the phone. "I don't know. Come over tomorrow." Brent said okay. He had felt a strange kind of numbness, or tingling, just as he had hung up the phone the first time, the time Alex rushed away because of the crash. Brent had felt a kind of blanking out, then a sense of being up in the air, a little dizzy and floating. It hadn't lasted long, and it hadn't been scary. It had given way to argumentative thoughts. Yet when he wondered what Alex was concealing, Brent felt this tingling again. He had vowed to ask Alex about it as he hung up the phone the second time, but by today he thought little of it. Alex hadn't volunteered anything—he was more silent than usual, sad about young Jeffrey. Brent left him pretty much alone today.

Brent and Alex had played with little Jeffrey just a month ago when Mr. and Mrs. Romer brought the kid down to the lagoon for a swim. Little Jeffrey had squinted up at old Donnell Wight's house and asked his mom about the huge brownwood structure. His mom, a sad-looking woman, thin and stiff but with big boobs, told her son the old man was said to be strange. Jeffrey, pondering the house on the hill like he was set for *Larry King Live,* said seriously: "It's a house where angels live." Mr. Romer said, "Could be, son," and the mom, whose name Brent never learned, laid out the picnic, responding not to her son but politely to the presence of her neighbor, Alex, and his friend, with an invitation to fried chicken, potato salad, and pop. The older boys refused politely and went farther along the trail to a more hidden spot where they resumed diving, swimming, and lying out on the hot rocks like seals in the sun.

Today they had begun their journey into the river forest along a deer trail that led to the suspension bridge. They crossed it and jumped into the underbrush at the other end, climbing to rock cliffs fifty feet above the water. At first, they met a man there lying naked on his large, hairy stomach. Every once in a while they met someone at this remote spot. Today, the man became disturbed by the presence of the teens, as if he were looking for privacy and just couldn't seem to get it. He donned his shorts and packed his fanny pack and water bottle. Alex, so typical, apologized to the man for bothering his nap. The plump man waved off the apology and started away.

Brent pondered if perhaps today he could find the courage to do what the man, whose hair had been glistening wet, must have done—the fifty-foot dive into the water. Brent wanted to do the dive more than anything, but he froze whenever he looked down from the high point. The green water reflecting gold on the surface where the sun touched and black in the shadows—the rock formations all around and across—the roar of water in the middle of the river but the stillness below these cliffs: all made him feel like a scared kid who let water and rock and distance and fear turn him into a nervous turd. At least, being with Alex, he didn't feel one-upped. Alex, even more a nervous kid, wouldn't contemplate diving this height.

Watching the man receding, his hairy back, his paunch, his fatty ribs, Brent pulled his own shirt and shorts off, proud of his nakedness. Where the man, like Brent's father, had lost hair in patches at his knees and calves, Brent gained it with a glistening blond fullness. Where the man's cock and balls draped under flab, Brett's hung from a flat stomach and pelvis. Brett measured his erections every few weeks, always at the moment his masturbation brought him to just before the explosion—

figuring that at this moment his cock would be largest. He had reached 6½ inches, measuring from the tip to pelvis, and 6 inches when he measured from the scrotum.

He longed to ask Alex if he measured his organ but hadn't wanted to risk admitting his own sexual vanity. Probably Alex, because he was black, was going to end up with a bigger cock anyway. Why should he measure his? He and Alex hadn't talked about their bodies in about six months, since Alex stopped stripping at the river. The coming of manhood drew the boys farther apart, not closer, at the time when they needed each other more than ever, more than, Brent often thought begrudgingly, they needed anyone else.

"Look at the hawks." Alex squinted, pointing over toward Donnell Wight's house.

Brent looked up, following his friend's gaze. There were seven or eight hawks gliding up there.

"I've never seen so many!" Alex exclaimed. "Jesus Christ."

Brent, too, had seen four or five at a time, but never this many. They circled high up along the invisible currents in the lakes of air above the plateau and the huge house.

"You remember the poem Mrs. Quinn taught us last year," Alex said. "About the hawks."

Brent lay down on his stomach, the sun's heat on his back and buttocks arousing him with a slight quiver. He looked upriver where last year a spot fire had burned a bunch of acreage. Now the blackened trees were a dull brown, almost a gold in the sunlight.

"Remember, man?" Alex said. "It was a poem called 'Hurt Hawks.' "

"Yeah, I remember. But these hawks don't look hurt."

"I was thinking of Jeffrey," Alex said. Alex was so deep, always thinking, always feeling things. Brent tried to feel as little as possible about Jeffrey. He couldn't believe he had seen a tear come to Alex's dad's eye when he talked at the house about the dead boy. Everyone loved Jeffrey like they loved Jesus or someone.

"Jeffrey was pretty cool," Brent begrudged, closing his eyes. The birds chirped all around. He enjoyed the sound, remembering his mother's quilt when he was little. She made it for him herself, a patchwork of meticulously sewn robins, blackbirds, and sparrows. She always loved birds, keeping at least ten bird feeders in the yard. This was one of those things he had come to love about his mom and hated about her at the same time.

"Jeffrey was an old soul," Alex sighed, sitting down in rocky grass some ten feet away. Brent opened his eyes. How weird Alex had become lately.

"How come you sit way over there, man?" Brent squinted an eye closed against the sun's glare as he cocked his head up to look over at his friend.

"I don't know," Alex murmured, squinting upward toward the hawks. Brent turned again too, following the sound of a hawk's high whistle. All but one hawk seemed to have settled, for the moment, in a tall Douglas fir. Two crows or ravens—Brent never quite got the difference—flew at a lone hawk that must have gotten close to the crows' nest. The big black birds darted and cawed, the hawk finally tiring, returning to its buddies in the fir. Brent saw clearly the hawk's brown-white talons as they fastened onto the high branch. Just as they fastened, quivering the tree, three of the other hawks rose up, spreading their wings and ascending in spirals. For a good three minutes, Brent found himself watching their gliding. They cried out a few times, regal, smooth on the air. He found himself envying them. He felt they wanted to tell him something. It was a strange feeling.

"How far down do you think that is?" Alex asked. Brent brought his eyes back from the sky to follow Alex's gaze. His friend's blood-white eyes looked over the fifty-foot cliff.

"Nine thousand feet." Brent grinned. Alex always asked how far down the water was. Brent always added thousands of feet.

"If the hawks can fly," Alex said out of the blue, standing up and brushing off his bottom, "I'm going to fly."

"No way!" Brent laughed.

Alex pulled his glasses off, placing them on a rock. He pulled his shirt off, revealing a brown, muscular, and shiny chest, hairless and touched, between the pecs, by a bead of sweat that the sun hit just as Brent's eyes hit it, giving the skin under its glass bead a momentary color of white lavender, like a liver spot on black skin. Alex left his sockless tennis shoes on but pulled his khaki shorts and boxers down over them. Brent tried not to look at Alex's genitals, but his eyes went to them and he thought a second, "I'm bigger than him." But when Alex moved purposefully to the cliff edge, poised, his eyes upward toward the hawks, Brent rose up on his palms, like a push-up, then came to a sitting position.

"What are you *doing*, man! You really gonna do it?"

The naked half-boy, half-man did not look down or around. He said, "I see such a beautiful light on those hawks. It makes me want to fly. I see something else too. It's so strange, Brent. I'm seeing . . . someone . . . so clearly." What was Alex talking about? Alex kept looking up at the hawks, as if they spoke to him. There was some kind of light illusion going on:

Brent thought it was as if strands of electricity shot through the air near the hawks and Alex. He seemed to be nodding his head, even murmuring. What was that light?

Then Alex put one hand to his nose, clamping the nostrils, the other over his genitals, and stepped off the cliff.

"Holy shit!" Brent cried, jumping up and rushing to the edge. Alex screamed his way into contact, disappearing into a foaming, volcanic splash, the slap of his feet and hands on the water echoing up to his friend, who thought for a second of drowning and death and a body washing up into the cliffs. Then the body rose and Alex shouted, "Oh man!" shooting up through the surface of the water.

"Oh fuck that was intense!" Laughing, Alex slapped the water twice, fast, then swam back toward shore.

Knowing he must now jump too, Brent felt paralyzed with fear. If he didn't jump, everything would be screwed up. Everything he had thought about himself and Alex—Alex the brave one, he the wimp. Brent felt nauseous as he looked down. He looked up at the circling hawks, finding no inspiration in them nor the reflection of light any longer, only an increase of giddiness.

"Fuck!" he hissed. "I'm a wimp!" A hawk screeched as if in answer. Alex had reached the shore. He looked up at his friend but said nothing. Brent looked out at a car on a road far off to the north.

"I see a light on those hawks," he said, as if his friend's words were the magic words of courage. "It makes me want to fly."

The words did nothing for him, so he closed his eyes and let out a terrified yell, and jumped.

The air, inconspicuous until his moment of flight, now

suddenly became palpable. Brent grabbed at it, groped at it, flailed at it, his body, like a baby's dropped by a mother, grasping and careening and falling away. When in split seconds it felt as if the air would hold on to the flapping arms, the air always let go, and before the descent could be corrected, Brent's whole being smashed into the calm glass and was consumed, exploding into a mass of cold, his lungs caught in the moment just before drowning, but the body kicking up, propelled by frantic movements, into the air again.

"Holy fuck!" Brent screamed, twisting his head so his hair flew off his eyes. Naked, pausing in his climb back up the rocks, Alex laughed with his friend. Brent swam hard toward him, happy to see a smile he hadn't seen all day, happy to be in one piece, happy to be alive. Touching shore, climbing up, peering at his friend's hard, brown-black buttocks above him, Brent couldn't stop grinning. He felt as if a huge old burden had lifted. He thought he heard whispers around him, tiny voices. What the hell was that? Shoving a finger in his right ear, he tried to get the water out. He didn't listen any longer, yelling up to Alex, "You're crazy! Alex, you're crazy!"

"It's the light, and the hawks," his friend responded, breathy from the climb. "And it's Jeffrey. I have to grow up." Alex made it up to the top, disappearing over the ledge up there. In a few moments, Brent got there too. His friend lay supine, glistening in the sun, his elbows propping his torso up. Seeing Brent, he grinned.

"I'm shrinking!" Brent shrieked, looking down at his own cold-tiny genitals and pointing to Alex's.

"Me too!"

Brent dropped down next to his friend. He felt the strange urge to hug Alex, or something strange like that. The urge sent a shock wave through him like he had felt when, a few years back, he had his first sexual fantasy involving a guy. He knew from sex ed it was normal, but its strangeness had a taste, a touch, a feeling all its own, as if his body had wanted it deep down in its hidden nature. Brent had asked Alex two years ago when they talked about such things, before Alex got silent, if he had dreams about guys. Alex confessed he did.

For some reason, Brent saw himself on the bema, at Temple Beth Israel. He was reading the passage he had read for his bar mitzvah, about Cain and Abel. He was thirteen. He had two sisters but no brother; the story of Cain and Abel did not apply to him. He lay on the cliff but saw himself reading the Hebrew on the bema. *"In the process it came to pass that Cain brought of the fruit of the earth an offering to the Lord, and Abel also brought the firstlings of his flock, and the Lord preferred respect on Abel's offering but not to Cain and Cain became angry at God. . . ."* He felt Rabbi Jacobson next to him. Rabbi Jacobson had said the story of Cain and Abel was really about humility—Cain failed the test, he wasn't able to be humble and patient; he let his ego rule him. "You don't want to be that kind of man, Brent."

Brent closed his eyes to the hot sun, overwhelmed by the reminiscence—himself at his bar mitzvah, gliding the silver quill over the Torah, everything lit with radiant light. Fuck! A huge and terrible shuddering moved through Brent, like a terrible feeling of evil, a dark feeling, a shame and a rage and a sadness all in one.

Brent felt a breeze on his wet skin, a shrill sound of hawk, heard himself pray silently, *"Baruch attah Adonai, Eloheynu Melech Ha'olam . . . "* reciting the prayer of forgiveness, then *"Ve Yisgodal, Vey Yisgodah, sheymey raboh . . ."* the prayer for the dead. He could not stop himself from praying, or from seeing Jeffrey floating over the meadow. Brent saw the boy there and was filled with a sense of calm, as if he were watched over, guarded by the boy. Jeffrey was completely healed. No wheelchair. Brent felt Jeffrey's presence, and he felt something dissolve his armor. From within it, he returned to himself, opened his eyes. This was the strangest moment of his life so far.

"That water was *cooooooolllld!"* Alex grinned.

"Oh mama, hold me," Brent whined, "I'm coooollllld," a sweet mocking whine, accompanied by arms embracing himself. He was back to himself. It was like he had been dreaming of Jeffrey and his bar mitzvah—it was like a hallucination. Jesus!

"Jesus, look!" Alex cried.

Brent followed his friend's eyes; all the hawks were coming straight for the low cliffs. Attracted, perhaps, by the noise of the boys, they had all taken to the air, flying at three levels, in random groupings.

"What the hell is going on?" Brent gasped.

"It's a blessing," Alex said. "They know I'm okay. Muhammad was here. Muhammad and Jeffrey are telling me I'm okay."

"What are you talking about, bro?" Brent frowned. "Muhammad?" He started to say, "I saw Cain and Abel, and Jeffrey too."

The hawks flew over the boys with two screeches. The screeches were whistlings, so close, so loud, not thirty feet above; the hawks circled—Brent saw that one of them had a broken black wing, like a comb missing a tooth; all the hawks with white necks and hooked beaks.

"I've never seen them so close!" Alex exclaimed.

Watching the hawks in a wash of vulnerability that was foreign to him, Brent thought of Jeffrey—"it all started with him, man." All those years of cancer, and he didn't ever seem scared.

Alex pushed himself up, opening his arms upward.

"What are you doing, man?" Brent whispered.

Alex said nothing, just stood naked, his off-color cock and balls small in his cold groin, his arms up like Moses or Jesus, the hawks circling above him.

It had come with goose bumps, as she read the end of the interview with the psychologist. She saw a man carrying the little girl's body toward a cave. She saw a church and she saw a mosque behind him. This didn't make sense, because she was sure that the cave she saw in her mind's eye was across the way, where those teenage boys, Alex and Brent, were climbing. How could there be a mosque with a single spire, and a church with a steeple near a cave in the river gorge?

And the hawks—the hawks seemed to fly above the boys and the cave and the man carrying the little girl. It was all one scene in her mind, and it made her shiver. Beth took the binoculars, stared into them across the valley, searching for the cave. She couldn't see it along the cliffs the way she saw it so clearly in her mind's eyes. It wasn't there. Nor of course, were the religious buildings. The teenagers were there, yes, and she knew she had seen, in her mind's eye, a cave, just under the cliff the boys had climbed, yet a cave her reason and memory confirmed was not there. She and Nathan had walked and sunbathed in that area three or four times before. There was no cave. Was she now hallucinating? Was she seeing images in another person's mind? How could she see this girl being carried to the darkness?

Beth felt she was caressing up against a terrible darkness.

Nathan wanted her to talk. "What's going on?" he pleaded. She knew she mustn't talk yet. She shushed him and moved away, closing her eyes. She saw the man again now, not his face, but his body—he seemed muscular, medium height, wearing jeans and a hooded windbreaker that was blue like the jeans. He carried the girl over his left shoulder toward the entrance of the cave, inside of which there was a glow from a lantern or flashlight.

The pain began behind her eyes again, spreading through her head and down her back, like a shock wave that passed through her and out. The vision left her mind, the man and girl gone, replaced by an emptiness for a moment, a sense of purity that somehow pulled her to Nathan. This lasted moments, then a terrible sense of loneliness propelled her away from him, back into a kind of inner flight over the river valley, toward the teen boys. She had lost any sense of self, felt only that she was floating or flying, like the hawks, buffeted in direction of instinct or service. She seemed to be gliding directly to the teenage boys, who needed her somehow. She was pulled to them like water filling a container. She wanted to see more of the man carrying the girl. She tried to see him, but felt so pulled to Alex and Brent.

She saw Muhammad and Cain and Abel near them. Why was this? How strange! These ancient people from religious stories were standing near the boys, behind a kind of veiled light, like a doorway large as a wall. The religious men had come from the church and the mosque? She had only questions, but was not afraid.

"Keep the door open," she whispered silently, "please." With her spoken words she returned to her own body on the grass, leaving some other part of herself in the air. She felt pulled to raise her arms to the hawks circling, a tingling growing from the base of her spine moving into her torso, biceps, even fingers. She spread her arms at the boys.

"Beth," Nathan whispered, "what's up, for God's sake?"

She didn't answer, staying focused, closing her eyes. The tingling began to recede, then release. When she opened her eyes, she felt lighter. She had no doubt that her soul had been taken into flight. She had once been a heavy body, but for a moment had flown free. She had no doubt she had helped the boys, as an electric current lights a bulb; exactly what the help was, she could only guess. She felt power in herself, power building and teaching her, gradually, how to be powerful.

"I think I left my body," Beth said. "I saw things. Nathan, listen." She told him everything she could, wishing for the feeling again already, the feeling of being completely aware, and free, and flying, and able to change things around her. She got chills along her arms again, and the back of her neck. Her hair stood up for a second, as if someone had blown on the tiny mane of fuzzy hair weaving down between her shoulder blades. "I want to call the police. I'm sure there is a cave somewhere. I'm confused but I'm sure I'm seeing this killer. The newspaper article stimulated me. I'm sure of it."

"What would we tell the police?" Nathan asked reasonably. "Can you describe the man?"

"Not his face," Beth said, feeling a frustration that saddened her with its edgy reality. She was experiencing some kind of altered state here, on this day, at this place, in these hours, one that promised everything pure and holy; yet it would not pulse without darkness pulsing too. She could not escape the pulls of all the worlds.

"Look!" Nathan pointed with a shout.

The hawks were coming across the valley like a wave. They had flown over the cliffs but now came across the river, toward Lucia Court, toward Beth and Nathan.

"They're exquisite," Beth exhaled. They flew without formation, about a dozen of them.

Could Alex and his friend see them?

Beth knew she was not in flight with them anymore, but they came as if for her, yearning for her to join them. Beth reached her left hand up. The hawks, high up, flew over and then further east.

"So beautiful." She grinned. Her head was buzzing, her body tingling.

Nathan put his arm around her waist and she his, as they lost vision of the birds to a bank of high ponderosa pines far past Greta's house, in toward the city. Turning back to the river valley, Beth bent and picked up the binoculars. She found the teenagers, watching the hawks themselves, Alex standing at the cliff's edge. Beth could see his nakedness and felt a sweet electric attraction to his youthful frame, and to his genitals.

She put the binoculars down and said to Nathan, "The paragraphs and sentences that are coming automatically to me are being written by the killer of the children. I know this just as I know I was reading his mind with those religious images, Muhammad and Cain and Abel."

"You're sure?"

She looked down at Greta's envelope of clippings on the grass, reading "The Light Killer" in Greta's wavy handwriting on the flap. "All of what's happening today is possible because this killer exists. I don't understand it, Nathan," she said, "but everything is interrelated, interwoven. There is a plan, Nathan. Evil is part of the plan. It's so . . . sad." Beth felt a sudden wave of exhaustion, and emptiness.

Nathan said nothing, listening for more, but Beth had no more words. She was silenced by physical exhaustion, as if after flight, and sadness at what she had just said, that evil was necessary. Gone to Wal-Mart for Trudy's medication, she was supposed to be home any minute. "I'll just be gone a second," she'd said. Where *was* she? There was so much to share with her. If only Greta would get home.

"How can I feel so one with everything, and in a second feel so far away?" Beth said to Nathan, her voice choking.

"Donnell," she whispered. "Where is your soul now?" She looked up toward his house, toward his white curtained windows, drawn to them. She sensed evil from behind those curtains, which made no sense to her at all either.

"Beth," Nathan said, "you've changed in seconds. You're just so . . . flat now. Are you okay?"

She sat down, waiting for Greta, Nathan asking her questions, her answers coming in words but her heart tired from the terrible journey of having flown across the universe, only to return to the confusion of being so utterly human.

Clothed, dry except for hair, the two young men walked down the deer path toward the bridge, then along the bridge toward the other side of the water. They did not see the man who, in the afternoon sun, watched them walking there. He had seen them from a distance—first seen them climb, then seen them naked, now clothed. The black kid reminded the watcher of a young man from Ghana he had known, who wore an embroidered cap on his head, and knew the Qur'an by heart. The watcher had first thought of two brothers, the darker Cain and the lighter Abel, as he watched the young men, and the birds of God above them, gliding. Then the watcher thought of the Muslim people as he watched the black kid jump—a brave group, led by Muhammad, a prophet of both bliss and doom. The watcher stood in a kind of meditation, hoping to take from the young men what strength they possessed, and trying to envision the sources of their strength in the characters of the old texts. There was much strength in the old texts, and the watcher already knew all of them by heart, from the Bible and Qur'an to the Upanishads and the Lotus Sutras. Now in the world there was also the coming of new revelations, not recorded in those old texts.

The watcher, in his meditation, avoided the nagging presence of Other—the woman—and conjured a picture of these young men as younger children, picturing them with a deformity or illness on which the light could shine. As the black kid and his white friend walked across the bridge, the watcher felt the sun, blazing above, like heat in the shape of a cap beneath his hood, on the inside of his skull. It was already beginning—the headache and the next wave of healing heat on his hands. As he had watched the black kid jump off the cliff, he had thought of death, how sweet it would be to die, to fly into the center of all things. He saw the white kid jump and wondered how soon it would be before he himself died. He had no fear of death. The Light knew all, gave all, took all away. Thus far, it had given him immortality, and immense power. Soon he would control more than a laboratory in a cave.

Why, then, the strange feeling that he would die soon?

The young men had crossed the bridge now and stopped at the river there, turning to look back from whence they came. The watcher stood behind a tree, hidden, and again, as he had done so often today, slipped into the shadows as he watched the Light build.

Stopping at the water's edge, the two young men looked back up at the cliffs, admiring the bare rocks and admiring themselves still up there, jumping into summer air that would not hold them. When they resumed walking, their footsteps on the dirt path as if on loud paper, the rush of water just behind them, Alex thought with wonder of how he had seen each of the hawks lit up from within, like flying bits of reflecting glass. As if his prayers of the last year had been met, he saw the prophet Muhammad floating in the air above the cliff, telling him to take his clothes off and jump. Muhammad had been sitting on a horse, his eyes quiet with long death. "You must always know that God is great and God is with you, no matter the evil in the world," Muhammad said. "Naked, you will jump from the cliff. When you have jumped, your life will never the same, for you will be a man in God's eyes." Muhammad had been surrounded, like the hawks, with the same white-gold light as Jeffrey had been, lying there on the grass.

Alex felt pulled to talk to his friend at the mosque, Ahmed Al-Habat, and yet he felt even more drawn to Brent. Could he confess to Brent that he had seen a vision? It hadn't been just imagination. It couldn't have been! The prophet was so real, floating there. It had all started last night, with Jeffrey and that light.

Alex had been walking a little ahead of his friend, but now

Brent came up beside and Alex felt an arm around his shoulders. Brent, who had been so strange and distant for the last few months, stopped Alex in his tracks, and hugged him in a big bear hug. "I love you, man," Brent said into Alex's neck. "Even if you are brave!" Brent pulled away, beaming. "I love you too, man," Alex said, turning his head away a little as he said it. "You're . . . well . . . you're my best friend. Even if you aren't Muslim!"

Brent started walking again, "Even though you *are* Muslim, you're my *only* friend." Brent laughed a loud echoing laugh. Coming up out of the gorge after Brent, looking up Henderson Street to the north, Alex saw two younger boys on skateboards—one looked like Sammy Range—and a young girl, Sally McDonald, watching them.

He said to Brent, "I'm glad I'm not twelve anymore."

"No shit!" Brent agreed. "Whatdoyawannado?" he said, as they crossed the street toward Alex's house.

"Stop a minute," Alex said. "I gotta ask you something." Brent stopped, turning to him.

"Up on the ridge, man," Alex began, looking into Brent's brown eyes, which were bloodshot from the water, and a light shine of water still on his brown eyebrows. "Okay. Did you . . . like . . . *see* anything? Like, even if was from a story or something?"

Brent lowered his head. He had kinky, curly hair, not as kinky as Alex's, but kinky brown, with tiny empty spots in between roils of hair.

"I saw some stuff," Brent confessed, raising his head again. "It was weird. I was, like, back at my bar mitzvah, you remember?" Brent described everything, laughing it off, but forced, by the intensity of his hallucination, to describe all of what he'd seen.

Alex felt the courage now to talk about the vision of Muhammad. "It wasn't just me jumping off the cliff," he said. "The prophet helped me."

Usually when Alex brought up the prophet Muhammad Brent rolled his eyes and closed his heart, but not now. He just listened.

"We gonna tell anyone?" Alex asked, turning his head back to the skateboarders. He just couldn't look into Brent's eyes for too long. Brent had lowered his head, shaking it now. "We gotta think hard about telling anyone, man. They'll think we're fucking out of it, man."

Alex thought of Greta and then of all the neighbors at her house. When Brent left after dinner, he might tell Greta. She probably wouldn't think he was weird. Her house was filled with things from every religion. She always said she enjoyed listening to him talk about his faith.

"You gonna tell your parents?" Brent asked.

"Maybe." Alex doubted it. They were not happy about his conversion to Islam. His father worried that it would affect his grades. It was like how parents didn't get that a sixteen-year-old might fall in love. They had worried that Alex's older brother's grades would be ruined by his "puppy love" for Christine, his girlfriend. Now Stuart and Christine were at Georgetown together.

"If we'd been stoned," Brent said, "it woulda made more sense."

"Yeah." Alex had not smoked dope since becoming a Muslim. The experience today had been like being stoned, but even more than that.

"Let's go to my house," Alex suggested, stepping down

onto Henderson to cross, stealing a quick glance at the Romer house, and the spot of the accident.

"Wait up, man." Brent caught up to him, and the two young men walked up the driveway together. Alex thought silently that there was so much in life he could not understand. And he knew that although he could not see yet how to do it, he must strive from now on to look more clearly than he ever had into the dark.

8

We Are as Gods

Expert, Parents and Clergy Beg Light Killer
To Return Children
Spokesman-Review
June 9, 1992

"There is a Light that shines beyond all things on earth, beyond us all, beyond the heavens, beyond the highest heaven; that Light shines also in our world." So begins the latest letter received by the Spokesman-Review, purportedly authored by the now infamous "Light Killer."

Claiming to quote the Hindu text, the Chandogya Upanishad, the author also claims to have abducted and murdered three children, each of whom has a disability. All three children are between the ages of 9 and 11 years old.

"I have found a doorway," the purported Light Killer writes, "a simple opening to the Light, guarded by the most loving angels. Why must the devil live there too?" This he claims to be a quote from the medieval mystic, Hildegard of Bingen.

Scholars at Gonzaga University have helped to discern the accuracy of all texts quoted by the Light Killer. Dr. Alfred Hecht, Professor of Philosophy and Comparative Religions, and formerly a practicing psychiatrist, headed a team of scholars until he left for a six-month sabbatical in Japan. This team rates the killer's understanding of comparative religions to be good to excellent. However, he seems to fill in blanks, according to Dr. Hecht.

"The quote from the Upanishads is accurate," Dr. Hecht explained in a recent interview, "The Hildegard quote is fabricated." Dr. Hecht believes the killer was brought up in a strict religious household, probably a Christian denomination, then rebelled by pursuing other world religions.

Hecht said, "I believe he is one of those persons who suffer from a dissociative personality, as well as schizophrenia. I believe he is killing each of the children in some kind of ritual way, some way in which he perceives that religion would sacrifice individual humans in order to heal humanity."

Hecht has an international reputation and is the author of several noted books. He and Dr. Adelle Tourtellotte, of Eastern Washington Mental Facility, are consultants to the Light Killer Task Force. Hecht's duties are ending as he prepares for his sabbatical in Japan, but Dr. Tourtellotte will continue to consult with the FBI profilers from the FBI's national headquarters.

Hecht was the featured speaker at a South Hill neighborhood meeting, held at Sacajawea Middle School last evening. Parents and clergy spoke after his presentation.

"We are terrified enough," said Mary Lesh, mother of

three. "We don't need to hear how the killer is sacrificing children."

Rev. Randy Lester, of First Methodist Church, came with a group of his congregants. "New Age religion is the cause of this madness. This killer is reading all sorts of material outside the Christian domain, and this New Age religion is fueling his distance from God."

Larry Mathewson, owner of Moon Children Books, a self-proclaimed alternative bookstore, told reporters that he is on the lookout for the kind of man who fits the profile Hecht detailed for his audience. Mathewson also said, "We are getting flak from the Christian Right. They might want to look in the mirror when it comes to bizarre practices."

While the town meeting last night was peaceful, tensions are running high as a city faces the loss of its children to what experts agree is a careful, brutal, and yet devout killer.

The feeling started in Beth's lower spine, just after she looked at the sun, which had moved past the height of day toward the west. It was like a nodule of heat at the top of her pelvis, and it made her stretch to rub back there instinctively. It went away for a second when she touched it, like pain going away when rubbed, but when she removed her hand, the heat began spreading up her spine, in branches along the backs of her ribs. She closed her eyes.

Unlike before, this time the heat moved through her without pain. She laid the newspaper clipping on the file envelope, her eyes still closed, Nathan lying on his back beside her, holding the stone he had brought up from the campsite. She felt as if the newspaper articles were alive, trying to communicate with her; so was the stone. Everything was trying to communicate with her.

The heat spread up past her shoulder blades, along her neck, raising her hair slightly, into her brain stem, into her brain. She saw the young girl in the WSU sweatshirt sitting on a boulder, holding out her right hand. In it was the piece of cloth. The girl had gray eyes, blond hair. She looked numb. Unhappy. Her face was gaunt. She had suffered an ordeal. She was dead, Beth sensed, but still somehow able to communicate. The cloth in her hand was crumpled up in her cupped palm.

Beth waited. The girl looked at her, held the crumpled cloth. Beth was moved to reach for the stone Nathan held, hoping this was the signal the girl sent—touch the stone.

Nathan sat up slightly, silently relinquishing the stone, watching.

Beth touched the stone. Now the girl was gone. There was a jolt of electricity, and then she saw Nathan in the future, in a huge compound of buildings with grass all around, looking down on a city, as if the place was in the mountains; the compound of buildings was a laboratory of some kind. Beth said: "Nathan, I don't know why—but I think you will die young. It's a strange sense I have. Weird. Maybe it's nothing. I mean not too young, but not at eighty or something. I can sort of . . . see it. I see you in the mountains, at a laboratory. And I sense you're going to die young. I was seeing the girl, then I touched the stone. You're about forty, and someone shot you."

"Are you serious?"

"Yes," she said. "I wish I could communicate with the girl."

"You think I'll die young?"

"Yes. I think so."

Beth opened her eyes, returning to herself suddenly. Could she really have seen Nathan getting shot? Should she have said anything. She could see it stunned him. How could it be believed? By him, or even by her? It was too bizarre to do anything but plot one's life without death in it.

"Will I finally know who I am?" he asked, half in jest, half seriously.

"You will have a family, and you will know." Beth was sure of these things.

"Kids?"

"I don't know, exactly. I see one but I sense more."

"Will it be with you?"

"I don't . . . I don't think so. I don't know." Was this knowledge of her own future, one without Nathan in it? She felt breathless, and did not fully want to know the truth, as if it would kill their relationship now, right away, rather than whenever it was fated to end.

"Beth, are you really right?"

She dropped the stone. "I don't know. I don't know. But you won't die soon, I know that. Just not at a very old age, either. I'm sorry."

"There's Greta," Nathan said. Beth heard her car on the asphalt driveway in front, and the sound of the automatic garage door rising.

"Should we check on the boys?" Nathan said, distracting himself from Beth's prediction. He grabbed the binoculars up and searched the far side, then laughed. "Probably still naked as jaybirds," he cried, even though he did not see the boys at all now. "Let's get naked too," he cried, pulling his shirt off.

"Nathan!"

He had a muscular and wide torso, with tufts of blond-gray

hair at the nipples and navel. Beth did not for a moment think he would, right here in Greta's backyard, take off all his clothes. But now he took off his shoes, then he took off his pants and underwear and he said, "Look at me, I'm naked, I'm the new human, I'm Adam! No! I'm Adam II! And before I die too!"

"Nathan! Not here. You're just doing this to shock. Greta will be here any minute. And there's the old people next door."

He stood, unself-conscious, a stripped tree, cupping his genitals with his right hand and grinning at her. Beth reached down for his shorts and he grabbed her up, raising her and kissing her. She pulled away, feeling his midriff against her, his genitals bounding against her hip.

"Nathan!"

"Kiss me," he whispered, "and I'll put my shorts back on again."

"You promise?" He must be terribly unhappy, or confused, by her predictions. He did what he often did—feign happiness.

"Cross my heart and hope to die." He did indeed cross his heart, leaving his large genitals exposed. She reached up and kissed him and he made her kiss him harder, a long kiss, full of tongue and juice. She enjoyed it, which seemed to satisfy him, and he pulled his shorts back on. I wonder why I can't see his aura, she thought suddenly. She had not seen the girl's aura, either. She had seen Harold's and Laura's, and seen a glow around their visitors. Was there no order to what she saw, what she experienced? All random?

She saw only the Nathan of wide body and handsome face and gray eyes and blond day-old beard. She sensed somehow that his energy, his personality, its frenetic quality, its inner dialogues that he tried so hard to conceal—all this he always carried in him somehow blocked or distracted her powers away from deeper observation of him, making her insights about him quick and brief.

Shaking herself loose, surprising herself, Beth slapped his bottom hard and grinned. He laughed, turning around for her, grabbing her, and wrestling her to the grass. Now he kissed her again and she felt a stirring in her groin. She felt his thigh there and kissed him harder.

She felt a presence suddenly, a presence outside of him and her. She stopped kissing him and he, sensing her sudden shift, raised his head.

"What's going on?" he asked.

"A . . . dark feeling . . . something, someone."

"Where?"

"Here. With us."

They wrestled free of each other and looked around—the Svobodas' yard, the river gorge, the high fence to the west. They saw nothing except the natural surroundings.

"It is a . . . a spirit?" Beth whispered. "Like a . . . a dark spirit of some kind?"

"I don't feel it."

"It's like one of the visitors, but something harsh. Like it's watching us, like it's pulsing just enough to be felt by us, but then recedes away.

"It's too much to think about." Beth shivered, embracing herself as she continued scanning. "It feels like being telepathic but not being able to turn off the power. I see some things, but not others. I see the girl, but she goes away. I must be defending myself somehow, not letting things in. I feel like if I really let it in, I'd be able to feel and see so much of the terrible stuff.

Do you feel it! I just felt it again. Cold. Very cold. It takes the heat out of me. The heat's gone."

"It's a ghost or something?" Nathan whispered, putting his arm around her.

He closed his eyes. Beth couldn't bear to close hers. She kept them open, hoping the malevolence would not show itself to her if she did not let her mind dream. She stared at the sunny valley, the pine trees, a hawk flying.

The back screen door squeaked and shut with a small slam. Greta was here!

"How are you both?" Greta asked, leaning on her cane.

"Greta," Beth said, "I'm feeling something so dark, something evil, or very mean, a presence, right around us, in this proximity. We thought maybe it was a . . . ghost. Something like that."

"Do you still feel it?"

"I don't know," Beth responded. "Not as much." Beth saw, in her mind's eye, dots of light, atomic particles of spirit, everywhere around her all the time. Closing her eyes, she watched an amazing dance of lights.

"What do you see?" Greta asked.

Beth said, "I think I see gods and angels? That must sound so stupid." Beth opened her eyes, embarrassed a little. If only Greta and Nathan could see the lights everywhere, lights fading as the sun hit Beth's eyes.

Greta, her sunglasses dangling on a silver chain on her chest, blinked against the sun and smiled. "Gods and angels," she repeated. "An old professor of mine once told me something. He said, 'Think about the Greek gods, the Norse gods, all the goddesses.' He said to picture Hermes flying about, or Zeus making lightning, or Coyote creating life from nothing except a tiny thought. Then he said, 'Now look at us humans.

" '*We* are the gods. We now fly, as Hermes did. We throw lightning and thunder, in our bombs. We can create life with our medical technology. We can conjure up dreams and visions, as the gods did, in our movies and television. We can travel in space, as they could, in our spaceships. We can communicate instantaneously with others of our kind, as they could, through our satellites and the Internet. There is hardly anything the gods and goddesses could do in legend that we cannot do now.

" 'The writers and diviners of the ancient stories of gods and goddesses were early *Homo infiniens,* perhaps, who predicted the future as much as they explained the mysterious past. The future is not only now, but we can almost say, as the new millennium comes, that the future depicted in the legends is *behind* us. We are becoming even more powerful than the gods and goddesses were imagined to be. And we will have to be as responsible—or perhaps *more* responsible—than they were. Especially as abilities like yours, Beth, become more commonplace.' "

Nathan was looking up at the blue tinted sky. Beth followed his glance to watch a magpie, black and white with a blue face, cross Greta's yard.

"Greta," Beth pleaded, "what do I *do?* There are things happening to me."

"She's changing," Nathan said.

Greta took a deep breath, drawing her sweater in with her tiny, thin hands. "Once in a while, old souls like you, in a lifetime, have a distinctly sensorial apprehension of the unembodied strings, energies, call them spirits, that are everywhere.

This is what you, Beth, had at the Svobodas' next door. This is what you probably have in your visions . . . your sensings. I think you will learn your clairvoyant powers and teach others."

"I think a dead girl is trying to communicate to me, give me something, but my fear is stopping me from . . . connecting. Could this be?"

Greta raised her eyebrows in wonder. She pushed her wispy gray hair back with her left hand. "If there is truly no death, and truly there is not; and if this is truly an endless universe made up of infinite beings and dimensions of experience—which it is; then what is most important in everyone's life is right before us, and just needs to be noticed for what it is. There's nothing to be afraid of. But accomplishing a fearless state: this is the hardest spiritual work possible. Few are able to do it. Today, you are becoming more able, and I have the privilege of watching it happen. I wish it was not coming on the heels of Jeffrey's death, of Donnell's, so much pain . . . but there is a plan. I believe this. There is a plan."

Beth got up and embraced Greta, who hugged hard, like hugging her own child, and did not seem to want to let go. Beth had the feeling of being a well drunk from by a thirsty soul.

When the embrace was done, Nathan said, "Greta, it's good to know you. You know?"

"And you." Greta smiled.

Nathan said to Beth, "We need to get back down to the river. That rock with the seam—where I got this stone." He picked it up off the grass. "We have to try to see what's going on there with the lights. Don't we?"

"We do," Beth agreed. It was about 2:00 or 3:00 P.M., the afternoon waning. Beth wanted to get back down to the river.

She had been feeling the pull. It was as if Nathan read her feelings and tried to guide her. "Nathan and I have to go back to where we saw the lights. Will you come down?" She described to Greta where the camp was in relation to Greta's house.

"I might come down to the river later, my dears." Greta smiled. "Depending on my energy. I'll check on all the neighborhood kids, then get Trudy's dinner." Greta's eyes had moved to the motion of children on the street just south.

Beth turned to see Sammy Range and another boy on a skateboard, and she saw Sally McDonald, watching them from a seat on a boulder. The second boy let out a loud "Yay!" as he made a jump on his board.

Nathan smiled. "I was about their age when I broke my leg skateboarding down a friend's driveway."

Beth came up beside him. The boys were graceful in their dance along the air. Sally, a little older, seemed to be studying the boys, wanting to play with them but wanting, first, to be asked. Beth imagined that the girl was watching spirit visitors who hung near the boys. As she imagined this, she found herself shooting through a tunnel and ending up sitting right next to Sally. She overheard the girl talking, in her head, to the older boy, Sammy. "It must be hard for your dad to die," Sally was thinking to him, as he sailed on the skateboard.

Then, suddenly, Beth shot back through the tunnel to where she was beside Nathan.

"Jesus," Beth exhaled. "Another kind of . . . I don't know. I shot through a tunnel over to Sally, hearing her thoughts, then shooting back here."

"Telepathy—like before, or different?" Nathan whispered.

"I don't know." Beth closed her eyes, trying again. Nothing happened, so she opened her eyes. Sally turned and saw her,

Nathan, and Greta; she waved and smiled. Beth and Greta waved back, Greta pushing up out of her chair. The three adults began walking to Sally, who, seeing this, got up from her perch and came over.

"How have you been, dear?" Greta asked.

"I've been thinking a little about Jeffrey," she said, "and dead people. Hi, Beth," she said. She smiled at Nathan, knowing him less well.

"It's been a confusing time." Beth smiled, stepping closer. "Has anything unusual happened to you in the last few hours?"

"Like what?" the girl pondered.

"Like perhaps seeing the light from last night again?" Greta asked.

"No."

Beth felt a kind affinity for the lanky, blond girl. She must have just started puberty, her breasts budding. Beth remembered how remarkable and how difficult that time had been for her. She wished Sally a better time, a close relationship with her father.

Nathan touched Beth's shoulder. "We've got to get back down to the river. All my stuff's down there."

"You go, dears," Greta prompted. "Sally will help me back to my chair."

"Sure," Sally agreed.

Beth kissed Greta on the forehead, then gave Sally a wink, moving with Nathan back to their things in Greta's yard. Beth grabbed up her journal, Greta's file folder, storing them in the pack as Nathan put shoes and shirt on, then followed him back down the hill of the river gorge. As she walked, Beth sensed she would see Sally again, and missed her already. Crossing over the line of consciousness to telepathy, in so many different ways, had not yet overwhelmed her. This surprised her. How elastic the brain must be. And could it be that she had been slipped drugs somehow? But how?

The sun moved lower in the sky yet, still hot, broke an immediate sweat on Beth as she walked down the incline of the gorge, following Nathan. As she walked among the pine trees on the trail she caught a smell of pine sap and stopped to put her nose to the huge tamarack at the trail's edge. A honeysuckle bush sat next to the pine, emitting the wonderful smell of a hundred white flowers. Beth sucked in its sweet draught.

She lost sight of Nathan, wanting to call him back to smell the amazing, syrupy tree and bush; yet she welcomed the peace of just leaning there, her face half embraced by the flowers. Then she returned to the tree side, pushing her face into syrupy bark. She put her arm around the tree, embarrassed for a second to be hugging a tree. But no one was around.

"Who is to say," she thought, "that this tree has no soul? If this tree does not, then I do not. Doesn't this tree grow and bend in whatever direction the sun is? Isn't that the same as my growing toward my own source of light?"

She closed her eyes and let the soul of the tree envelop her in its aroma. She let the soul of the resounding river envelop her. She let the soul of the air envelop her in its invisible well of oxygen she sucked in, over and over. She knew herself to be lost in an immense embrace of sentimental love for the world. She saw the eternal deep space as a womb, and the earth as a fetus in the womb. The smell of the tree sap, the honeysuckle flowers, the sound of the river, the air in her lungs, the vision of space and birth filled her with a remarkable sense of peace. She felt loved. She did not feel afraid.

When she opened her eyes, she pulled her journal out again. Some words were forming over and over in her head. The same words. She slumped down beside the tree to write them down.

"Everything is simple—I am breathing, and that is all I need to do.

"I am secure, here, on this earth.

"I am at peace."

The words came, over and over, and she wrote them like a haiku repeating itself, and when she was spent with writing them, she felt her grandmother Rachel's presence, and she felt utterly forgiven for not having spent enough time around her grandmother. What a beautiful feeling! Thank God for the feeling. Was this a moment of fearlessness? Was this part of the plan?

Beth Carey breathed in deeply, and spread her arms like a bird. She grinned and heard a kind of moan from her own throat.

Then she got down on her knees and bent her body to the pine needles and moss beneath her and did something she resolved she would do, from now on, every day.

Driven to the ground in the greatest act of humility she could imagine, she bent her face to the loam under her, and she kissed the earth.

Who was this woman? the watcher wondered. This woman seemed quite lit up. What was she doing on her knees there?

The man with the birthmark, who'd been with her on the trail, was her consort—returning to her, wondering how he'd lost her on the trail. This man with the birthmark had picked up the stone, given it to her—it must be in one of their pockets now. At first, the watcher had wanted it to affect these others. He had bestowed it, after all, after great concentration in the spirit of experiment. But now he wondered if his experiment was being too successful. This woman walked in such Light!

The watcher steered clear of her and the man with the birthmark, continuing on his way to find access of another kind, near the children up on the road. Though he believed himself invisible in an unexplainable way, nonetheless he kept his hood on, his head covered.

This large woman and the man with her had been first to the boy, Jeffrey. Were they touched by the Light? In this valley now, was there a motion of Light he himself was supposed to acknowledge or include, in his plans? Was the Light being shared with others? The watcher had not felt afraid since he had begun, months ago, to listen to the Voices, and to fulfill the Mission. But today, seeing this woman, he became a little frightened.

Was she the Other he'd been feeling? He had begun to feel watched.

Since boyhood, he had been a genius. Everyone knew it. Only because of illness at ten years old, illness of the mind and of the body, had he been stopped from great accomplishment. Things had changed last fall, though. Vision had come, the Voices were clear. He was Healing himself. He had found a way to keep the Madwoman out of his head.

But he sensed her again today. Would he need to accelerate

his Mission? The old man at the House of Light had killed himself today. This big woman and her friend had gone up there, and after that the old man was dead. Was she the angel of death? She seemed to have power. Why were the Voices not helping him to better understand?

9

THE OSPREY

PERCHED ON A boulder, facing half into the river gorge and half into her street, Sally McDonald gazed at the two boys skateboarding. It would be dinnertime in an hour. She'd have to go inside by 5:00. Her mother put dinner out earlier than any other mother. How long could she just sit here on this perch, Sally wondered. Sally was twelve years old, caught in the limbo of her age. She wanted to play with the tireless boys but couldn't, didn't want to play with them but, as if her muscles spoke for her, nearly rose up to enter their fray.

"You're just about out of your cocoon," her mother liked to say. "You're not a little caterpillar anymore, but you're not quite a butterfly either."

It was sure nice of Beth, Nathan, Greta, and then Trudy, to ask how she was. Greta had been nice yesterday, too, wondering how Sally felt after everything yesterday. Mom and Dad had both called Sally from work twice during the day today to make sure she was okay after the terrible accident and the strange light.

After seeing Jeffrey so bloody and broken, Sally had felt a huge feeling of love for her parents, and also for everything and everyone else. It wasn't just "hormones," as her mother liked to say about everything she felt these days. She had told her parents about the light when they talked to her after Jeffrey's accident. Her mother then her father held her as she cried.

Had Sammy Range told his mom? The older skateboarder, Sammy, carried his dead father's name. Sally already saw the boy as a man—large, garrulous, well-liked, an image of his father. Samuel Sr., a commercial roofer, had fallen from eight stories two years ago. In Sammy, Sally had already noticed his father's love of heights and the open air, noticed it not quite consciously, but like an idea a friend has. She noticed it now as Samuel Jr. propelled his skateboard over the curb and onto a makeshift ramp, then rode the empty air as if it loved him, then landed on the sidewalk again, knees bent, arms out, a surfer on ocean waves of concrete.

"Radical!" the younger boy, Josh, called out. He tried the same run at the ramp, but lost his skateboard in the air.

Touched by a shadow, Sally turned and raised her eyes. An osprey—a riverhawk—glided onto the second highest branch of the second tallest pine tree on the far side of the river basin. Sally watched as it pulled its deep brown wings into its white body with the grace of a dancer's arms in a plié. A breeze touched the bird and the branch. Sally turned fully away from the boys, toward the sight of the bird. For a long while yesterday, she'd seen it here too.

Sally spent hours every week in the river gorge, pursuing

the love of nature she shared with her father. She couldn't really express all the things she felt in the gorge, but she knew that her father, too, had a private vision of the woods. With all the kids getting taken away up on the north side of town, Sally was glad to have such a safe area of the river to wander in, where nothing had happened of a bad kind. Everyone in the neighborhood was so glad.

"You see what you're meant to see out here," her father liked to say. "And you only make it other people's business if you want." By this he meant, "You're becoming a young woman. You can share what you want with me, but I won't try to pry things out of you."

Letting the breeze touch her eyes, Sally watched it touch the slow river like breath exhaling over embers, the undersides of birch leaves and the surface of the river going from shades of green to shades of gray then, as the exhale finished, returning to verdancy. Sally rubbed her palms together between her knees. Bleeding as she was only for the second time in her life, her maxi-pad felt like one of those McDonald's ketchup pouches stuck down there. She had not eaten McDonald's ketchup since she made the ketchup/menses and the McDonald/McDonald's connection in her mind. Even more bizarre to her was the scent of marjoram in her own menses. The boys on skateboards would never know what a girl could smell.

Sally jumped off the boulder, shaking off torpor. She thought of little Jeffrey, whom she had baby-sat a few times. He would never skateboard. Though maybe he was skateboarding in heaven, she smiled. Maybe that light had been a pathway to heaven for him to walk on.

Sally descended the gorge, a gooseberry branch slapping

her arm. Using a pine trunk as ballast, she launched her right leg off a rock the size of a football. She dropped like Sammy, knees bent, onto weeds and pine needles, propelled herself farther down the incline then, nearly losing control, ran the rest of the way to the river's edge. Panting at her destination, she looked up into the pine across the river—the osprey sat stoically there, staring upriver.

"What do you see?" Sally asked the bird, looking upriver. What was up there? Sally had not slept well last night, unable to free herself of nightmares in which Jeffrey's bloody, broken body lay in her own bed. Last night, and now, she kept hoping he would reappear, little Jeffrey, miraculously brought back to earth by a weird light, like in a movie.

But she saw only trees, wilderness, more river. She moved a few steps to see further. On the heels of a squirrel's complaint two sparrows lit onto a nearby honeysuckle bush, chirped something to each other, then flew off. Sally walked the few feet to the bush, dipping to pull some burrs out of her white ankle socks. Choosing to stay squat, she pushed her knee-length, denim skirt down between her legs, squatting like those African women she saw on The Discovery Channel, and smelled the lower terraces of the rows of honeysuckles. She watched an ant on one of the honeysuckles, moving as if without purpose, stopping nowhere, finding nothing, just moving, now on the pistil, then in the couched palm of the inner flower, then out on the skirts of the petal, then down underneath it, along the stem. Its progress took ten seconds of Sally's life. How long, she wondered, did it use up of an ant's life?

Pushing herself up along the flowery valence of honeysuckles, Sally breathed in the wealth of fragrance. It filled her with a kind of dizziness. Standing among the smell and the purling water and now again the breezy rustle of leaves, she felt almost like she levitated above the scene at that place just off the ground where the scene really transpired. What an effect honeysuckles were having today. Sally let the fragrance completely in.

Exhaling, Sally turned from the honeysuckles. There on the pine branch, the osprey still sat looking upriver.

"Are you brainless, or regal?" Sally asked aloud, her hands on her hips. She had never understood whether large birds could stare so unequivocally into space in one direction because they were pea-brained, or because they had an assuredness reserved only for divine creatures. Especially today, Sally chose to think they were divine. She was not at the age yet when she could make herself happy by shattering her own illusions.

"I saw the osprey again," she reported to her parents at dinner just a half hour later.

"Same place?" her father asked from lips half-hidden inside his dark brown beard.

"Same place. Two days in a row now."

"There's no nest there," Sally's mother pondered. "What's it doing there?"

"Before it gets too dark," the beard said, "let's Sally and me check it out."

Sweet electricity shot through Sally's body, a tremor like the tingling after a hot bath. Like a boy, she wolfed down her food.

Her father, his beard, hair, and thick eyebrows all a deep brown, his body bearlike, was certainly not a woodsman—he managed a Radio Shack store—but he lumbered down the incline into the pine gorge like someone accustomed to holding the forest in the palm of his hand. Years before, he had held his hand out to Sally when he pulled ahead, offering to bring her forward into his pace. Now he let her hang back. There were other ways he opened to her, she knew that, other more subtle interactions appropriate for a father of a girl becoming a woman: She knew to be watchful for them, watchful from a place within herself that was still young, unsure of adult signals. Slapped by a low pine branch as he just was, he would have stopped a year ago to hold the branch open, like a door, for his little girl to pass through. Now, he just pushed through and moved on, letting Sally fend for herself. This was a sign. She knew she must take new steps of courage toward the independent adult world whenever she could but not move too quickly, for the adult world seemed full of problems. Sally wasn't as anxious for its rewards as many of her friends were. She preferred the river to cars and boyfriends. Watching the Romers yesterday, how Marti was screaming, Sally didn't want to grow up too quickly. Crying so much like she did after the accident, shaking and sniveling in her room, she didn't want to grow up and have a kid and have him die.

Sally came up beside her father as he stopped at the river's edge. Father and daughter craned necks to look for the osprey in the trees across the river, but saw nothing. Her left arm tickling, Sally looked down to see a hairy horsefly sniffing at the blond fuzz below her elbow. Then she saw a mosquito light on her father's hairy arm.

"Daddy." She pointed. She had always known that the world did everything in twos—if people would just notice. Just as her father had not opened the branch for her minutes ago, Sally now noticed her own chance to grow up, to be different than, say, a year ago, when she would have swatted the mosquito off her father, giggling, her father crying, "Yowie," grabbing her and tickling her till they both wrestled, her father's smell on her lasting into sleep.

Watching her father swat the mosquito himself, she said, "The osprey's gone, Daddy."

"Looks like it." But he started walking, jumping low rocks, pushing through bushes. He hunted and Sally followed.

Beth wrote in her journal and felt heaviness, like an ache in her shoulders and neck. Nathan was solicitous, examining her eyes and her vitals twice in the last half hour.

"What is really going on?" he asked. "Describe it."

"I feel like I'm getting signals from everywhere," she responded. "They're beautiful, but I think they give me waves of tiredness."

"Maybe there's some amazingly huge miracle about to happen to you," he said, "like the burning bush or the sky opening?" He said it as a joke, but also needily. Until that moment, Beth hadn't realized how conditioned he was, or perhaps she and everyone was, to see miracles as great dramas, rather than small lights. Her miracles the past few hours were small ones—weren't they?

"Did you hear that?" Nathan asked suddenly, his head cocked upriver.

Beth heard voices to the south, a man's and a girl's, shifting in and away on the breeze. Then she heard a louder sound, the shrill call of an osprey. She looked up to see the brown-white riverhawk flying downriver, as if toward the voices.

Beth's eyes felt very heavy, like she was being hypnotized.

She couldn't resist closing them, nor wanted to. Her mind opened. She saw Sally in her mind's eye, sensing in the girl a vast ability to know the beautiful, and a vast ability to feel the hidden spiritual physics of the world. That girl, Sally, was definitely an empathic sort. Beth saw her older, in a hospital. She was a doctor or nurse, bending over someone. Beth looked closer and saw her bending over a dog. She was a veterinarian. Beth saw this more clearly than had been the moment of telepathy with the girl earlier. No tunnel in this vision. Just the girl's future, free and clear.

Then in her mental vision, Beth saw a second bird, already dead. "There's another osprey, this one's mate. I can see it. It's lying dead." The achiness and heaviness coursed through her body like a heat. "It's like I see . . . wait, Sally and her dad aren't finding the dead one. They're supposed to find it."

"Supposed to?"

"I don't know what I mean, really. I just have an overwhelming feeling that Sally and her father are meant to find the dead osprey. It's like the light is talking to me. Oh God, how weird that sounds!"

"We're beyond weird!" Nathan frowned. "I'm going to find a way to study the kind of thing going on in your brain, Beth. I promise you that."

"I don't know why," Beth murmured, "but Sally must see the osprey. Something . . . I don't know. Honeysuckles? I smell honeysuckles. Why? It's related to the osprey. I don't know. But I know I have to help her see the osprey." Beth saw the palpable light between herself and Sally widen until it was the width of a tree, then a yard wide, then even larger, like a field of light expanding until it swept in the osprey. Just as the light touched the osprey in Beth's mind, she saw Sally hesitate, turn, look up and see the bird! And the wide light disappeared as soon as Sally set eyes on the bird and called to her father. Then the light disappeared, its work finished somehow. Beth no longer saw Sally, or her father, or any of the far scene. Her eyes opened, still heavy. Her body shivered. Beth felt as if she somehow had controlled time and space with a power not her own.

"I don't know what I did," she whispered, "or how I was part of it, but I helped somehow. Using the light."

"Like with Alex, and Landry?"

"Kind of." There was something else. Something else there. What was it? Beth felt very attracted to the dead osprey.

"Do you still have the achiness?"

"It's getting less, really fast." She felt his fingers on her wrist again.

"I wish I could check your blood pressure. During these bouts, there's some kind of rapid titration in your cells."

Now they heard voices again, on the changed direction of river wind.

"I don't want that girl to suffer," Beth said. "Sally. I want everything to work out for her in her life." Beth felt an openness in herself, an openness to the girl, as if she could reach out and embrace the girl and save her from all harm. Beth was aware of heaviness and lightness mixing in her, a palpable internal state undefinable except to float with it.

"This new human," she said, "this *Homo infiniens.* She will be capable of fully trusting the universe. Do you see that?"

Nathan nodded placidly, a kind of smile on his face like someone who has simply decided to come along for a nice ride.

"Let's not bother Sally and her dad," Beth whispered. She

was almost glad nothing more had happened than just seeing people fifty feet away through the trees, the dusk sky giving just enough light for them to be visible. Pushing herself up, Beth moved with Nathan to between two pine trees, hidden away. She saw Sally's face as she saw the dead osprey in the dirt.

"Nathan," Beth whispered. "We need to go there after they leave."

"Right where they are?"

"I don't know why yet, but remember that spot. We're going there."

"Okay," he murmured beside her, committing the place to memory.

Beth closed her eyes. Why was she certain that they would go to the spot where Sally was now standing? Beth yearned, in her new power, to see inside Sally's mind again. She closed her eyes more than once, frustrated. She opened them to watch the people, closed them again to try to see better. She couldn't control the telepathy, but she knew in her heart that the visioning would return. Even with the achiness in her back and neck that the telepathic seeing brought her, it almost felt more like seeing than when she saw with her open eyes.

"There it is!" Sally called. Impressed by the shadows of the bird for the second time today, Sally's eyes moved left to the river. The wide-winged osprey glided over the river to just twenty feet out of Sally's reach, then rose upward toward the height of a pine. Perching there, it stared upriver as it had before. Sally and her father strained to look in the direction of the bird's gaze. Her father started walking in that direction and Sally followed.

"I'll be damned," Sally heard her father mutter. He squatted as Sally came up beside him. There, at their feet, was a female osprey—wingspan probably four feet, head to tip of tail about eighteen inches long, its head snapped back, neck broken, its eyes open, half eaten. Inside its beak were tiny white honeysuckle flowers. Wow! Flies buzzed around the gorey carcass; black beetles climbed it; worms and maggots dug in. So many ants attacked that its pinkish talons had all but disappeared in a thin, shifting black. The brown regal feathers were matted with a caul of dried blood, crusted dirt, and insect juices. The bird looked as if the mouth of death had wetted it with a grotesque, drying saliva, then spit it back out onto the earth.

Sally dropped to the ground next to her father. She was crying. Her father had reached for a twig. Wanting to reach out, hold the bird, yet disgusted by the bugs, she held back her tears as her father poked the bird with a twig, shocking the insects. With sudden jolts, tiny things shot every which way, beads off a necklace.

"The boys hit her with a rock," Sally said.

Her father shook his head. "Nope, someone strong broke her neck. An adult. Pretty unusual, though, for an osprey to get caught by a human. The human would have to be very quick, or mesmerize it somehow. I've never seen a dead osprey down here like this." He lifted the bird with the twig so its white underbelly showed. He let it drop again and turned his head to the osprey in the tree.

He asked, "What do you think he'd want done with his mate?"

Without pause, Sally said, "He'd want her buried."

"We'll bury her then." His eyes glowed with a light that

came from more than the play of sunset upon the pupils. His eyes glowed with silent love.

"We'll do it together," he said, pushing up from his knees.

Sally joined him in a search among the rocks for branches suitable for shoveling. To the surviving male osprey, she said silently, "We'll take good care of your mate, Daddy and me, we'll do it just right." She had known deaths among her relatives before, but maybe because she thought God must be giving her a sign—Jeffrey dying and now this osprey—she felt alive in the bird's death, enlivened in a way that a funeral could never do. Her father had begun digging with his hands. Sally joined him.

"Daddy," she asked, "do you think the male knows what we're doing?"

He nodded. "He knows. He feels our kindness." Dirt gloved her father's hairy hand as he dug. Her father, a man who could wear a coat and tie and smile and be patient with Nintendo-drunk boys and bulk orders from restaurant chains, was really best here, in the woods.

"I'm gonna wash her off." Sally wiped a band of sweat off her temple with the hard back of her hand. She was uncomfortable with the motionless bird, especially the insects on it, but she felt a passion for its dying that was bigger than her fear. She lifted the corpse gingerly, its tail feathers smooth in her two fingers. She moved quickly to the water, before too many insects found her arm. She was aware of wanting to hold and cuddle the bird, but shuddered at how gross that would be.

She dipped the bird in at the water's edge, like dipping a baby in a bath. Bravely, she reached her free hand in and washed the bird. Panicking insects used her arms as life rafts. She withstood them, even her sudden self-doubt as she realized a hundred living insects were drowning so she could wash a dead bird.

At that moment—not, as Sally would think later, at the moment of burial or prayer—the male osprey in the tree spread its wings and, gliding above Sally's concentration, flew away. When for the third time in one day Sally felt the touch of the bird's shadow, she lifted her eyes.

"He's flying away, Daddy." Sally pointed.

Her father, who had dug the hole, looked up too. "He can say good-bye now, I guess." Soundlessly, the osprey disappeared around a corner of trees.

"Good-bye," Sally said. Her nose ran just slightly, sadness returning to her neck and head like a warmth, as if the back of her neck and shoulders hurt a little. She brought her left hand up to her nose, smelling the river, the loam, the tiny carnage of insects, the scent of the dead bird.

"You about ready?" her father asked.

"She's in our care now," Sally said, liking the responsibility of it. Her father stepped to the grave. She followed, laying the bird in it. Together, on hands and knees, father and daughter put dirt into the hole. "Let's say the Lord's Prayer," Sally suggested.

"Let's do that, sweetheart," he agreed.

And they did.

Standing back up when the job was done, Sally looked south again along the river. At first she thought she was looking for the male, but then she realized it wasn't that. She didn't know what she was looking for. Something. Jeffrey? That was it. She was looking for Jeffrey. She thought he was right here, if only she were not blind to him.

"Better get back to your mother," her father said.

"Maybe I'll show her the grave tomorrow," Sally said.

"She'd like that." But Sally knew, and she knew her father knew, her mother didn't enjoy these woods like her husband and daughter did. She never came out here.

Giving the grave one last look, Sally stepped away. She found an opening in the trees and started up the incline toward the road. She heard her father following her. Night was rising, the world around her darker than the blue up in the sky. Even through the tops of the trees she saw the blue hue. She thought of the osprey flying toward a new life. She thought of herself.

For a long and graceful moment, she envied no one in the world nor had any worries. Everything fit together. The trees, the squirrels, the river, the osprey, and everything invisible. It all made a kind of sense. She couldn't form a thought about it, but she could feel it in her bones.

"You know, Sally," her father said, stopping at the edge of the road at the top of the incline. "That osprey—so unusual to see one dead like that, unprotected, and the mate just waiting for us."

"I know," she agreed.

Sally saw in her father's face a deeper consideration, an idea trying to form that just didn't get formed. He shook his head and thick beard. His brown eyes twinkled bluish in the late dusk light.

Sally hoped tonight she would sleep better. She hoped she would dream of osprey.

"I think I was an osprey in a past life," she joked with her father.

"There are worse things," he said logically. "My mother,

your Grandma Irene, who died just before you were born, she and her family raised peregrines—hawks, falcons, and osprey—before she married your grandfather. Kind of interesting, you know, us finding that osprey. It's from her I learned things like how osprey go high up to die, they don't come down to the side of the river. Your grandma, as she was dying, she said she saw Jesus holding his hand out to her. I was right in the room, you know. Right there, holding her hand. I didn't see anybody, but she was mumbling in her confused way, and she said, 'Yes, Jesus, I'll tell them.' And then you know what she did?"

"What?" Sally had not heard this story before.

"She turned to me and my sister and the nurse, and she opened her eyes wide like she was very conscious, very alert. She said something like, 'Jesus has brought the light. He is here. He wants me to tell you that inside you there's the real truth and the real kingdom, nowhere else, not even in Him.' Your grandma was a very Christian woman. We didn't think twice about her talking to Jesus. Since she was a devout Christian, we figured she just must have gotten the message messed up a little."

Her father looked up now, toward the sky. Sally waited, unsure of her father's train of thought. She had seen old pictures of Grandma Irene—her middle name had been Sally. She had died just four months before her granddaughter was born. Mom didn't like the name Irene, but she did like Sally.

"Sweetheart," her father said, stopping just at the front door. "When you ran out to be with Jeffrey yesterday. . . . Was it really hard for you?"

She nodded then noticed her father's eyes straying behind her and turned to look. Alex Bass had come out of his house and was going toward Greta's. Her father waved to him and he waved back.

"Wasn't Alex with you yesterday?"

"Yes, Daddy," she replied.

"Come on, let's ask him if he's had any strange things happen today. 'Cause something is really going on today, I just feel it."

Sally followed her father toward Alex, and toward Greta's house, which was lit up in nearly every window.

"Hey, Alex," her father called out. "Wait a minute, would you? I've got a question for you."

Sally looked up as she walked, thinking she saw the osprey again. Or had she just seen another shadow, some movement? What was that? She stared into the woods as she moved with her father. No, nothing there. Certainly not the osprey; it must have flown far upriver by now. Sally imagined her grandmother was around, having visions as she died; maybe Grandma Irene had something to do with the dead osprey. The thought warmed her, as she and her father caught up with Alex, who started talking about something that had happened today, involving him and his friend Brent, on the other side of the river.

They spoke, standing together, near a boulder that sat like a perch just up from the river gorge. They didn't know that among them was another presence, both watching and listening. He was shuddering as he heard how indelibly he had been able to use his telepathic ability. He was becoming a Master of the Light. The black kid seeing Muhammad, the other kid seeing Cain and Abel. The watcher listened to his mind revealed in the world of these people. He had seen the religious figures in his mind and been able to plant them in the minds of the boys. How much stronger he was becoming! The experiments were working. The girl, Sally, and her father revealed the osprey. Even in this he must have a large part, as they had buried the osprey he had killed, and buried it over one of his own children's burial sites. As he had watched them there, he'd been worried for a few moments that they might discover more under the earth than they expected. He'd also been amazed that they chose that spot to bury the bird. It must all be part of his power. Oh, tonight would be good! It was just an hour until dark, when he could act. His head throbbed with pain and his neck ached. How he dreaded the building of the pain, but how he yearned for the action, the motion, the work. Not this Sally but another girl waited. His early feeling of his own death was gone.

As the small talking party broke up, the watcher moved away. There had been so many deaths today. Would he touch the new girl tonight or tomorrow? What would the Light tell him to do? Should he move now to his car and away from here, toward his quarry, or should he perhaps find the big woman again?

The watcher moved silently through the forest back toward the big woman and the man with the birthmark. Why not find her? He had time. What would she do next? Would her power grow? Could he get to know her? Would she go mad as everyone must believe he had gone mad?

He held his head, his temples exploding with pain. He hated this part. The pain.

He stopped, leaning against a tree, everything leaving his vision and consciousness and feelings except the terrible pain. Have to wait this out. Have to wait this out.

Part IV

The Mirror

10

The Handkerchief

Serial Murderer Receiving International Fame
Associated Press
June 26, 1992

Spokane—. This mid-size American city in the Pacific Northwest has become the center of international attention as it joins the ranks of cities combating the bloodshed of serial killers. Previously known for the serial rapist, Kevin Coe, Spokane has always seen itself as a family-friendly place, according to Mayor Tommy Kaas.

That has changed.

An alleged killer claiming to be led to child victims with disabilities or illnesses through hallucinations involving intense light, has claimed to have abducted and killed three children, most recently a ten-year-old girl. Her name is being withheld. Letters have been written by "The Light Killer" to the Spokesman-Review city desk. No authority has yet communicated with the killer by phone or any other means.

"I am somewhat like the profiles say," the killer wrote in his most recent letter. "But as if you are looking in a mirror. And I will not be found anytime soon. I watch, I listen, I am among the Hidden. I have powers you cannot imagine."

The Light Killer Task Force, headquartered in downtown Spokane, is directed by Police Chief Todd Harrington and FBI Special Agent Bernie Washington. At a press conference today, both men discussed the unsuccessful six months of investigation, involving nearly forty full-time local and federal personnel.

"We have no hard evidence," Special Agent Washington cautioned community members. "We have no bodies, nothing to make clues of. Each envelope has multiple fingerprints from being handled by USPS personnel. Each letter could come from any number of computer printers. While experts have analyzed the language we have arrived at perpetrator profiles that can fit thousands of men."

Harrington said he does not know how long it will take to apprehend a suspect. "This is uncharted territory for us. We don't have a handle on what we're dealing with," he said.

Washington concurred. "We have not yet been in the position of stopping a killer who never lets us see his victims. To us at the task force, everyday is a memorial to a lost child. We are religious and humble people, most of us parents ourselves. We are doing our absolute best."

Parents and friends of the new victim, as well as the children previously abducted and presumed killed, have asked that donations be made to the Spokane Child Victims Fund, care of the Spokane Police Department. The Department has so far collected $159,000 from locations as far away as Madagascar.

In the Light Killer's most recent letter, announcing the death of the latest child, he wrote of his place in the universe. This is a common subject in his correspondence:

"How can you stop me, Citizens of the World? I cannot be stopped because without my efforts the Universe would shrivel into Darkness. Do not think me an individual in this, nor that I have the ego to believe my death will end the Universe. This is not what I mean.

"I mean that I am part and parcel of something far greater, so deep is my service to the Universe. Were my body to die, my sweet soul would continue to measure the light and the darkness, without end.

"You cannot keep your children from me, for I live with the bidding of God, the Creator.

"Citizens of the World, you may know me as the devil incarnate, but you have been wrong to think God hates me. Like Lucifer, I serve God. Like the serpent, I am of God's design."

Based on this new letter, experts have asked the public to pursue the possibility that the killer is involved in devil worship or a satanic cult.

For Spokane, each new theory gives new hope.

But the emotions of many were expressed by the mother of the latest victim. "Why is God letting this happen?" she asked.

Beth put down the clippings.

She was thinking: Sally and her father must be gone from the spot now. We can go there.

She was thinking: How could this killer's language sound so similar to mine?

She was thinking: It was right we didn't keep watching daughter and father, like voyeurs, but now let them be gone.

Something happened to Beth like an explosion, and like the coming of a terrible peace.

The heat flashed through her body and she cried out.

"What is it!" Nathan jumped.

Then Beth felt as if she were going to float. The feeling made her turn toward the boulder with the earth-seam from which lights had come earlier. She felt herself grin, said she was all right.

She stood, and Nathan stood. No light emerged from the rock, even though she had felt pulled to look there. She touched the stone Nathan had given her—no heat or light on it. The sun was setting, twilight reflecting off water, the rocks, the shiny leaves on tree branches, the moon rising.

"We don't always need the hidden light to show itself," she said to Nathan, the words barely her own. "We are following it even when we don't see it. The light is happening all the time. I kind of see why the crazy killer uses a capital L. The Light is always and everywhere, if we'd just see it.

"Nathan," she said. "Come on."

He walked with her through shrubs and then to a deer path. Though it had gotten darker, the moon brightened the forest. Their destination was the spot where Sally and her father had buried the dead osprey.

Beth kneeled down at the grave, waiting. She knew there

was a reason the osprey had died here, there was a communication, in another kind of language. She would not force it. She would wait. She squeezed Nathan's hand, lying now on his knees as he kneeled with her.

"Shhhhh," she hissed gently. "We can't speak."

Then it happened. The girl in the maroon WSU sweatshirt appeared. She walked as if out of a background of light. The girl held a tiny white cloth, crumpled like a stone in her fist. She walked toward Beth almost animal in her hesitancy.

"There's no reason to be afraid," Beth heard herself say, words she had used to reassure her younger siblings.

The girl walked closer, raising her hand, holding out what Beth now saw to be a handkerchief, a man's creamy white handkerchief, monogrammed with DLK in small gold-tinted, subtly raised, brocade. Beth saw herself take the handkerchief in her own hand.

Then the light disappeared. The young girl was gone.

The "trip"—the happening—was over.

Beth opened her eyes and studied her empty hands, half expecting the handkerchief to have materialized there. "Describe what's happening," Nathan suggested. "Something about your hands?"

"There's heat on my hands, but . . ." she told him what she had experienced, and what she had expected to see in her hands.

He took her hands in his. "They are warm, for sure."

Beth looked at the slightly mounded osprey grave.

"Maybe it was a hallucination," Nathan analyzed, "neurally stimulated by the warmth in the cells of your hand."

Beth saw the osprey in her mind, saw how painstakingly it had been communicating with Sally. She saw Sally bringing her father here. She saw herself involved, through some sort of strange touch, in bringing the dead osprey together with the humans. She saw the burial. Beth saw the little girl in the sweatshirt back by the river bridge earlier in the day. She saw the cave of her earlier vision. Beth saw the osprey fly out of the cave, then saw the shadow of a bird flying over the river.

"Don't think," she murmured. "Let the heat absorb you, let the achiness absorb you. Don't analyze it. Don't be afraid of it."

Then she saw what she had not seen.

"Help me, Nathan," she cried. She began to dig in the dirt for the dead bird.

He began to dig. "We're supposed to dig the bird up?"

"We have to dig under it," she said, feeling the poke of the wingtip as she dug deeper. Nathan had the head, holding it by the beak. She moved the brown-white speckled, wet, and insected bird into Nathan's hands, and he put it on a small rock. It overwhelmed the rock like a canopy.

She dug. When she had gotten about eight inches down, Nathan digging beside her, she felt either a large wet leaf, or moist cloth.

Nathan pulled it up. "Is this what we're looking for?" He held it in his right hand, the hand ringed with dirt as if with a glove. It was a very dirty, white handkerchief. Nathan's eyes widened as he said, "Jesus, Beth! It *is* what we're looking for. It's the handkerchief from your . . . hallucination. Whoa."

"It doesn't belong to the girl," Beth said, looking around in the stumps, shrubs, dirt nearby. "But she held it in her hands." Was there a body buried here as well?

She reached for the handkerchief, feeling a dark sense of evil as she touched it, like she felt earlier up at Greta's. This time, as if she were a little used to it, it didn't overwhelm. In fact, she realized that she no longer even questioned the veracity of her experience. She knew now that this handkerchief was related to the missing children, but it was not a child's.

"I think it belongs to the man doing the abductions," Beth said. "I don't know why I know this."

Nathan studied it as it dangled between two of his fingers in front of them both. Caked with soil, it smelled of loam. A tiny worm peaked out of some of the caked dirt. A black spider climbed along its bottom rim, then dropped off.

"Shit!" Nathan exclaimed, dropping it. "If all this is really happening, then this is the murderer's property, and it should have his prints. He dropped it or something. We have to keep it untouched for the pathologist."

Could any of the children still be alive? Should we call the police? Would they believe us? Thoughts overwhelmed Beth as she saw the reality before her. She had received a communication after a day of trying, like a letter that someone had been trying to deliver for years.

"I've got my cellular phone in the pack," Nathan said, standing. "Come on."

Beth stood up as Nathan grabbed a stick to carry the cloth. She moved over to rebury the osprey and Nathan hissed, "Don't! What if there are prints on other things here. Rocks. Stones. Let's just move away."

Beth moved away with him even though she did not feel the presence of the killer here, in this area. She only felt it on the cloth, which she was glad Nathan carried.

"I wish we could wait to alert anyone," Beth said, as they walked back to their campsite. "I feel like more will come unless things get . . . chaotic with people."

Nathan was ahead of her. He came to the pup tent and

moving into it like an animal on all fours, he came back out with his pack, pulling the big, gray, rectangular cell phone out.

"Something's been happening all day," Nathan said practically, "something real, certainly real to *you*. It's led you to this piece of cloth, which you think belongs to a psychopath. I know how we can get the police's attention, and how we can *prove* the rightness, the realness, of what's happened to you. Think about it, Beth. We get ahold of this task force and we tell them you saw a girl with a WSU sweatshirt. That's not a detail that's been in any papers."

He was right. If no girl had been abducted who wore a WSU sweatshirt, all this would have been some other experience, mixed into what she had been reading about a sick man hurting children. But if there was a girl, who must now be dead, who wore a WSU sweatshirt, and if this girl had been abducted, then the police would have to believe her. Beth shivered to think what it would mean if they did. It would mean so many things. It would mean this day was fully real.

"Call the police," Beth pressed.

"I can call 911 or call a friend of mine who's a pathologist?" Nathan was staring at the phone, weighing his options. "You remember Kenny Rosenthal?"

"Rosie?" Beth remembered. Rosie was a tall Jewish doctor of about thirty who looked thirteen.

"I'll call 911, try to get through to the task force. If I can't, I'll try to get Rosie. He knows everyone."

"Or you could call Landry. Or we could go see him?"

Nathan nodded, already pushing 911.

Beth knelt at the handkerchief as Nathan spoke into the phone, giving the dispatcher his physician's credentials, then describing himself as a friend of Dr. Kenny Rosenthal. He spoke precisely and finished by saying he had information about the Light Killer.

She let her hands hover over the cloth. She felt no coldness or pain or evil. It was as if her mind was no longer in another kind of consciousness. It was thinking out practical issues, and thus not free to see or feel beyond the problem.

Nathan got through to someone on the task force. Beth listened to him describe the strange events of today (leaving out the light above Jeffrey, leaving out Donnell Wight), describing the visions his girlfriend had had regarding the missing children, especially a girl, about nine or ten, blond, hazel eyes, dressed in a maroon Washington State University sweatshirt. Nathan described as best he could—and he admitted it sounded crazy—how his girlfriend had come about finding the cloth. It had been found just below Lucia Court, near the Spokane River, he said. The WSU sweatshirt hasn't been released to the public, Nathan said, so this would prove veracity.

"Oh," she heard Nathan say, hearing surprise in his voice. "Are you sure?"

The conversation was short-lived after that. Nathan said good-bye and hung up, his forehead furrowed in a frown Beth could now barely see in the late dusk light.

"No girl with a WSU sweatshirt," he said.

Beth stared at the cloth. Something was going on. Something was missing. "What a journey we're on," Beth sighed aloud.

Nathan dropped down beside her. "I'm sorry . . . about the police."

"It's kind of a relief," she told him. "It's okay."

They held hands, sitting on their knees beside the cloth for a moment, then rose in tandem, Nathan carrying the cloth back to the hole downriver where it had come from.

He got onto his knees, pulling the hole further open with digging fingers, his muscled arms flexing in the dusk.

Rather than digging, Beth bent at the osprey, then felt pulled to look at the river. She saw lights on it, about twenty of them, hovering. Then she heard an old woman's voice.

"Jesus," she murmured under her breath. She got a picture suddenly of Nathan in a large yard next to a huge building, like a university or institute. She was seeing his future again. His hair was grayer and he stood with some other women and men, posing for a picture. It was like a class picture or something, but not a medical school graduation. Nathan was in the center of the picture, a leader of this group.

"Nathan," she said, "something just happened again. Jesus, my mind just won't shut off."

He came over and took osprey in his hands. "What happened?"

"A voice. I don't know. I saw the lights on the water."

He looked out at the water, saw nothing.

"We're going crazy, Beth," Nathan laughed, and brought the osprey to the hole.

Nathan's hands were bloodied with dirt and mud, and the hole was almost a foot and a half deep. Beth came over to him, and a silence fell and she and Nathan put the cloth and the bird on top of it, into the hole.

"I'm hearing voices now," Beth said. "What if I'm losing my mind or something? Some kind of temporary schizophrenia?"

"No," Nathan assured her. "It's not that. I don't believe it's that. Yes, you seem to be 'insane' from some sort of social standpoint. I mean, we could probably diagnose you with multiple diagnoses from the PDR and DSM V. But I'm here with you and I know you're not going insane."

Beth nodded, engaging his eyes. "Thank God," she said, embracing him. So as not to dirty her, he held his hands out away from the embrace, but he let her hold him as long as she needed.

Then, the embrace done, they bent again to their task. "We'll know the . . . evidence . . . I guess that's the word . . . we'll know it's here," Nathan said, "we'll know just where it is if we need it."

"And it won't be near our camp tonight." Beth imagined the kinds of nightmares it might give her, as electrified as her mind had been the last hour, so sensitive to different kinds of touch.

Giving the moment a piece of silence, Beth and Nathan stood over the grave. Then, moving toward the river, they squatted over the water, and washed their hands.

When they returned to their camp, Beth said, exhausted, "Read me some poetry, okay? Light the fire then read to me. No killers. No visions except beautiful poetry."

Nathan had laid the fire earlier, with twigs and branches, ready for night—Nathan, always ready. Now he pulled matches out of his pocket, and lit an old piece of newspaper at the bottom of the tepee of kindling. The fire lit immediately.

They sat side by side in the firelight so Nathan could read. He picked a book she'd brought, the poetry of W. B. Yeats. He opened a page at random and read.

Beth listened and looked out at the river. As Nathan read, it seemed to her that the river, too, curled its swan's neck up to listen. Her eyes drifted on the faint hope of sleep. She heard words, then saw the book not in Nathan's hands, but in the hands of Sammy Range. The boy held the book in his hands, opened it. This was happening tonight, at the river. Beth saw that she was handing Sammy Range the book tonight, here.

All thought of sleep left her. There was a moth near Sammy, touching him. Beth was sure Sammy was around here. He was coming to her.

Everything today somehow had to do with children.

11

THE MOTH

WHEN SAMMY HAD turned to look at Sally, hoping she admired his skills with the skateboard, she was just turning into the late afternoon sun, pushing up on her hands and starting down toward the river gorge. He stopped his board and thought about following her. Josh, ten, two years younger than Sammy, wore what he always wore: the sullen look of a boy who hates his family. But he loved to skate. And Sammy did too. Sammy saw him fly over the curb and into the air, the back of the skateboard shooting high, the front tip dropping toward the concrete but Josh righting it, twirling, airborne for a second, then landing on the street, feet cocked on the board. He braked, popped the board upright with a foot, like a monkey flipping a stick, and started again.

"What're you starin' at?" he dared.

"Sorry, man, thought you were a girl." Sammy retorted.

With a "Fuck you!" Josh embarked again on his little skateboard ship.

Sammy wished he had followed Sally. For a few weeks now, he'd been noticing her. Other girls, too. More than once he had thought that her company would have been better than Josh's. Without saying anything, Josh skated down Lucia Place, giving Sammy some time to go the other way. Sammy took it. He skated out past Greta and Trudy Sarbaugh's house, no destination in mind. He tried hard not to look over at the spot where Jeffrey had been hit, though he saw it and felt his throat seize up.

Six Mile Road spread like winding fishing line far off across the river toward the dam many miles north. Sammy had been in an airplane once with his father and had seen his own neighborhood and the dam from up there. He and Sam Sr. had gone with Mr. Jackson Hess, who was teaching his father to skydive. Mr. Hess and Sam Sr. made Sammy swear he wouldn't tell his mom, and he didn't need swearing. He knew how much his mother didn't want Sam Sr. or Sam Jr. in danger.

Up in the plane, all was forgotten except the beauty of the world. Sammy had never thought life could be so cool, so big, so full of things. He closed his eyes and heard the prop engine and the roar of the wind and became, for a moment, something else.

"Being up here," he yelled to the two men, "it's like being a fish in the ocean."

"How do you figure that?" Sam Sr. laughed.

"Maybe we're not really flying, see. Maybe the sky is really an ocean, but made of air, and we're, like, fish in it." His father, who could always be counted on to enjoy most whatever his son said, teased back, "So if I'm a fish, I won't need a parachute when I jump!"

At his son's sudden pallor, he belly-laughed.

The skateboard under him, its wheels churning on the concrete, the wind in his face, his arms out like a bird's, Sammy remembered his father's death and then Jeffrey's with a pain inside him so vast he could only notice it again for a second, then glide through and hope, when he stopped at the top of the river gorge, it would be gone. If it wasn't, he would keep skating and keep skating until it receded back to its source, waiting for him there, but waiting till he was older, perhaps much older, and capable of meeting it the way Father met things—his father, that boisterous, life-filled, risk-elated man, deep voiced, flawed only in that he feared nothing.

When Sammy came to a stop thirty feet above the river trail, he felt quiet, almost angry at something. But what? He looked up and there was a man coming toward him, wearing jeans, hiking boots, and a hooded windbreaker. A white man, his eyebrows were brown and shadowy under the hood. His lips were small and closed, his eyes lowered. Sammy stepped out of his way so the man could pass. The man walked in a kind of loping way, and hardly made a sound on the footpath. Sammy stole a glance at the man's back as he moved farther into the forest, and then was gone.

Turning back to the front, Sammy now saw to his left, at about forty yards, the fleeing white butts of a deer and a fawn. He heard the mama snort. Snorting in his own way, he flipped his board into his hand, and slid on ski-bent feet down the incline toward a path that cut through the birch, pine, holly, and gooseberry bushes. He heard a *screeee* and lifted his eyes toward an osprey flying south. The trail would take longer to the water than just running down the rocky incline, so he ran and fell on his butt and ran some more and ended up, finally, at the water's edge.

He walked along the river toward a fallen log his father had shown him when he was ten. It stretched, along with another log, into the river, seeming to Sammy like a king's colonnade, from which the ruler could see his watery domain. Flashy reddish orange in the dusk, a fish jumped. Looking upward at the sources of color, Sammy saw two jet streams, like dissolving white train tracks, going in both directions. Sammy followed the white streams with his eyes till he hit the horizon of heaven. He had never seen beyond that. Mrs. Sarbaugh once told him it took a soul forty-nine days, or something like that, to get to heaven. Jeffrey had forty-eight days left. Sam Sr. had gotten there long ago.

"Papa," Sammy murmured, "I won't forget you." It was something he said often these days. He had begun to forget his father's face after a year. His mother, he knew, had begun to forget too. Another man had begun to fill her eyes with new pictures.

"Samuel, we have to bury the dead," she had said a few days ago. "We just have to move on."

"So who's stopping you," he said with a glare. "I'm okay with it if you are."

She didn't believe him. Her clenched hands, and half-hug and awkward sigh said something like, "Poor Samuel Jr., I wish I could make it better for you."

How do you convince your mama you're fine, Sammy wondered, feeling the weird anger again for a second, like a fist in the gut. It had been coming between him and his mother for a few weeks now. He had felt it even more since seeing Jeffrey lying there, dead. Sammy remembered just panting and trying not to cry while the adults ran around. Then there had been that strange light, so big, it was really there. It felt good.

Sammy picked up a stone and tossed it into the water. "Like a bomb hitting a fish that's really a plane." He smiled to himself, dropping down onto the dirt, his knees drawn up to his chin. He imagined himself skating across the water on his skateboard, right across. A skateboarding Jesus! Closing his eyes, he leaned back on gravel-pocked palms, his mouth opening as if in sleep and the cooling sun reddening his face. To the watcher, he looked like an angelic boy drawn in orangish-reddish hues in a pastorale. Too old, though. Developing just a little fast. And nothing wrong with him—at least nothing obvious to the eye, nothing found even in private places. Sammy lay back on his elbows, then all the way back, dozing off in the sunset.

When his eyes opened, Sammy looked at his watch—he had slept almost a half hour. His shirt was up above his belly button, pulled up by the breeze. The top button of his pants was undone and his zipper only half up. He didn't remember undoing his pants. Had he peed while he slept and not realized it? Sammy buttoned up, zipping, looking around and seeing no one.

Rippled circles of water lapped onto shore, one by one, and disappeared into the foamy tufts of algae at the water's edge. Sammy bent forward toward the water, feeling a sudden urge to press his face into the lapping river glass like a god looking down into his domain. Closing his eyes, Sammy felt the water hit his face, fill the crevices of his closed eye sockets, open nostrils, closed mouth. It outlined his hairline and neck, just above the ears. For a second, he enjoyed the closed-eye embrace of the water. It made his face into a mask. He was God looking into the world from heaven. Opening his eyes, he peered into the algae-rich water, seeing rocks, green moss, dots of algae in the layers of water like tiny moats of dust caught in beams of sunlight. All fish, all other movable creatures, would be gone, frightened by the huge peering presence into their world. Sammy pulled his head out, took another deep breath, then descended again, his cheeks puffed like a blowfish's.

Pulling up out of the water, he shook his head the way a dog shakes himself after a swim. Droplets fell everywhere, making stains on rocks and on his jeans and blue T-shirt and ripples on the still edge of the river. Wiping his eyes, he peered upward again toward the blue lake of heaven. He closed his eyes, soaking the twilight onto his cooled face. Eyes closed, listening to his own heartbeat in his ear, his own tingling of consciousness, the murmur of the river like blood through open veins of the earth, Sammy saw Jesus in his mind's eye, saw him riding on the back of the great blue heron with Jeffrey next to him.

"Jesus, Son of God, King of Mercy," he prayed aloud, "teach me how to be good, and not miss Papa. Teach me to make Mama happy. Jesus, please take care of Jeffrey, Jesus triumphant." A tear brimmed his right eye against the river-wet there. With deep breaths he smelled pine resin and the rich algal odors of summer. He looked into the sunset, then closed his eyes. On his arm he felt a tickling. Opening his eyes he saw a moth. Startled, he blew it off him. It flew for a second but couldn't quite right itself against the force of his breath. Toppling, it hit the water.

Sammy stared at it in the water just four feet in front of him. Brown, it had a wingspan of nearly an inch. Its black dots got tinted by the dusky light. It struggled, its right wing heavy with water. Sammy leaned forward into a kneel, moving uncomfortable gravel out from under his knees. He watched the moth struggle, water droplets running off its wings as off a roof or raincoat. Everywhere it struggled it made tiny ripples in the water. For a second it alighted, but then fell in again. Now it had struggled to another foot farther out. Sammy thought he saw a white-goldish light on the moth, like the light near Jeffrey yesterday—but then it was gone.

An owl hooted upriver. Two squirrels carried on in a pine just to the left. A fish jumped. Two ducks rose into the air with the sound of a squeaky propellor. An angry voice from deep within Sammy, a voice neither his mother's nor father's nor anyone's he knew, but very mean, whispered to him, "Watch it die; let it die; its time has come." But then another voice, equally powerful—it sounded like Jeffrey's!—whispered, "Save its life; you must." Sammy thought of Jeffrey, whom he couldn't save, and of his father, and of Jesus on the cross. How bizarre his mind had been this whole last day. So much in it. How weird to hear a voice.

He put one foot, still shod, into the water, keeping the other out. Dipping forward, he cupped his right hand under the moth, brought the insect upward with a palm full of water. Stepping back onto shore he set the moth on a small rock. Its wings immediately stuck there. Sammy felt a warm tingling in his legs and arms, then in his body and head. It was like a million insects on him—it was a tingling like he felt when he was getting goose bumps, but it felt really good, too. While he felt it, he petted the wings of the moth with his huge finger, then he pried the wings' edges off the rock with his fingernail. The tingling started to go away, but just as it did, the moth seemed to light up, with that white-gold light. Sammy looked to see how this could be, how the reflection of white light could be created. It couldn't—there wasn't enough sun. Sammy felt a little scared. The moth just kept glowing. It was really like last night, it was like that glow above Jeffrey. Was Jesus here?

"You can do it, go ahead, fly, you can do it," Sammy thought. The words were in his head but they couldn't come out. He reached out to touch the light on the moth. Just as his finger seemed to touch the glow, the moth fluttered on the rock, then rose, then flew off upward toward the trees, avoiding the water this time, flying up. Wow!

Sammy watched the light disappear into the forest, heading west. Then he heard something near the water. Underneath the water he saw the light forming again, underneath the water near the rock. It was as if the river were lit from a flashlight dropped down into the water. Sammy was sure he stopped breathing for a second. Could he reach in and get the flashlight? He started breathing again, thinking it must really be a flashlight. He leaned forward, without thinking much, and pushed his hand in the water. He dipped his face in too, feeling fearless, wanting to get closer to the light down there.

Once he touched the water with his face, the light seemed to push out into the water, toward the center of the river. He lifted his dripping hands and face and looked toward the river's center. Now he saw something he thought he would never be able to tell anyone about: he saw his father and Jeffrey, holding hands, like lit up angels floating over the water. They were holding hands and smiling at him. They both looked happy, like being dead was okay.

"Papa?" Sammy said aloud. He found himself entering the water, his feet suddenly wet. He got up to his thighs when the light, and the two people, disappeared. Stunned, Sammy looked around, looked everywhere. What had happened? He stepped back out of the water, turning all around with looking. He heard the wind, the trees rustling, the water purling.

He heard voices. He turned west. Two people were upriver. He heard a woman and a man. The voices sounded like the big woman, Beth, and her friend Nathan, the doctor with the big red birthmark on his neck. How far away were they? Had they seen anything?

Sammy walked out of the water and picked up his skateboard. He started back in the direction of the two people, walking around a group of pines, and then a maple. The breeze must have played tricks with sound, because the two people were a ways off. Walking with drenched pants, he sounded slushy. He saw them again, Nathan, gray-blond in the night glow of moonlight, and Beth lying back in the dirt near a tent and a fire.

"Hello there—Sammy?"

He wanted to say, "I just saw my dad and Jeffrey, did you?" but he didn't know what to say.

"Come here, buddy," Nathan invited.

"Sorry," he said, smiling, "I got wet."

Beth said, "The water has been breathing today, so loud we've heard it, we've watched its chest rise and fall. Have you felt God's breath like that?"

"Yeah, I feel things like that." He almost mentioned the feelings he'd just had. It was like she'd been inside him.

"Have you been okay, Samuel?" Nathan asked. "Since . . . since yesterday."

"I'm okay," he answered quickly.

Beth closed her eyes, the firelight making her large face a

pale kind of orange. "Your father liked to fly. I see him up high. He was a big man. He liked it high up. And the spirits here at the river liked him. He stayed around here after he died, trying to get your attention. He wants to make sure you are safe and growing up right. He's very active today, actually. Have you seen him?"

"What do you mean?" Sammy asked, fingering his skateboard. How could she know?

Beth smiled. "He's a beautiful spirit. Doors are open today because there have been some important deaths today and yesterday. Some sort of perfect symmetry of suffering and joy. They've pried a door open—I know you'll think it sounds weird, but it just is, you just have to believe, that's what the light was about—a torn seam in the Veil. There will be more discoveries tonight. Some of them very sad. But not for you, Samuel."

Sammy didn't remember Beth ever talking much. He remembered Nathan talking, but Beth seemed like the teacher now. She pointed to Sammy. "There are so few boundaries. I feel like a sheet of rice paper. I see a moth on you, Sammy. I see a white moth near you, Sammy, and you are with it near the river."

How could she know? She must have seen him save it, and she was pretending to have this weird vision. She and Nathan must be on drugs. Unconsciously, Sammy brushed at his hair, feeling as if the insect clasped his hair with its feet.

Beth sighed and smiled. "I see that you're going to live a long time. You're okay. You won't die like your dad. Have faith that you'll always be taken care of. He'll be with you as long as you need him. He'll always take care of you. And you have the gift of flight, you know," Beth said, "like your dad. You'll do something having to do with airplanes."

"How do you know?" he asked. She was like a psychic or something, a New Age person Mama's preacher hated.

"I don't know. I just see you flying airplanes. Very clear."

Sammy didn't know what to think. "I gotta go," he said.

"It's gonna be okay," Nathan said. "But be careful. Go back toward home. You don't want to stay alone down here when it gets dark."

"Okay," Sammy said reflexively. Sammy turned, his skateboard bouncing against his right side as he picked up speed, walking down the path and out of earshot of the two adults.

"Wait!"

Sammy stopped running. Beth was right on him, holding out a book.

"Take it," she said. "Whatever you do in life, be like your dad. Don't be afraid, okay? Everything happens in a beautiful plan."

"Okay, thanks," Sammy murmured, raising his hand. Beth placed the book in the smaller palm with her puffy hand.

"You're welcome." She grinned, and bowed just a little, like maybe she was from India, then turned on the path and started to walk back to her boyfriend and his fire.

Sammy jogged along the river trail, toward the incline trail, and then the street. He looked at his watch. His mother would be waiting for him to eat and change and go to evening church.

Could Beth really see him in airplanes? Would he be a pilot? A thrill surged through him. Was Papa always around? Had Papa been proud he saved the moth?

"Papa," he whispered, speeding toward home. "Papa, are you there?"

The sound of his wheels, a loud truck out past Five Mile Road, a screen door closing behind the Romer house—the blue wavery light of the TV in Alex Bass's second-story room, the smell of cedar from the Sarbaughs' cedar tree, then the flits of gnats circling his head and letting him pass—all of it seemed like his father's hands upon him, answering "Yes!" Could that really be?

With hope, Sammy closed his eyes, riding the wind of his wheels, arms out like wings.

The river valley, and the watcher within it, gazed with rapt attention at the flight of a boy awakened to the air. He became the whooshing sounds of a child pretending to fly. He heard, too, the low hum of another sound—his own voice imitating the whoosh, the hum, the wind as evening turned toward night. Because of the waning daylight, the watcher could not see the whole boy there, not every feature, but more a moving silhouette, a figure of flying. And he already knew how the boy's body felt; he had already inspected it for illness, touched its soft skin, yearned to go deeper into the pants of the boy who stirred there by the water.

The boy noticed nothing but his own vigor, and did not seem to mind being watched. There was no desire about him, only play, and the joy of meeting lost love again, as if it had never gone—his father lived, completely, in his life right now. The watcher could not mistake joy.

The boy ended his song of flying, closed his arms, and kicked the skateboard up into his hands. He listened and walked, the faint sound of the river in his ears, the lights of the houses around him, reminding him that he was not altogether free.

So much to ponder. The watcher looked on as the boy walked past the house where the two old women lived, then toward his own house. One of the old women, the one with the cane and tiny glasses, came out her back door, crossing her grass toward the river.

The watcher turned away. His head was hurting more and more each minute. It was coming closer to the time when he must leave the valley and gain his prey. The watcher walked, contemplating this boy—vaguely remembering himself, in Syracuse, as a child. This boy was one of those who had seen the Light yesterday. What part would this boy end up playing in the drama of Light? The watcher had had the Light to himself for months, but now it was being shared with all these people. He had had the urge, earlier, to kill them all. But this, he knew, was not the Light's plan. It was not the instruction that came with God's Sound. There was much going on here, a big lake of Light and Experience he must master. He had things to do. He had things to learn. And he suspected he had to hurry.

In his next letter, he resolved, pulling out his pocket notebook to write, he would tell people more than he yet had, especially about Healing. His head was hurting, throbbing, and this would be the Call to action. The new girl, anorexic, would be in his arms soon, and she would inspire so much wisdom about Hunger and Healing. She would give Grace to his Appetites. He would Teach her then Touch her and Heal her. This time his power would fully accomplish its promise. He felt urgency like never before. Tonight was very important!

A crow emitted a loud *cawww* above him and he looked up to see a black spirit in the shadowy sky. The sound of the river was loud as he moved toward it. He stopped to write:

"When the Light is our friend, we become a prophet. New rules apply to us. How else could it be? We are the masters of true Freedom. No one can find me unless I wish to be found.

"When a Prophet emerges, the emergence begins with a period of awakened senses. The Prophet is generally someone with a history of gifts. Always the Prophet can see the Light! I can see the Light! There are Mirrors everywhere. The awakened ones are Mirrors, as I am.

"The Prophet faces praise and opprobrium both, and fears neither because the Awakening moves aside the individual ego, melding the Prophet with the source of Prophecy.

"There is nothing as powerful in a lifetime as feeling connected to the source of one's own Power. The Prophet usually has to begin with or ends up with certain healing Powers and Empathies. I must take more children, must Heal them. The true hidden Power of Healing is mine. It is the Power of the Light. The Light promises me that."

The watcher looked up into the full moon and saw God's eye looking down at him. He stowed his notebook in his pocket, turned back toward the campsite of the big woman and her friend. What should he do with them? Should he kill the big woman? Could she become too powerful?

12

The Healing

"Greta, you've come to share the night air with us." Nathan opened his arms to her and did a little bow.

"I needed to talk to you both. I'm glad I found you." Beth rose to hug her, and spread out the towel for the old woman. Greta saw a rock and walked the distance to it, leaning, as usual, on her metal cane. She was a little out of breath.

Beth watched the old woman with the kind of admiration she felt for a mother. She was glad to see her old friend. There was so much to tell.

"We just saw Sammy," Beth said. "He has a beautiful spirit. He seemed a little overwhelmed, confused by intensity of experience, but I think he'll be okay."

"I think I'm afraid," Nathan said, looking down at his hands now, and the little stick they held. "I want to say it aloud."

He prodded at the fire, its light in his eyes. Beth was surprised to hear him say things like this, so hard for a man to say. Why, suddenly, now? He had been sitting with her peacefully. But now he was . . . well . . . so honest. Beth felt a surge of love for him, and at the same time a terrible fear, as if some part of her preferred never hearing him admit the weakness she had always known was in him.

"Being with Beth today," he said to Greta, "seeing all the suffering around us today, hearing her tell me I'm going to die young. . . . How do I explain this? Joy and delight don't move me like the vibrations of terror move me, not at the deepest levels. What I'm most attracted to somehow, what I most want to analyze, is the serial killer. The darkness. I'm disappointed the police didn't recognize what Beth knew."

"The police?" Greta asked, looking at both Beth and Nathan. "You called them?"

Nathan explained.

Beth saw a dark aura on Nathan. Was he experiencing, in his way, communication from spirits around here, dark spirits that grazed against him? He seemed to have changed in the last ten minutes or so. Was it just that a day of Beth's visions had worn, finally, on Nathan's ego? Or did he see in the boy he must have been once? Was that it?

Beth turned away from Nathan to Greta, and, as Nathan paused in his retelling of the events, stepped in to tell her old friend about Sally and her father, the dead osprey, the burial, then the cloth, then the call to the police. Greta listened, asked questions. She wished aloud that they hadn't reburied the cloth.

Greta said, "What if there is something *we* can do to save those children?" And with this Nathan's mood suddenly lifted. He came alive again, laying out all the options, as he had thought of them all. "Without more information," he pointed out, dropping his stick in the fire and sitting in the dirt next to Beth and Greta, "we don't know anything. No location. No perpetrator. Beth can't just turn on the visions like a spigot. She may not get another single vision about the killer or the children. Not one. We just don't know. But we can develop a sense. . . ."

Greta looked up at the cloudless sky and a sea of stars and said, "Those poor children. Is no one safe today? I'm old, and I have finally learned that life is safe, not something to fear. And soon I will die. That is a puzzle. Well"—she turned back to Beth and Nathan—"I'm thinking about Adelle. I don't know what can be done for the abducted children. I left Adelle a call earlier. I think I'll call her again—maybe she can advise us regarding the police.

"Let me tell you what has happened this afternoon while you were down here. Then I'll go call her."

"Did much happen?" Beth asked.

Greta smiled. "How do we define 'much'? I've received calls from Alex and his mother, and talked to Sally and her father. Nothing like what you've had, Beth, but things have been happening for everyone. Annie has not said that anything has happened to her in a metaphysical way, but all the others have—they've either had dramatic incidents, like Harold and Laura's visitors, or 'big feelings'—this was Alex's word, or as Mr. McDonald put it, 'Everything just feels strange.' He told me about burying the dead osprey. This is very unusual, to see an osprey dead on the ground. As I've been thinking about all the reports, and listening to you both, I'm thinking that Beth seems to be involved in everyone's experiences. Do you notice that?"

Beth thought back to each person and recognized herself playing a part of some kind. She nodded. Nathan had already seen it, or thought of it in that way people have who don't realize their thoughts till others speak them. "Definitely," he said. "She's woven into everything."

Greta nodded. "Everyone who saw that light has been having experiences that go beyond all boundaries of previous experience. It has been such a shock to some of the mental systems here—Mrs. Bass was worried that we've been exposed to some kind of experimental gas—such a shock that we are not going to be able to keep this to ourselves for much longer. Word is going to spread. We should all be ready for that. You, especially, Beth. I don't know what you will do from here, but you will never be the same."

Beth shivered. "What should we do? Is there something we're supposed to do, or maybe we aren't supposed to try to control it at all?"

"We have to try to contain this, at least for a while," Nathan said, his eyes radiant against the night. "We have to study it. What we should do is get MRIs and PET scans as soon as possible, tomorrow or whenever I can get people in, to see what has happened to our brain functioning. We could complete the scans of everyone in, say, three days. When the papers or TV get hold of our experiences, who knows what will happen to us . . . or to the integrity of the experiences themselves?"

Greta touched Nathan's arm. "This is a new awakening for all of us. Who are we to say we should try to control its effects on the world? Heaven has visited us now, heaven on earth. We have to be careful how we greet her, but we shouldn't keep this a secret any longer, certainly not any longer than the forty-eight hours we all agreed on."

"I disagree," Nathan said, like a lawyer going on record.

Beth found herself rocking back and forth, like a Jew davening over scripture. The purling sound of the river just thirty feet from her, the slight sound of the wind, the memory of the honeysuckle and vanilla smell—each moved in and through her, giving her a feeling of calm.

"Nothing can go wrong," she said aloud. "No matter what happens, nothing can go wrong. This is all larger than we are."

"I know it is," Nathan said. "But how do we best play our part? How do we best serve this moment? We have a responsibility to do our part well. If we don't, if we don't protect this . . . light. If we don't understand it, don't we open it up to something terrible?"

Beth thought of her journal. At least there was that record.

Greta grinned that odd grin of hers, glaring white newness of dentured teeth against an ancient, wrinkled face. "You have always liked a debate, Nathan."

"I will take that as a compliment," he grinned back.

Beth saw a tiny spot of food between Greta's teeth and yearned to touch it away. Beth tried to see when Greta would die, but saw nothing except the tiny spot on the teeth.

Then Beth lifted her hand, asking for quiet; a shimmering had begun. It had started over the water, a golden shimmering in the dusk-blue light over the green water. A ball of light for a few seconds, it spread out over the river like moonlight covering the surface. It was golden light, and it seemed to be communicating.

"Do you see it?" She pointed.

"What do you see?" Nathan asked. Both Nathan and Greta looked out at the water with her.

"I just see moonlight on the water, dear."

"But it's gold," Beth said, "and it started out as a ball of light. Wait, now it's becoming white again, moonlight. How beautiful!"

"Is it like the lights from under the rock?" Nathan asked.

"Yes."

"Angels?" Greta said, coughing then recovering. She started coughing again, a deep and raspish cough, like a cigarette smoker's cough. Yet she was not a smoker. Some of the fire smoke must have caught in her throat, Beth thought. She coughed again and breathed in with difficulty.

"Greta?"

"I'm fine—" But she coughed again, as if there were something climbing in her throat. She pounded on her chest with her open palm. Nathan rose, went to her in two steps, and bent over her. She leaned on her cane, coughing ferociously. Nathan gently pressed her back with an open palm. Her face was turning a little bit blue, then golden, golden like the water had been golden. Beth cried out when she saw the gold on her friend's face. She pushed up and went over and when she got to Greta, holding her other shoulder, she saw the golden light pull away, like a bat flying off into the night.

Greta's coughing subsided.

"You're doing fine," Nathan said, calm and encouraging. "Take three shallow breaths, then a deep one." Greta took the four breaths, and the coughing diminished considerably.

"Thought you and I were going to get to kiss," Nathan jibed, miming a mouth-to-mouth resuscitation.

Greta couldn't talk yet, but she did smile.

Nathan and Beth both sat down on their knees in the sand next to her. "Are you all right?" Beth asked.

"I'm fine, dear," Greta said at last. "A tickle in my throat."

"It came onto *you*, Greta. I saw the light come onto *you*! Then, as if it was done with you, it flew away. And you got better."

"Some kind of healing is going on. Or is going to go on. Soon. Here. Or near here. I think some spirits came to get some energy from me to use for a healing of some kind. That's what I think. It's just an intuition. Often this has happened with Trudy, where she's feeling badly, and I cough or feel constricted, then she feels better."

"But you're all right now, Greta?" Beth insisted.

"I'm all right, dear. Though I think I'm a little tired after all. Nathan, would you walk me home?"

"Okay."

He stood up to help her and Beth stood to embrace her. "I'll see you soon," Beth said. "Maybe I'll come up for a shower."

"Just come by when you can." Greta smiled, still finding her voice. "I'll call Adelle. I don't know if she'll be in yet—though you'd think she would sleep some time." Beth watched Nathan help Greta walk up the path: The muscular young man walking with flashlight beside the skinny old woman. It was a sweet picture of life's variety, and success.

Beth stared at the fire, meditating on its colors and dreams. She sat down and rested, confined and confirmed by the beauty of the breathing night. Drifting at the fire, falling back and nearly dozing off, she heard a voice, the same voice as before. It seemed to fade in and out in some strange way. Not like a radio signal, but like a memory.

"Who are you?" she asked the night.

"I'm hearing voices again," she lamented. Yet, she had the feeling she had when she bent to kiss the earth, a sense of herself being transformed from a creature of fear and ego insecurities, to a creature given over to the habit of kissing the earth and serving the forces of light and love.

The voice came again. Electricity coursed through her, and Beth began to feel herself drifting, floating above the fire. She felt herself meld with the golden moonlit energy-light that had gone toward Greta. She saw herself getting larger and smaller as the world required, as if she were light itself. She saw herself floating in the forest and then coming to a beautiful, dark portal. Hesitating there, like a dragonfly wondering whether it will lose its colors if it enters, finally she chased the light into the dark and there she suddenly submerged in blinding light.

Then a face. A man's face. He was in his early thirties. He had a jutting chin, thin flat lips, and a flat nose. He had gray eyes, a protruding forehead, gray eyebrows and hair. Beth saw him sitting at a table, in a small room, walls of wood, writing, murmuring. He was dressed in jeans, a white shirt, and a blue zippered windbreaker, the hood draped on his back, the zipper half down to his chest. She saw him stand up then disappear for a moment, only to reappear on a rock between two trees, writing in a notebook.

Beth shivered. She knew who he was. And she knew why Nathan had become strange before; this killer's presence, this evil soul, was communicating. How? Communicating while writing? The words he was writing in the tiny notebook came to her, like the automatic words had come earlier in the day. She knew immediately that he wrote hundreds of pages of words, far more than he put in his letters, and she knew, too, that she and he were connected somehow, had met, and were of the same family.

Clearing her mind, she listened to him, watched him through this remote viewing, hoping his location would come to her.

"When the Light is our friend, we become a Prophet. New rules apply to us. How else can it be? We are masters of true Freedom.

"There is nothing as powerful in a lifetime like feeling connected to the source of one's own Power. The prophet usually has to begin with or ends up with certain healing powers and empathies. I must take more children, must hurt them and then heal them. The Power of healing, not just the power of hurting, must become mine. The true hidden power of Healing. The Light promises me that. How many children will be sacrificed?"

Beth wept at the fireside as she quickly wrote down what she had been able to see of him. She had to get everything down just as she'd seen or said it if she was to help find the children. A duck flew by then the duck disappeared and became three butterflies covered in the light—the healing light from before. Beth felt a bizarre urge to rise up and twirl her arms. It was as if she were hallucinating. She had the presence of mind to say, "I'm not myself," but twirled anyway. When she stopped, she fell onto her knees again. She could hear Nathan returning down the path in a rustle of leaves and breaking of twigs thirty or forty feet out of camp. She felt almost desperate for Nathan to come so that she could tell him about these last moments—of the feeling of being somehow naked in the human garden, a fright to others because of the powers her nakedness possessed. She felt the urge to stand up, brush the dirt off her knees, not show Nathan her dirt-lined humility, and thus be better able to join him where he was, an accommodation. But she could not stand up.

Nathan came into the camp.

"Nathan," she whispered, "I'm opening up, inside out. I saw a man. The children. We have to save them."

"Tell me!" Nathan came over, dropping down beside her.

"A healing is occurring or will soon occur. Those butterflies."

"Tell me what you mean."

"The children. I'm sure I'm seeing them. And him."

"The man who is taking them? Tell me!"

She tried to explain, holding Nathan with the full force of her body. He began to pull away, and she clutched him closer. She was drifting in a mist. "I have to come back here," she told herself. Nathan pulled away and tenderly guided her down to the sand, where he lay next to her, muzzling his face into her chest like a small animal. "Are you okay?"

"We have to save the children," Beth said.

Before he went away to find the girl he had seen in his visions—the girl with the purple sweatshirt—the watcher listened to the big woman with the thick glasses and her friend with the birthmark talk to the old woman. As he read in Beth's mind a yearning to save the children, the watcher moved away. How interesting, that she could not see how the children were already dead. How interesting that she could not see what was happening with the Light, how it talked to people like him. Yet, though she lacked these abilities, she had others so powerful. She must be the voice of the Madwoman. He had heard it before. He knew. She could easily become greater than he. She could grow in power instantaneously. Light moved differently in dark matter than in ordinary matter. Only 4 percent of the universe was ordinary matter. He was finding his way into the other 96 percent. What if Beth was following him into these realms?

What should he do? He knew. He would have to kill her. But not now. He had to get the other child.

The watcher crossed the suspension bridge and returned to a position across the river from the firelit campsite. He closed his eyes and envisioned golden Light on the water, letting it grow there then, when it was potent, sending it shooting toward the big woman. As if she caught it instead, the old woman choked with it. How strange! The watcher fell to his knees. This was definitely another Sign. The big woman could deflect his power. The Madwoman was gaining.

The watcher had been practicing on the children. He practiced how to use the Light for healing, learning to direct the Light, to use it in order to alter children's moods (then he would alter adult's), to send Light where he wished so that he could hurt or help anyone he chose at any time. Still, with none of the children had he found complete success or Power. To take on the Madwoman, he would need more Power. Could he gain it, tonight, with the new child, the anorexic girl who would be wearing a purple WSU sweatshirt?

Part V

The Power of the Light

13

The Crippled Woman

Annie would soon be crippled. It would begin gradually, in waves of pain so severe she would yearn for the time when she felt only twinges, then the pain so diminished into dead nerves that she would yearn for anything again, including pain. Today, her usual tears of defiance mixed with tears of sadness for Jeffrey and his family. She had cried so much today her face felt like it was bleeding. Now, late afternoon turning to evening, her cheeks and lips were chapped, her wet cheeks dry in the warm wind, as if a film of glue were thinly attached to the corners of her lips and jaw.

"I'll be back after dark," she called to her brother.

"Be careful," he called out the window. "You going to Trudy's?"

"Yeah. I'll go for a short ride first." He didn't know that she hoped to meet Jake there, her lover. He only knew she had been grooming Milky, her gelding, and weeping through the communion. Tom was a loving brother and gave her both embrace and distance, as she needed them.

"I'll just come to Spokane for a few weeks," she had told him, from Japan, six months before. She had not wanted to burden her brother with her own debilitating condition, yet she felt called back to Spokane as if by a voice more powerful than her ambition, pride, or shame. Ushi, her Japanese boyfriend, gave her up to her journey back home in the same way most people let her go. She was a free spirit, talented, adaptable, resolute. People knew this.

As she finished Milky's saddle, she remembered her last days with Ushi. Four years in Japan had built to them. On their last night together, she recalled Ushi running his fingers like sweet insects down her spine. The memory compelled her hand to run down Milky's nose as he chomped his second apple. She had not admitted her fear of her own physical pain to Ushi, but last week, sitting with Trudy, having had two unsuccessful operations already, she whispered, "Oh God, I'm afraid, Trudy, Oh God." She had wept with the blind woman who had become, in the last year, a true friend.

Annie checked the saddle one last time and then struggled onto Milky. Wincing in pain, she got herself right, then began the horse in a slow walk. She guided him down toward the river trails, passing away from Lucia Court, along a stretch of open trail. She saw a fire down at the river twenty or thirty feet below the trail, and she saw Nathan and Beth sitting there. She had talked to Beth a few times, Nathan once. And of course she had seen them yesterday, with Jeffrey, when that strange light had reflected off the pavement and into the air.

Nathan was staring up into the sky and Beth was writing in a journal. Both looked up at her and Beth smiled, calling upward, "Hello, Annie." Annie asked how they were doing. Nathan came over and asked if she had had any unusual experiences in the last day or so. She hadn't. He said Beth had been having unusual experiences, but then he didn't elaborate. Milky fidgeted, and so she said her good-bye. Milky moved forward, further north on the trail, and toward a clearing he sought almost by instinct. She waved a second time to Beth and Nathan, then she encouraged Milky to let himself go. "This may be the last time we ride together."

Her doctors had already told her not to ride anymore, and the pain sometimes numbed her senses. For weeks she had planned today's last trip, girded up today with an abundance of Naproxen. Especially after Jeffrey's accident, she wanted to do this. Still, she winced as Milky navigated the trail. Milky could find his way on any of these trails, even in the dark, and he seemed to try to walk gently for her, as if he understood her atrocytoma, her syringalmyalia, the pylocytic nonmalignant grade-four tumors all over her spine, filling with fluid and cutting off the nerves. But the trails themselves were pitted, and he could not compensate completely.

"Whoa." She pulled at the reins, wincing again as she entered a copse of crabapple trees. Horse and rider sat a moment, hearing each other's breathing, then the river breathing, as twilight took hold around them, and Annie's pain receded a little in the stillness.

Feeling self-pity and disliking it, Annie thought of Jeffrey. Little Jeffrey whom everyone loved, that little boy she had watched in his wheelchair—so broken and vulnerable, rasping, bloody, a piece of carnage. He lay there with his leg and arm bent inward, his blond hair red, his eyes closed. He was the child she would never have, and he was slaughtered.

Annie got off her horse and stumbled over to a huge spider's web woven between a living, vertical tamarack and a dead horizontal Douglas fir. In the dimming daylight, Annie could see the spider unmoving in the middle, surrounded by dead flies and mosquitoes. The green and brown of the living tree contrasted with the grayish-white horizontal trunk, stripped of bark long ago, spotted brown in places like large liver spots. The web, about two feet in diameter, was one of the largest she had ever seen.

Milky came with her on the reins, and seemed to join her in examining the scene, but only for a moment, before dipping for some weeds. Annie placed her hand on the fallen log next to the web and rubbed it there, then brought it to her nose, smelling the log's earthiness. Milky raised his head and snorted, his huge exhalation quivering the spider's web and awakening the spider and one of the flies. As if to protect her web, the spider lifted her tiny head. Annie pulled Milky back and over to the other side of the fallen log, dropping his reins and cooing at him. He settled there, chomping, and Annie sat on the log next to the spider's web watching the spider settle down again.

As she watched and listened to the river world, Annie saw a monarch butterfly flutter about eight feet away. It had come from behind her, maneuvered in the air, then turned to her, flying toward the web, a catastrophe in slow motion. The butterfly hit the web and the web shuddered. The butterfly became frantic, its left wing completely caught, its right wing out in the air. The spider moved, not toward the butterfly, but alert, waiting for the shuddering to ebb.

Without hesitating, Annie stood up and moved painfully to the web. Sympathetic to the spider, she said, "I'm sorry to rob you of a meal, but I've just got to save the butterfly, it's so beautiful." She tried to calm the butterfly: "It's okay, it's okay, I know this feeling. I know." Her back and legs buckled as she reached over the log to the web. She had to stop, getting a knee propped against the log for ballast so she could free the beautiful insect. "Come here, come on." She clamped the two wings and gutted the gossamers around the butterfly. Pulling gently, she freed it, mournful for the hole she made in the web. "I hope it gives you something to do," she said to the spider, rationalizing her destruction. "I hope keeping busy is good for you." The butterfly was as distraught out in her fingers as in the web, struggling so that Annie thought it would break itself apart. Annie wanted to get all the white gossamer off of it before the butterfly flew away, but the frantic insect did not want to wait.

Annie let the butterfly go, watching it fly through motes of dust before becoming swallowed up in the greens and browns of the forest.

Annie looked up at the sky. It must be around seven o'clock now, the full moon rising white into a golden sky. Instinctively, she caressed her hands together, as if finishing with the spider and the butterfly. A gossamer of webbing held to her right index finger like a white tendril. After she had freed it, she wanted it back.

"Come on, Milky," she murmured. She got his reins and looked one last time at the spider's web. The spider had not moved from its waiting place near the center.

"Did you see Beth and Nathan at the river?" Trudy asked, after Annie had tethered Milky outside in the small field and come in the backdoor. "They've been having quite extraordinary experiences today."

"I saw them," Annie reported. "Beth was busy writing, but Nathan and I chatted. He said they've been having weird experiences."

"Yes, so I hear from Greta."

"Is Greta around?"

"She's in her study. Tell me how you're doing, dear." Trudy turned her head as Annie dragged the desk chair over to the bed. She caught her own breath from the pain, emitting a moan, but hoped Trudy would only hear the scrape of the chair on the hardwood floor.

"Not so good, Trudy," she said honestly, sitting and taking the old woman's hand. "You won't ever die, right?" It was kind of a ritual comment between them. Trudy always smiled. "Not yet, I don't suppose." Annie thought, a little shamefully, "At least don't die till I've gotten used to being paralyzed." Trudy, a great-grandmother already, seemed eternal; both she and Greta were such spiritual searchers, speaking so gracefully a language of eternal orders and patterns—much of it strange to Annie, but nonetheless reassuring.

"Tell me about your ride," Trudy prompted. "I'm surprised you took a ride, after what the doctors said."

Annie ignored the admonition. She spoke instead of the butterfly and the spider.

Trudy said, "You'll have to take Jake to see the spot."

"He's a good friend," Annie said. She suspected that Trudy knew her grandson and her neighbor were lovers, yet it never came up in conversation. Jake, twenty-two, had become Annie's lover during his spring break from the University of San Francisco four months ago, when he'd been back to Spokane to visit his grandmother and great aunt. Annie had gone over to San Francisco once to visit him, then he had come to Spokane to work for summer break. Annie had not told her brother she had a lover, especially Trudy's grandson! She thought he might balk a little or be jealous of Jake's youth or act strange as men did when they wanted to protect a woman.

Holding Trudy's hand now, Annie felt the many edges of what anxiousness could be—both anticipation and fear. She felt so lucky to know Trudy, who, blind and paralyzed, seemed to have transcended her fears. Trudy had become paralyzed and then blind in her fifteenth year of marriage. About four years later her husband had asked for either a divorce or an open marriage. Trudy turned her eyes away as her husband saw other women—but after five years of that, she divorced him and moved in with Greta.

"The river spirits were speaking to you with the butterfly, don't you think?" Trudy asked.

"Yes," Annie said, wishing that she herself had a mind more deeply carved for spiritual things.

"Few on this earth," Trudy said, "have known fear as you know it now. Perhaps only mothers dying in childbirth or men going to war."

"I wish I could feel I'm in an important drama like that," Annie sighed. "I just feel numb . . . lost . . . I feel like I'm being punished, or something. I know, rationally, that's wrong, but I feel like I'm being asked to find courage I may not have. Today I was thinking about what cops do when they put guns to their heads and commit suicide."

"You won't kill yourself, Annie. Don't say that!"

"No," she admitted. "I won't. But I don't know how strong I am."

Annie listened to the hum of the refrigerator, the ticking of two clocks, the hiss of a vaporizer on the floor on the other side of the bed. Sometimes Trudy went silent for a while, as she did now. Often Annie was aware, as she waited for Trudy, of feeling abandoned by her—just as often, of being sanguine in the pleasant silence of women.

Trudy exhaled loudly. "Today is a day of miracles," she said, squeezing Annie's hand. "You watch for a miracle today, all right? I've been hearing the language of the birds all day. And Greta said that Beth has been learning the language of light today too. Greta says there's something very important happening around us right now, right here. Little Jeffrey's passing—that is a big part of this. Jeffrey must be quite an old and powerful soul."

"The language of the birds?" Annie smiled politely. "I've sometimes thought it would be neat if birds could talk. Like in Disney movies."

"It's a very real thing." Trudy smiled, but did not explain.

Annie pulled her hand away from Trudy's, hearing a sound out front. Her hand sweated despite the coldness of Trudy's elderly hand.

"I hear Jake's car," Trudy said, a smile crossing her face. "You're relieved of me."

"Oh, Trudy," she laughed. "I can never get enough of you. Don't say that." The truth was, Annie felt herself going deeper into self-pity the last few minutes. She wanted Jake's body.

Annie rose, kissing Trudy as the front door closed and Jake's booming, low voice intruded, like a longing, into the gentle world.

"Today has been way-out, weird stuff," Annie reported as they rode into the forest on Milky, watching the moon rise. "It started last night. It was so sad. You heard about Jeffrey?" Milky picked his way perfectly in the moonlit dark.

"I did. I'm so sorry, Annie. I know you loved him."

"We all did." She told him everything she could as they rode. Jake massaged her thighs, then up along her waist. She could barely feel his physical gestures of affection, though she saw his hands on her. She took him back to the spider's web, and the spider had moved closer to the wound in the weblines but not yet ministered to it. She reported the rescue of the butterfly, and then she realized they had passed where Beth and Nathan had been. Where were they now? By the time she maneuvered Milky to a small meadow by the water, Jake's hand was unbuttoning her blouse. He jumped off the horse, gently helped her off, and then sat on the loam, on his knees, her against a pine tree, his hands finishing her blouse. The night was here, and she was glad for its shroud of darkness and privacy.

Annie closed her eyes, wanting to feel, whether in physical body or in her active mind, every moment of touch. She found herself thinking of blind Trudy, and what sensual things a blind woman might feel in lovemaking.

Jake seemed tentative as he unbuttoned the last button, pulling her thin, cotton shirt out of her loose jeans. She sensed that he invited her to lead. He usually gave her this early invitation; if she did not take it, he took over with beautiful force.

Without opening her eyes, and through the pain in her legs and back, she said, "Love my body, Jake, let me just keep my eyes closed and *feel* it."

His hands moved with assurance to her ribs, her back, leaning in to kiss her as his chest pressed hers. She felt the sweet pressing moisture of his lips. She felt his big hands on each side of her upper back, reaching to undo her bra. She felt the round of the pine tree just touching the top of her spine like an evening beard on her soft skin. The air had gotten duskier, and only slightly cooler, as some stars joined the full moon above.

She breathed with Jake, chest to chest. She kept her eyes closed and let herself swim in the passion, the deep body passion his youth gave her. She felt tears of grief and loss well up awkwardly, suddenly, as they often did when she did physical things. She felt a tingle in her loins and focused on it, pushing the tears away. She had to focus on those tingles with all her mental power to make them stay.

His hand searched down with soft fingers toward her pants. He unbuckled her, unlatched her Levi's buttons one by one, fast, popping sounds merging, momentarily, with the sound of breathing. She felt hotter, wet, and squirmed with his hand, excited by his tongue in her mouth. His hands gripped both sides of her jeans. She leaned, pelvis up from the tree, spine still attached to the tree. She withstood the pain with a wince. He pulled his face away and bent down in the same motion, pulling her jeans and pink panties to her knees. While he struggled with her shoes, he buried his face in her hairy pubis, and she felt a sting of electrical current. In the numbness it was just a sting, yet it was something, a blessing, the form of his face in her flesh. He had her right boot off, then the left. He had the pants and panties off now. He pushed his tongue inward and she spread her legs to him, sitting against the tree open-legged, the bark touching her back as if far away. She could feel his tongue near her labia and pushed her pelvis to meet it, but she felt so little there, the numbness overwhelming—in just three weeks she'd lost more feeling than she could tell him. "Oh God," she moaned, "Oh no—"

"What's the matter?" He lifted his head out, moisture on his chin and lips.

"No—don't stop." He was so kind. He pressed in again with nose and chin, but then he rose again toward her face, running fingers up her naked legs, a tactility she could barely feel. Her legs would give out soon—the thought enveloped her and closed her in. She felt stirrings of passion recede and was aware that she had to plan this sexual encounter so as not to fail at it. She wanted to lie flat, hoping it would help circulation to the nerves.

"Jake?" He looked and she pointed at a sandy spot. Lifting her, he moved her there.

"Please," she pleaded, pulling her shirt off. "Take off your shirt and let me kiss you."

He pulled his shirt off and kissed her right nipple as she dropped her bra. She had C-cup breasts with dark aureoles that had been immensely sensitive since puberty. He turned his body up and over her, brought his chest over her face and she licked at his copious black hair as his lips moved to her other aureole. She felt the aureole's fire down toward her groin. As if following her energy, his hand moved to her clitoris. She spread her legs for him and saw Milky, in her mind's eyes, come over to lick her clitoris with his huge tongue. She'd had that fantasy more than once.

She closed her eyes and felt Jake's hand leave her clitoris to go for his own pants.

"No no," she whispered. "Let me." She pushed him up off her face and breasts and, pushing through the pain that shot up her spine, she sat up too. His face was red and his breathing harsh, arms still out, pants bulging. She undid his Levi's and lowered his zipper. He wore no belt and no underwear. His penis, surrounded by black hair, popped out as she pulled the pants down. She put it immediately in her mouth and he moaned. Sucking it gently and deeply, she undid his shoes and helped free his pants from his legs.

In an immense, loving vulnerability, he murmured, "But, Annie, this is *your* time. I'll do everything for you." She touched his testicles with her left hand and raked his left leg with her right and he called out loud, shocking a crow, who cawed back at the humans. Annie realized she was scared to put him in her vagina—she knew how much less she would feel today than last week. She knew she would cry from the grief of him inside her. But she wanted him in her desperately, one of her last inclusions of a man in her that she would *feel*. A last time she would feel the liquid squish between her legs and even drip out throughout the evening, a time of scent both man's and woman's. She had learned in her recent months of research that paralyzed women developed sexual needs. She suspected she would try to turn some man, later, into a kind of necrophiliac, conning him into lubricating her useless vagina with Vaseline and entering her. But that would come later.

Jake was moving to take her, already to his knees, kneeling like a spiritual lover, his large penis erect, waiting for her to fall back so he could enter missionary style.

A bee flew suddenly into the concourse, interrupting her flow of backward motion. Yellow and black, its rump pumping on Jake's leg, it looked up a moonlit moment from between black hairs, then flew away. Annie pulled up and over on all fours.

"From behind," she said, "and please, please, while you're fucking me, please kiss my scar, my spine, please." She felt how weakened, how dependent she had become over the months of grief and fear, so that she felt almost like a beggar after tiny gestures of sensual love.

"Oh yes," he moaned, his arms and hands helping her place her tingling legs in an open position. In an act of love so generous he, in his youth, would never know its meaning, he bent to kiss her scar *before* searching for her vagina with his penis.

"You're my treasure, Jake," she murmured to him. "Give me yourself, please." He pumped into her and she felt the throbbing and it lasted, then he jolted with the pure electricity of loving, and cried out into the river's mind, and fell forward into a shuddering, graceful end.

"You're the bravest woman I've ever met," Jake whispered, pulling off of her so his weight would not hurt her. He lay down on his back and she cuddled beside him on her stomach.

"They must have been attracted by your yell," Annie whispered. "Look!" The crow that had complained once now had company. Five others, or maybe more, up in the shadows. "Greta says crows are guardian spirits."

"Don't move!" Jake whispered.

"What?"

"There's a spider. Man, this is wild."

She turned her already upturned head as far over as she could and saw, from a pine branch twenty feet up, a silky thread glistening in the light of the clear night and the moon—there was a brown spider at its end, dropping downward toward her back. It came to about four feet from her.

She replaced her head down in the sand and said, "See if it

comes all the way. Don't disturb it." It looked like the same one from before.

"It's gonna touch you," Jake whispered. "I hope you're not scared of spiders."

She assured him, also in a whisper, that she wasn't.

"Can you feel it?" he asked ingenuously.

"Is it on me?"

"Yeah. On your right buttock."

She felt nothing, imagining a phantom tickle.

"It's going off your leg onto the dirt. What the hell!"

"What?" She squirmed, looking up. His eyes had left her back and buttocks and focused on the air above. Annie twisted her head upward to see a huge monarch butterfly in the air!

"There's a . . . no, there's *two* butterflies!" Jake hissed. "Don't move. They're coming closer, like there's a light on you attracting them. Or maybe they think you're a log or something. Jesus. Now there's three of them!"

Annie couldn't twist to see and so returned to the blindness of her face in the earth. She didn't want to move for fear of destroying the contact.

"One's coming to land! Annie, can you feel it at all?"

Annie said no but just as the word came she thought she felt a clasping tendril on her back, at the base of the scar near the third lumbar.

"Oh man, another one!" Jake whispered. Annie barely felt another soft prickly communion at the fifth lumbar, then another up on a thoracic, as if the three butterflies needed the spread of two vertebrae each for sitting room. Annie strained to hear fluttering wings, but the rolling river noise was too much sound.

"I can barely feel them," she whispered.

"One of the heads just went up, no, it's gonna fly, no it's staying. Yeah, all three—staying, fluttering. Annie, it's so beautiful. Just don't move."

Annie heard the words "Just don't move" as if in an echo chamber. She breathed lightly, so as not to disturb the universe.

"You're crying," Jake whispered.

She felt her crying rock her body now, pulsing it, moving it, overriding the tiny nerve endings of the butterfly legs with her own crying. They're going to fly, she thought, stop crying! But the tears came, and the butterflies remained.

"They love you, man," Jake whispered, so full of sweet innocence and with it, the spontaneous expression of great truth. "They fucking *love* you!"

Annie's rocking ebbed. She rubbed her sniffle on her right wrist, slowly, carefully. The butterflies remained. They are healing me, Annie thought inwardly. They are angels and they are healing me. My hardware is going out, but they are going to protect my software, my heart. They are healing my heart.

"One of them," Jake reported, "the middle one, has, like, a wound on its wing. Like it was so delicate and got stuck in a tree branch maybe. Maybe in the spider's web you saw today. Wow, that would be such a fucking coincidence. But . . . oh shit, there goes one, oh shit, the second one. They're going. They're flying."

The phantom feeling of tendrils lifted, and Annie squirmed to look now and there they were, three monarchs, brown and gold and black washed in moonlit white and each one large with the ripe earth, flying up into pine branches.

Annie nodded. "Three butterflies on my dying spine. My God, how bizarre. Have you ever seen anything like that?"

"I'll never forget tonight." Jake leaned in, kissing her forehead. "I've never seen anything like that. I'll never forget you, Annie."

Annie smiled up at him, curling her head into his chest. She thought wistfully how she would have forgotten Jake quite easily in a few years time, as she had forgotten all but a few snippets from many lovers since she was eighteen; she would have recalled him, at best, like an old picture, or a TV show. Except that he had been here for her final lovemaking before paralysis. Long after she forgot the feeling of his penis in her mouth or vagina, she would remember his "Wow!" upon seeing her butterflies.

Annie led Milky home in a different mood than she had set out just a few hours before. She thought of the butterflies and their transformation from cocoons. Her pain, especially because of the physical task of lovemaking, had increased in the upper body, which compensated for problems in the lower, and the lack of pain, the numbness in the lower body had increased too. She needed to get home for more medication. Yet she didn't want to leave the river. She didn't want to go back to the house, to her brother, to conversation. She wanted to be lying still with Jake. In a day he would leave town again for college; he would leave town and not return until after she was in a wheelchair.

At the crest of the trail, at the edge of Richardson Street, up at Lucia Court, she looked out over the river gorge at night. "Annie?" she heard. It was a calling voice, a woman's voice. She turned around and saw nothing. She brought Milky back to the edge of the gorge, and retraced her steps, but still saw no one. It sounded like the voice of Beth. But

Annie did not see her, and the breeze changed, making her think the voice could be coming from anywhere, even across the river. She stayed still a moment, but the voice did not come again, and she went back toward home. Her brother was up and waiting for her.

"How was your last time on Milky?" John asked sweetly, taking the saddle off for her in his strong arms. He wore his usual Dockers khaki slacks and white golf shirt.

She told him she had been lying naked and three butterflies had come onto her back. Tears came again for the tenth time today. Her brother held her, and then she went into the house for medication as he finished bedding the horse.

In the bathroom, she swallowed four naproxen, then wobbled down the hall to the wheelchair her brother had recently purchased. In immense pain, she sat down in it, wondering if she was in fact feeling Jake's leaking sperm between her thighs, or feeling nothing. She closed her eyes, feeling the chair as best she could, waiting for the painkillers to kick in.

"I'm just going to doze for a second," she murmured. Then I'll call Trudy and Greta, she thought: I'll ask them about butterflies. Alone, she sat dozing in some of the worst pain she'd known in a long time, unable to sleep, but her eyes closed. To her brother, watching, she seemed to inhabit the face and crippled posture of an old woman in a wheelchair, sleeping upright, as if to lie down was to be defeated. John pitied her, though he knew pity was just the opposite of what she needed.

Annie's mind was half in the other world as her brother opened the door and came in from outside. He kissed her on the head and she moaned slightly, "Thank you," and continued on her way to a world of dreams where pain became ecstasy and where she was not crippled but healed, dreaming clearly of butterflies and herself flying with them, as if they made a trail of color against a clear, white sky. She did not wake up to call Greta or Trudy, waking up instead, as did everyone in the neighborhood, in the middle of the night, when the sounds of sirens began.

14

The New Human

Beth and Nathan had crossed the footbridge that hung, suspended, over the river. They were trying to figure out how to save the children. They felt called to move, walking along the pathway talking and following Beth's intuition until they came to a place near a small riverside power station, a yellow brick building on the east side of the river. Nathan asked, "How long will these amazing experiences of yours last?" Beth was aware of feeling the way he did—feeling exhausted yet not wanting it to end. Yet she felt a second wind, as if she had many wells to drink from, and she wished her intuition gave her a way of finding the children. She felt, somehow, that the man in the hooded sweatshirt was close, hiding here, in this river valley. Yet she had no proof of this.

"Maybe we should call the police again?" Nathan said for the fourth time. "You can give them a man's face now, his clothes, his build." But they both knew these new details weren't enough. The police would probably not even talk to him this time. Nathan called Greta instead. Greta promised to pass it all on to Dr. Tourtellotte, who was coming over, and to Landry as well.

After the cell phone call, Beth had felt drawn to a spot in a small meadow where it seemed that the moonlight gathered. There, she and Nathan became silent, watching Annie and Trudy's nephew making love. Even despite some embarrassment, Beth felt mesmerized by the beautiful violence of the act. When she saw the butterflies, she suddenly recalled seeing butterflies with Annie just after Jeffrey died. As she watched the butterflies actually alight on Annie's spine, Beth felt a pressure in her head, like a hand moving around inside her skull. She thought she was getting a headache, then a backache. This newest ache had been coming on since she and Nathan left their little camp across the river. Like the aches throughout the day, it climbed along her spine but also, as if in an equation, the more fascinated she became with Annie across the river, the more her own back ached. This ache went even deeper than the aches before, as if she were becoming crippled like Annie. Strangely, she wasn't frightened, but neither could she remain still.

Nathan whispered, "Look at you. You're twisting around."

She was moving on the sand like someone tossing in a nightmare. As the pain in her head moved almost completely into her back, she heard herself moan. She lay face forward into the sand, vocalizing into the sand and pebbles, hoping not to be heard by the lovers across river.

Nathan grabbed her by the shoulders. "What's happening?" He took her pulse.

She could not speak. The pain overcame her completely.

She pulled the front of her blouse into her mouth and used it as a gag, moaning into it and twisting. It was Annie's pain in her, she realized. She was becoming Annie somehow, healing Annie. Knowing this soothed her.

Beth closed her eyes and saw her grandmother, Rachel, in her Ford Fairlane, driving off from her home. She was an Alzheimer's patient and should not have been driving. Why didn't someone stop her? Beth saw her lying dead. She had gotten lost, forgotten where she was, and lain down in a field where she died. There was a glow around her, white-gold like the light at the river. How beautiful to see Rachel again, see that she was part of the glow of light.

Beth opened her eyes. The pain was disappearing. She pulled her shirt out of her mouth. Nathan murmured that her vitals were okay. The river water purled gently. As Beth felt a clear dissipation in the pain of head, neck, and back, she saw Annie and the young man stand up, dress, present themselves again to the horse.

"Annie!" she called out as the two riders pushed up to the trail. Annie seemed to pause, listening. She could barely hear the call from across the river. She cocked her head, tossing the audible sound in her mind until she could not place it. She said something to Jake and pushed the horse on. Beth realized, suddenly, that she was glad Annie had not heard; what could she say to Annie right now?

"What's that?" Beth said aloud to Nathan.

"What's what?"

Beth sensed something else: light, very close, an invisible presence humming in her ear. "Someone's near us," she whispered. "Someone or something." She took her hand out of Nathan's, looking around.

"Where?" he asked, searching too.

"I think it's Gram," Beth said, not sure why. Grandma Rachel was near? "Gram?" she whispered to the night. Nothing but riversound came back to her. "It's not Gram," she said, hoping the correction would sound right. "It's the light . . . speaking. But it seems like Gram, too. What is going on?"

"*Now* what's happening?" Nathan whispered.

"Quick," Beth said, "get out my notebook and write what I say." Beth felt drawn to the name Rachel, and felt her gram's presence, but thought perhaps what she felt was something vast near her like her grandmother must have been to her when she was a tiny child.

Nathan plumbed her backpack for her journal and a pen. The full moon was a lone large org in the nearly cloudless sky.

"I'm talking in my own mind," Beth said. "Words are just coming. Write this down. Quick. I don't know what it means. It's like the . . . the thoughts I've been having today. Like there are voices inside me."

"Should I start writing now?"

Beth closed her eyes, sensing the man who sat in the darkness writing at the table, writing in the trees. Sensing, also, so much more.

"Write this. When the light came yesterday, how could we think anything but ecstasy? We did not think beauty could be ugliness, deformity, depravity. But God has a plan, and death calls to life like a child calls its mother. God's breath is the breath of thought that enters our minds when we think and feel. Write that, Nathan." What had she just said? It felt like a rehearsal.

"Annie will not suffer the way she thinks she will," Beth said. "I think she was being healed before. I helped her. I was used as a utilitarian part of the spiritual physics in the universe."

"You're saying, while your heart rate was spiking you healed her?"

"I don't know. The butterflies. They . . . were important. There's more than one thing at work here. More than one energy. And there's always the presence of an opposite. Why?"

"Beth, you are kind of in a trance," Nathan whispered.

"To experience love, this is the whole reason for life," she said. "And separation, or individuality, provides the motivation for love, for reconnecting. In physical reality there is separation, but when all the realities are taken as a whole, there is no separation. This is what *Homo infiniens* is now learning, and will continue to learn for a long period of human time, many of your centuries. Once that is learned, a new challenge will emerge."

"Many of *your* centuries?" Nathan asked. "Beth, you sound like you're talking as someone else."

"No," she responded. Here, in the moonlit dark, she felt the day collide with something greater than herself. Her body chilled, her mind awakened by night thoughts and a kind of electric current in consciousness, something that began as Annie and Jake made love, then built as the butterflies touched Annie, then exploded as the healing occurred—Beth knew she spoke not only for herself, but for other voices.

"I have wisdom regarding spiritual physics," she said. "Write this, Nathan."

"I'm writing."

"The experience these last two days has shown us the great energy field that is the ocean of existence, which we can, as we are able, see and feel. Now that we have seen the Field, life will get harder, not easier. We will have to evolve an understanding of spiritual physics."

"What do you mean? Say more, Beth."

"Your consciousness is layered in realities, and does not know all the realities because the physical reality, in which feeling occurs, cannot see into all realities at once, or it would be in constant explosion.

"The light you and the others witnessed at the death of the physical reality whom you call Jeffrey, the light reaching toward the home of the pilgrim you call Donnell Wight, this light is the primary element in the composition of the second reality, exploding in elemental vibration through the first reality by the deaths of the two powerful beings. You may ask 'why?' it occurred in this time, by this river. Do not ask these questions for the answers lie in the realities you cannot understand."

"You're saying 'you,' Beth. Like you're someone else."

Words continued to come despite his interruption. "Know only that occurrences of many realities-at-once are rare, and beget a mass of human vibration over time that you will have difficulty managing. It is not your job to manage it, but rather to let the vibrations permeate your human consciousness in physical reality."

"Beth—you have to stop a minute. I have to catch up."

As Nathan wrote, Beth formed in her mind the question, "Life in this physical reality is difficult and strange. Why must this physical reality exist? Why not just exist in the unphysical way of knowing *all*?" After a pause, in which the riversound mixed with the scratching of Nathan's pen, words came:

"For millennia, many religious teachers have spoken only

to the mind existing in those previous times, and so were required to simplify more than I must do today. Teachers have taught that when you die you become omniscient and omnipresent, perceiving all.

"This has been a myth. In fact, when you are dead and disembodied, you do not know what it feels like to smell a rose or cut yourself on glass, thus you do not experience those challenges, and do not learn their ways of loving. Physical reality must no longer be considered inferior to 'heaven.' In truth, 'heavenly bodies' are actually hungry, after they rest for a time, to be reborn into physical bodies. They yearn to be entrusted again with the joys of the spiritual physics."

Beth felt her mind go completely blank. She missed the words.

"Ask something, Nathan," she begged. "Keep me talking."

"Okay," Nathan said immediately. "Where does the spirit go after death? Is it all around? Is Jeffrey all around us?"

"Jeffrey is around us."

"Say more."

"Your mind may not be able to fully understand. To imagine what I am seeing, see a piece of energy, like perhaps a white stone, that is both here, in your hand, and also, at the same time, a million miles away. Then toss the stone away. You will notice there is nowhere it can land that is not near here. So it is with death. The dying do not leave us. To understand better than this analogy, you have to engage in physical experience—prayer, meditation, epiphany—in which you transcend this physical life, become one with it. In those moments of experience, you can imagine Jeffrey as both here, and not."

Nathan kept writing as he quickly spoke. "I can ask anything, right?"

Beth felt like a piece of cloth on wind. It was a beautiful feeling. She had never felt as happy as she did in this moment; it was a peace and vision that surpassed who she was, as if she had been handed the gift of life itself to hold, for a time.

"When did the evolutionary step to *Homo infiniens* as a species actually begin?" Nathan asked. "Can I ask that? When did *Homo infiniens* actually emerge?"

"Some of you have already emerged as *Homo infiniens*."

"Who?"

"Everyone in proximity of the light is the new human, for each person experienced other realities. The light you saw was a beacon to other realities, expanding cells in the brains of each of you. There is another who experienced the light as well, a watcher. You will meet him soon. There is always a watcher. In all physics, there are actors and the observer. This is the way of the realities."

"What was the light? Who is the watcher?"

"The watcher, who has experimented powerfully, will be condemned for his distaste of physical reality, but he is commended for his abilities to travel in many realities. His is the madness of heaven and hell both. I see that he has extra matter in his brain. Tumors. Yes. Tumors. Disease will always exist. There is always a watcher. Know that whenever doorways open to light, there is a watcher who commences new evolutions of the great wheel of life by trying to destroy the wheel itself. Your minds cannot yet know why this must be. They must grow further.

"However, you can know that the barriers to expanded consciousness are many because the need for expanded consciousness is still far concealed in most of your people. Most of your people seek the safety of the material world, where they hope what is known will not interfere with their 'material' nests. The other nests are more concealed, and thus tossed by your people into the bin of imagination, only to appear in dreams, or books.

"Nathan, there are some kind of . . . of lessons. Ask questions—that's okay. But make sure to write, okay? These seem to be truths I'm supposed to speak."

"Okay. Okay." He wrote in the moonlight as he asked, "Will *every* human being become the new human? Or will there just be a few people, like Jesus or Buddha?"

"Everyone. To think otherwise is to court evil, as the watcher, convinced of his singularity, will always do.

"What you call the light of God is unfolding everywhere at all times, bounding off the trees and clasping hands with our living souls. Experience, listen, let it unfold.

"If you avoid this intimacy, the mysteries will always remain distant things only the finest astronauts may see. This is not how God meant for divine spirit to be known. Complexity is for the intellect; it is useful. Simplicity is the intuition's vision into the truth.

"Keep things simple whenever you can." Beth saw the visitors in her mind who had come to Harold and Laura. She said, "Nathan, write this:

"Often the human community languishes, and just as often, it accepts the assistance of invisible aids. Hidden companions, the dead, angels, exist at all times everywhere. They anchor their affections in their experience of the deep feelings within each of us living in these bodies. In the same way that thoughts are God's breath, feelings are the breath of all those who have come before us, and linger near us. There is no intensity of emotion like that which we can experience in these embodied lives. All our ancestors, and all those in our energy clusters, are anchored on our feelings, and we feel not just for ourselves but for others. That is the amazing gift of life, and that is why we work so hard to live in families and communities that will allow us to *feel*, to feel *deeply*, and in so feeling, to know ourselves as the very breath of Being itself.

"Whenever we can find our way to absolute and authentic feeling, we will be visited."

"You've started saying, 'We,' " Nathan noticed.

Without responding, Beth continued. "Write this, Nathan. I'm like a flow of voices. Write!"

"Okay."

"Evil is as important for the development of the human mind as is good. This is a terrifying revelation. Good exists because it has evil to be vigilant against. Yet neither good nor evil is what we mean by revelation.

"I give thanks for each revelation, knowing that every vision, every bond becomes revelation simply by my feeling it in that certain, mysterious, divine way. Can there be anything more thrilling than revelation in the middle of an ordinary day, when least expected? Give me a hundred revelations of my own for every one truth someone else feeds me. Spiritual maturity rests in my own sudden contact with myself revealed.

"Am I 'channeling'? I don't know. I'm in other minds. I'm in the mind of unknowns. But I am completely myself. This is revelation. This is the feeling a person gets who 'speaks the truth.' "

"Write this down. Please, Nathan.

"Children know that we are all one, that every living being is interconnected. Children know this until they forget it and have to relearn it. People will ask for proof of the vast interconnection of all things, and seek those proofs provided by spiritual texts, or by teachers. Children accept reality without needing proof.

"Every human being, as the light of God works in their cells, wants *proof* that all things are interconnected, that he or she is one with all things. Instead, we should each be asking for proof that we are *not* interconnected, for all things clearly are one. Only he who wishes to argue that reality is not reality would think otherwise."

Beth felt a slowing down of her words. She paused for breath as Nathan wrote, the Bic pen scratching on the journal paper. She heard the sound of a siren climbing the road along the cliff side west of Donnell Wight's house.

Nathan looked up at the cliff with her, then asked. "Is religion necessary?"

Words came. "Don't be surprised if you take everything learned from religion, and take also all the icons of religion, and throw them together in the house of your childhood, and burn them all up. And then do not be surprised if, missing them terribly, you travel the world for ten years collecting each again, and building for them a shrine. Our spiritual lives are lived between the comfort of religion and the discomfort of religion. Religion is the beginning of our journey. It is never the end of our meaning."

"I'm getting this all down, Beth."

Beth was aware of more sirens on both sides of the river valley now. She heard Nathan write, and the hoot of an owl, a plane's dull roar far off and the passing of a car on a far road in the background. A fire engine siren seemed to be going toward Donnell's house. What would it be doing up there at this time of night? She looked up there, saw no blazing fire.

"Beth!" Nathan realized suddenly. "In this trance state, can you see more about the killer? Can you help the abducted children, their families?"

"I am having no remote viewing now. The police, EMS, the fire trucks are on both sides of us, but I can't see anything."

"I don't want to stop the flow of your words, Beth, but we have to find out what's happening up there." With her, he looked up at Lucia Court and over at Donnell's, lights flashing on both sides now.

Beth felt words, revelations, still coming. "Nathan, write this.

"Humans will discover 'timeways,' time pathways by which we will communicate with others across time. We will not discover how to *physically* travel through time. It is not possible to do so. But we will learn to communicate *telepathically* through time, thus to travel through time using our mental process. The first primary timeway will emerge between the year 2411 and this era. Communication between 2411 and this era will be vast, and change the human perception of the brain's capabilities."

"2411?" Nathan stopped writing. "Why did you pick that year?"

"I didn't pick it.

"We will become more and more telepathic, creating new linguistic problems and solutions over the next four centuries. This is the new human."

The feel of the wind was cool and sounded among the trees, one pine branch touching another like a knock.

Nathan asked: "Will we discover intelligent life on other planets?"

"Not 'people' like us. Also, our reliance on robots will become a reliance on artificial intelligence, which will further expand our definition of ourselves as a species, *Homo infiniens.*

"Tell people to learn how to play telepathic games. Our computer and other networks will one day join with telepathic communication. A piece of telepathy-sensitive equipment will be worn, as brain-plates, on the skulls of many people by 2411.

"M(2) X(2) = x2v2 = C(2) A(2). This formulation is very important."

"For what purpose, Beth?"

"I don't know. I just know in time it will become clear. The Light Killer knows it too. I don't know how I know that. It's not his voice in me, but I know it.

"Humanity will suffer greatly when a blue and white power emerges from the Middle East. And we will resurrect when a headless power emerges in the south. We will restructure our planet in the general energies of hot and cold, and create beings who can withstand the new earth, both hot and cold.

"All this will transpire and look like 'good' and 'bad' because the mind cannot understand too much at once.

"And now I will speak directly to you, Nathan, for you will study the expansion of space and time in the human brain, and become instrumental in human progress through that study.

"You must study the energy chemicals in the body, and discover how they are imbued by soul. Brain and hormonal chemicals are matters of *soul*. Beware the formula I have given you. It will lead and follow, and must be applied at appropriate times."

"What will you do in the future, Beth. Can you see?"

"I will become a healer for a long time, and then become barren. You will too, Nathan. Do not fear this cycle."

"Will we have children?" Nathan asked.

"People will ask this question of me, and many others like it, specific questions of oracular prediction. I will answer many of them, and often be correct. I will have to hope the seeker who asks is prepared for the answer. You are not at this time prepared for the answer to the question you have asked."

"Okay, okay."

Beth was aware of numerous questions, yet felt a blankness take her over. The lights and sirens were getting too overwhelming.

"Jesus," Nathan said, looking both toward Lucia Court and toward Donnell's house again, "We've got to call Greta, find out what's going on."

The flashing lights on all sides of her compelled Beth to close her eyes, and within closed eyes she saw in her mind's eye a palimpsest of steel plates, glowing—they were endless layers of spiritual steel, like "planes of existence." The vision receded quickly because it was too literal, too material. As it receded, it exploded into a thousand tiny pieces, then she saw each piece as a sliver of lit-up glass from an explosion, filling the universe of black space. She saw that there were invisible slivers too, and there were slivers within slivers. She saw her hand reach into space, trying to grasp a sliver, but the sliver slipped out of grasp, like a slimy fish.

". . . you see," a man's voice was saying, *"once the Soul leaves the Body it is not held in embodied form and so it explodes into a billion pieces of the Infinite, some of which remain communicative with someone like you, most of which are already re-forming to protect other new bodies. The Huge Soul is a mass of energy that protects the individual Energies as needed."*

Beth said, "Nathan, I am hearing a man's voice now, speaking through me."

"What?"

"Gram is still around here, but this is a man's voice. Write this down. I'm in the killer's mind for a second. He has been experimenting with something. Nathan! It's the killer's voice again. He's talking to someone. Is this a different kind of remote viewing, Nathan? I'm 'remote hearing'? God, I don't know.

"He says, *'We are not to reduce the Light. The big woman wants to reduce the Light to the many. Over the last year I've felt the pattern for seconds.'* " Beth felt the man's frustration in his voice. " *'I've seen the underlying pattern of the universe—but only for seconds.'* " Beth could tell she was immersed with the Light Killer because she felt a shuddering again. Something evil was happening. There was great pain nearby. The man's voice said to a companion, *"Intelligence, or Consciousness, is the end-goal of Creation. Intelligence of the pattern is the highest form. The Pattern is a flow of energy you will not understand for some time, you're still a little girl, but your seeking of it, with me, will become the Flow itself, pure Intelligence, and then you will understand."*

"My God, Nathan, he's talking to a child. I can't see her, but I see him. Write this down.

" 'Wild ginger is a promoter of peace in the world. The flower of the saint promotes inner peace. Sow and reap these plants.

" 'You won't die, Amanda. You'll know it for yourself soon enough. I have Power.'

"Nathan! I see it. He's in a cave, a set of rooms inside a cave. The cave doesn't open out to light. It only opens upward—an old mine shaft, a shed above. The shed is somewhere out behind Donnell's. Nathan, I see him, I see the girl with the WSU sweatshirt. She must be named Amanda. There's a shed somewhere, an outbuilding on Donnell Wight's property. The killer's got the girl in that cave down there, under the shed. There's a table down there, a bed, the girl's chained to the bed. He's talking to her. She's scared, in shock. He's lecturing her and writing notes in a tiny notebook."

"Beth, I . . . I want to believe you," Nathan said cautiously. "But the cops said he never took a girl with that sweatshirt."

"It's happening now," Beth said, sure of it. "This must be a new abduction. The sirens up there. The cops are up there. They know!"

"Jesus!"

"Why do I see these things? Why is all this in my head?" she hissed.

"Where's the shed?" Nathan asked, becoming alert. "If it's happening now, right now, we can do something. We've got to get moving." Nathan grabbed the pack. He shoved her notebook in it, flung it on his back, moving already. She followed him. They started toward Donnell's in the moonlit dark. They would have to climb the cliff side in the dark.

Suddenly, all revelations were gone, and she was blankly right here again, walking, following a scent of evil toward its source.

Nathan had pulled out the cellular phone, turned it on, and was dialing the police, who put him on hold. He hung up, dialing Greta's.

"What's going on?" he cried into the phone. Then listened, then turned back to Beth.

Hanging up, he said, "The police are coming to meet us at the suspension bridge. You did it, Beth, you led them to the killer. You just didn't realize it."

The insights, the cavalcade of voices inside her were gone, but the physical world was minutely with her, in sounds and lights, as she listened to Nathan tell her what he had learned. The killer had taken a girl, Amanda; the abduction had happened about two hours before; the killer was asking for "the big woman, Beth," who had been in his thoughts today.

15

The Watcher

It was the big woman, Beth—it had to be her who led the police to him. Donni Kozora heard the sirens and commotions far above him like he had heard his mother screaming into her pillow in the next bedroom, nearly every night, when he was a little boy. Mother, the madwoman, carried away by the white-coated ones in the sirens and light. Beth, with the thick glasses and the matted hair, the dirty jeans and white shirt behind which you could see a huge bra, the slightly dark skin and the glow about her, moving around in his mind, so smart, so able, so powerful. The Light was her friend. How could he have anticipated Beth's power? When Beth found the cloth—was this the clue? The head pain so severe, impossible to think straight.

The floodlights he had inserted onto the ceiling of the cave illuminated the girl, Amanda, who was gagged with one of Mother's white handkerchiefs, and chained to the bed. She was a mute girl, a listener, her hands handcuffed behind her, her legs connected by the ankles to the metal bed frame. She could lay on her back or stomach, or sit on her knees. He had let her off her chains to pee once, in the underground stream, listening to the sounds of her body for Signals, and upon returning her to her chains, returned to his desk, desk lamp, his writing, his teaching. Before the police came so suddenly, he had been preparing for the Healing.

"Lamentation of Loneliness. Listen now, Amanda. I saw you in a Vision of Light, and I have brought you here to be a part of the Light." Her white handkerchief gag was almost brownish-wet from saliva and tears. "The Light instructs me to cut you into slivers, and to bury you in a million places, and then to watch as the Light that you are reconnects. I observe that process, learning how to create it myself. Soon, I will lead others in Visions. You are the fourth child. You can help a great cause." He spoke and wrote, closing out the girl's whimpering. "All over this valley are flesh and bones I have been reconnecting with spirits. I think I know why, after Jeffrey died, the Light shared itself yesterday with so many. I must have accidentally caused that. Amanda, soon there will be a new beginning." Such a good listener was this Amanda, this thin girl. He had planned, in just a few minutes, to take her down the long shaft, along the tracks, to the operating room. But the sirens and sounds. If the police scurrying about above him turned off his electricity, he would know they knew his exact location below the shed. Beth, the big woman, was calling such darkness to him.

Amanda, her blond curls matted with sweat and saliva, tried to yell "Help!" or "Here!" into her gag. She choked in her efforts. Donni went over to her, slapping her back. He was glad she had worn the maroon sweatshirt, for it was cold and damp down here. Her little jeans, slightly faded, and her white socks and Adidas tennis shoes were already covered in red dirt, and the sweatshirt, too, was combined now with specs of red dirt like dried blood on the white-lettered "Washington State University."

"Amanda," he murmured, "stop yelling and you'll stop coughing." She struggled for the Breath. Donni listened to the slight sound of the underground stream.

"Donni Kozora!" he heard suddenly. A man's deep voice echoed in the mine shaft from above. "This is the police. You are trapped. Do you have Amanda with you?"

Donni said nothing. He was not trapped, though the police could not know that. Soon the lights would go out.

Donni returned to his table. "Amanda, don't forget what I've said. The Word is of value. Light moves in the Word. I will have to flee here, soon. I hate the sneaky ways, but there is no other way. Intelligence is the end-goal of Creation. Intelligence of the pattern is the highest Form. The Intelligent Pattern is a flow of energy you will not understand for some time, you're still a little girl. You will live, Amanda! How unlucky you are. I cannot take time to finish with you. But remember this, I beg you—there really is no such thing as death. Let me at least have taught you that, as I've taught the other children."

She began coughing again. Donni had the strange feeling of being watched, and again he saw Beth in his mind's eye. He stood up, walked over to Amanda, and slapped her back again. How children struggled so! The deep voice of another man, a policeman, called down to him, like an imitation of God calling down from above. God did not exist as people thought He did. One day everyone would understand that. God was not a person, but an infinite particle field.

Amanda lay back down on the bed, weeping; the lights went out.

Donni sat for a moment in the pitch dark. "It's okay, Amanda." He stood to move to his candles. He moved with the grace of someone blind. He lit a candle and called back up into the shaft. "There is a big woman. She's with a man who has a birthmark on his neck. Bring her here. I'll talk to her. Her name is Beth. And turn my power back on, or the girl's dead."

This was the next thing necessary: To meet the big woman. Adaptation. He must learn what the big woman knew, decide whether to kill Beth or try to take her with him. Then, through the tunnels, he would leave this place, which had been his home, the earth that exploded with light.

The night had cooled only a little. Beth and Nathan stood at the suspension bridge, watching the parade of flashlights coming toward them through the trees. Both the east and the west sides of the river valley were lit up from above, along the ridges, by flashing lights. Beth looked upward at the stars. She looked for a moment into the white moon.

Nathan held her hand. He spoke of things the police would need from them; of how they would explain her experiences. He wondered aloud if she was in fact actually seeing the killer, actually entering his mind simultaneously, via remote viewing, or if she was involved in some kind of a string of telepathy into the killer's future. Surely, he rehearsed, some of it was the future: "You saw the girl with the WSU sweatshirt before the killer took her."

Beth smelled honeysuckle. Then she smelled lilacs. It was midsummer. The lilacs were not in bloom anymore. Why this smell of lilacs?

"We're here!" Once police voices were near, Nathan called out. Bursts of flashlights moved toward the bridge.

Beth focused on Landry first. Then she saw another patrolman in uniform, two SWAT team personnel with semiautomatic rifles, and two men in suits, whom Landry introduced as Chief Todd Harrington and FBI Special Agent Bernie Washington. Overwhelmed by all the men and guns, Beth barely heard.

"Good to meet you," Chief Harrington said, "We'll explain on the way to the Wight place, Ms. Carey." He was a thin, wiry man. His face, flashing in and out of light, was shaved smooth, his hair crew cut.

Beth felt herself adapt to the flow of their walk, and felt, too, that Nathan was being pulled out of the flow.

"No nonessential civilian personnel allowed. We've left everyone nonessential in Lucia Court. Dr. Wondreski, I suggest you return there as well."

Beth felt as if a piece of paper were ripping inside her. "I won't go without Nathan. He's my partner."

"I'm a physician as well," he said. "I can help."

"We have a physician there already," Chief Harrington hissed. "No arguments. A girl's life is in danger."

Beth stopped the flow. She put her right hand into Nathan's left hand. "You are taking me to confront this man who has been in my mind," Beth said. "I'll go with you as long as Nathan is with me."

Special Agent Washington came to Beth's side. "I think

we'll take Dr. Wondreski, then." He walked away before anything else could be said. The others joined him.

"I'll show you the short route up there," Nathan said.

Beth asked, "Please tell us how you came to this moment. Please tell us when the man took the girl in the maroon sweatshirt?"

Chief Harrington came beside her, breathing without effort as he walked just in front of her on the narrow path. "He abducted her about two hours ago. Her father had been down in the basement watching TV, getting drunk. When he went up to her room to look for her, he didn't find her. He was sure something was wrong, given the news reports and all. He described his daughter to 911, what she wore. Somebody remembered the sweatshirt from Dr. Wondreski's earlier call. We tried to locate you. In this valley, Dr. Wondreski's cellular phone didn't receive our call. Since he gave the Greta Sarbaugh location in the earlier call, we proceeded there. Our consultant, Dr. Adelle Tourtellotte, was already at that location."

"Greta said she was going to call Dr. Tourtellotte," Nathan confirmed. The dirt trail, smooth in the moonlight, narrowed now as they approached the cliff side, so that the line of personnel had to move single file.

"The SWAT team is deployed at the top of the cliff," Chief Harrington said. "They'll drop some ladders when we call up our location. Will you be able to climb up, Ms. Carey?"

Beth nodded. Was the little girl still alive? If only she could see. . . .

"How did you discover that the killer is at Donnell Wight's house?" Nathan asked logically.

"The perp is Donni Kozora. He's actually the late Mr.

Wight's nurse. Do you know a Dr. Alfred Hecht?" the FBI agent asked.

"Yes. He was our professor in college."

"He's another advisor of ours. In Japan now. Before we arrived, he called Mrs. Sarbaugh. After she explained this whole thing you've got going around here with this 'light' and so on, Dr. Hecht suggested that all this 'electrical field activity'—whatever that is—would have to happen in the geographical area from Lucia Court to Mr. Wight's house." The FBI agent continued, his voice quieter now on the trail as they approached the cliff's edge. "It was Hecht who deduced that the Wight place was in play. We were at the Sarbaugh location and Ms. Trudy Sarbaugh—the blind woman? You know her?"

"Of course, we know her."

"She remembered there used to be a mine shaft over there, caves. She thought there was a shed over it. We got a SWAT team there immediately. Everyone is hopeful the little girl is still alive down there."

"She is," Beth assured them. She knew it now without seeing it.

"You know this—how?"

"The same way I've known other things today."

Harrington's cellular phone rang, the sound emitting from his waist. He flipped the big phone open, listened, then asked, "Still hearing from the girl?"

He hung up. "The team can still hear the girl's muffled cries," he said grimly.

On the cliffside above they could see the flashing lights and hear commotion, but the night made the top of the cliff appear far off, and now, as they approached the twenty feet of difficult climb, Beth knew the men in suits who would soon be as dirty-red as she and Nathan had been.

"They can drop ladders there," Landry pointed. Nathan was already heading that direction, to their left. The special agent, breathing hard, spoke into a kind of walkie-talkie, describing the location for ladder drops.

Beth listened to a hundred sounds as men congregated at the base of the cliff—metal guns against Kevlar vests, voices from the cliff above, movements of feet on dirt, the sound of the river now unavailable. She heard metal ladders dropping against rock. She looked up and watched them fall. Landry was beside her now. She touched his shoulder.

"How are you, Landry?" she asked him.

"I'm okay," he said. "Just adrenaline now."

Beth felt the adrenaline too, and something else. She knew she wouldn't die tonight. She was not afraid of Donni Kozora. She felt only that she was part of a flow, and she must move to him, intersect him. She sensed that he would not live through tonight.

She said none of these things aloud. Instead, she struggled to climb one of the ladders, the red rock face of the cliff scraping her knuckles and knees. Then she was up, into the hands of big men with alert eyes, who worked in silence to lift her, Nathan, Landry, the other men in suits, and their colleagues in vests and heavy belts of equipment. Nathan insisted on keeping his backpack on and she the fanny pack, which were silted in red now. Beth stared into lights everywhere, floodlights and flashing lights, police cars, an ambulance, a fire engine, so many men near a shed, to which they were all directed. Beth looked over at the Wight house and saw a large man and a woman beside him at the garage door. This must be Sandy and his wife.

"This way, Ms. Carey," the special agent directed, as other FBI agents—she presumed they were federal men by their suits and crew cuts—merged with their boss. She held fast to Nathan's hand until they came to a shed—more a small barn. Light emanated from inside. She recalled her vision of the cave earlier, when from Greta's yard, she had seen Alex and his friend. She understood now that the shaft went down from this shed and met the cave below. She saw now that Alex and his friend, without knowing it, had been on a lower cliff that, if they could have walked inward through rock, would have connected them directly with the cave that must be beneath this shed.

The FBI agent was saying, "We won't let you down there, Ms. Carey. Just talk to him from above."

"Just talk to him, Beth," Nathan agreed.

"Get him to release the girl, Ms. Carey."

They shoved her a walkie-talkie. An agent in a suit with black horn-rimmed glasses showed her how to push the button to talk, then release it to listen.

Nathan whispered to Agent Washington, "Why not just drop gas into the cave and go in?"

The big black man, still getting his breath, replied: "Kozora says he'll kill the girl the second the canister comes."

"We have backup scenarios," Harrington said, "but Ms. Carey is our best bet. Dr. Tourtellotte confirms this. Are we bringing Dr. Tourtellotte over to the Wight place?" he asked a man in a suit.

"She's on her way."

Beth saw a tall thin black man in a Kevlar vest standing near the hole checking his revolver.

Beth saw in her mind's eye, like a flash of a movie, that this man would shoot Donni Kozora. She saw herself standing with Donni and the girl. Beth listened to these men around her telling her to talk Donni into coming up, but she knew she would have to do otherwise. She had to meet Kozora down below. How could she explain this to these men? None of them lived in certainty, only reaction.

When Donni Kozora threatened to kill the girl if the big woman did not come down, she said she would go. This was not bravery—it was certainty. Nathan, the other men, all of them were desperate to find another way, to keep her out of the cave. But she closed her eyes, breathed deeply, letting the sounds of voices, of metal, of devices and equipment become one long sound. She saw a picture in her mind of the little girl, nine years old, trapped in what must, by now, be only a candlelit dark with a madman.

"How did you lead the cops to me?" the watcher asked, holding his gun on Beth.

"I don't know." She rubbed her hands together. Donni Kozora's hood was down behind him, revealing short brown hair. His eyebrows and dark eyes were lit from a candle on the desk. Amanda, six feet from her on the bed, whimpered. She was scared, but unharmed. The room was about twenty feet square with a ten-foot ceiling, its mud walls covered by gashes of white and gold paint, and on the northeast corner, there was a dark recess, a doorway that appeared to reach into a long hallway.

Beth said, "We have been part of a miracle today. We've been connected to each other. I don't know why.

"Why have you killed the children?" Beth asked.

Kozora scratched his forehead. "The Light shows them to

me and I go find them. I learn how to Heal them. I'm gaining powers all the time. I cut them into pieces and scatter them in this valley. I hardly sleep, watching to see how the Light recollects itself even as the body is disparate. It is the Reunion I am led to discover. Once it is discovered, I become the Prophet. Only you can be like me. Others can only follow. You might understand.

"How did you know to dig for the handkerchief?"

Beth didn't know what to do except speak. "This morning and afternoon this girl, Amanda, was in my visions: She led me to the handkerchief, told me to dig there."

"But I hadn't taken her yet!"

"I know." Beth nodded. "Can you please let her go now? You can have me instead."

His face illuminated by the candle on the table, Donni Kozora said, "Tell me everything you've understood about the light. I won't kill you, Beth. If you'll come, I'll take you with me. I have a way out."

Beth said, "You won't kill me, or the girl," seeing in her mind's eye the SWAT officer in the military gear. He was silently descending into the back of the cave. He would kill Donni Kozora. She shuddered as she realized it was she who would make it possible. There was no turning back from it. She knew that the bliss of today would not remain bliss. She saw that she would never have children, but instead choose another kind of life. Everything was clear to her in this moment.

"I don't know what has been happening today," she said gently. "I have seen you, and I don't know how. But I know you must let this girl go." Donni Kozora did not seem able to read her mind, to see the SWAT officer descending, death coming.

Donni Kozora closed his eyes and sat down in front of his notebooks. He was silent for a few seconds, seconds that seemed very long, seconds invaded by the cops above ground.

"You are like the Madwoman," Donni said. "Why is your name not Rachel?"

"Rachel?" Beth replied. "Rachel is my grandmother's name. Jeffrey called me Rachel when he first met me. Why is Rachel important to you?"

"Rachel is the Madwoman. You have immense power," Donni said. "There's no doubting that."

"Where are the other children's bodies?" Beth asked.

The SWAT officer, back in the tunnel, had touched dirt with his feet, pulling his revolver off his belt.

Donni said, "Can I show you my lab? Will you try to stop me? I can destroy everything in an instant, you know."

"Destroy what?"

"I've developed a brain plate, I wear it under my hood above ground. I try to heal others with the plate. Human society hates that I use children as subjects, but what can I do? Adults are hard. I'm a servant of the Light, as we all are, but I'm becoming a master of light. I'm not there yet, still becoming. My letters have been generous; I'm trying to keep people in the loop."

"Where are the children's bodies?" she asked again.

"All over the valley," he replied. "Betweeen Lucia Court and this place." He opened his arms, indicating a vast space. "I started seeing the Light when Donnell got back from India, about two years ago. I saw it even though I kept taking my medication. I think he brought the Light back with him from India. Amulets, crystals, little souvenirs he gave me, like ones my mother left behind when she died. The Light was on all of them.

"I saw the Light so many times. I stopped going to church because about six months ago I started seeing the Light here in the river valley. You owe it to me, you know, that the Light came to all of you after Jeffrey's wreck. You owe it me. I've tilled the soil with souls lit up by experimentation. Maybe that Light, when Jeffrey got killed—is that the Reunion I've been tilling in the soil?"

This vision seemed to give him pause.

"You are killing children," Beth said evenly. "You have a disease that makes you kill children. The Light you are seeing does not ask you to kill." Beth's head and shoulders felt very warm.

"Where are the children's body pieces buried?" she asked. "Can you tell me exactly, please?" The SWAT officer was so close now.

"How can it all change so quickly? Now *you* are the Teacher. The Light is on *you*. I know what you are doing, Teacher. You are the Madwoman. I see the cop through your mind." Donni reached behind him, pulling on a circular ring that hung on the cave wall, attached to a wire that spanned far into the long cavelike hallway. What was the wire? Why had he pulled it?

Suddenly, Beth knew. "Close your eyes, Amanda," Beth screamed.

Donni looked into Beth's eyes, then Amanda's, then turned toward the military man, his gun swinging over.

The crack of the gunshot deafened Beth. In the instant before brains and blood splashed against the wall of the cave, Beth saw a muted flash of white-red inside Donni's mouth as the bullet entered there. Donni's body hesitated a second, then fell against the table. Beth ran to Amanda, removed her gag and hugged her hard, not letting her go as the girl sobbed in her arms. The SWAT policeman came rushing to the body of the killer. Three men from the SWAT team were down in seconds.

Then there was an explosion from within the mountain. One of the policemen, who had gone to look down that long hallway of the shaft, flew back into the room, holding his ears, and screaming in pain.

16

THE MIRACLE

THE SWAT TEAM members moved to their fallen man. Amanda was screaming. One of the team found Donni's keys, unchaining Amanda, helping Beth and Amanda, who soon moved upward, inside the coughing of smoke and dust. Whatever equipment lay in the laboratory Donni had built far into the mountain had become rubble.

The flashing lights above were blinding for a second, then Beth adjusted, Nathan embracing her. The fallen SWAT team member's ears were bleeding. Beth's ears pulsed and rang. Beth and Amanda were covered in dust. Beth gave Amanda to a female police officer. Into a pandemonium of voices, care, and questions, Beth moved in shock, finally sitting down, held by Nathan, who pulled her head into his chest.

Then a debriefing began. Many voices, many questions. She and Nathan were whisked to the Wight house, seated around a table. Hello to Mr. and Mrs. Sandy Wight. Chief

Harrington's voice, "This is a cursory debrief, of the events in the shaft. Longer debrief at the station . . ."

Amanda's father arrived. He wept, "This is a miracle." That would be the headline the next morning—No, *this* morning, already 3:00 A.M.—for the press was there with notebooks and earpieces.

Dr. Tourtellotte arrived, helping Amanda and her father, then joining the debriefing. She was a huge woman, even larger than Beth, tall, 300 pounds. Beth answered every question, but she withheld from everyone, how she, Beth Carey, had committed a kind of murder, knowing the moment of death but not stopping it, unable to learn where the bodies were.

Only to Nathan would she tell the whole truth, hours later.

"Did I become evil?" Beth asked, staring into the moonlit shadows of the trees. After begging the police chief and the FBI agent to be allowed back into the river valley for the night—begging to save the station house for tomorrow (today, 10:00 A.M.); after Nathan had made them all see that if not for Beth, Amanda would be dead; finally, Harrington agreed to let Beth and Nathan put off the rest of the commotion of the world. Finally, Washington said, "There's a night's work here anyway without you two. You've saved a life. Go have a few hours." Finally, the first debrief done, Nathan and Beth returned to their camp, calling Greta, promising to come up in a couple hours, after dawn.

Nathan held Beth to him at the cooled circle of rocks, among the smell of ashes and, still in Beth's nostrils, the smell of cave, mold, brains, blood, smoke.

"Did I become evil in order to stop evil?"

"No!" Nanthan said. "You weren't evil. You may have been partly responsible, but that's not the same."

"I will never be the same," she said.

"We'll be together," Nathan soothed. "We'll get through it."

No, she knew, they would not be together for long.

How beautiful the day had been; now it was grotesque. Yet she had done the darkness into light. The child was saved. This filled her with some light. She understood responsibility, as if for the first time. And she was aware that whatever had happened during the last forty-eight hours was completing itself now.

"I feel like I've been in a dream," Nathan said. "I feel like I'm just waking up from a dream. That's what has happened to me, watching you, being with you, in the aftermath of that incredible Light. I've been in your dream."

"I've been swimming underwater all my life and I've just discovered breathing," Beth said, hearing the silliness of words. They explained nothing. If only she could see where the bodies were. Beth knew that over the next weeks and months—however long it took—she would try to help find those children's bodies. She felt that their souls were at stake.

"What do we do now?" Nathan asked, running his fingers through her hair. She lifted her head and kissed Nathan, power and electrical current flooding her immediately. She directed him, with her body, to lie under her. Making love, Beth looked up at the moon.

Sleep, when it came, was welcome. Once, while she slept, Nathan kissed her. She stirred, opened her eyes, feeling cold, reaching for her shirt, pulling it over her shoulders, Nathan helping her arms through the sleeves. She smelled of river moss and peat, dirt and bark. She pulled her shirt around her chest, then clutched Nathan in an embrace, glad her glasses were off, lying in a glare of darkness on a log. Nathan's companionship and affection brought a tear to her eye as she kissed him. She remembered her earlier sense that he would die young, a memory that gave her sadness, and she held him. Then Donni was back in her mind.

"Don't die, Nathan," she whispered.

He laughed. "You already told me today that no one ever really dies."

When Beth and Nathan awoke by the river, they saw the sun rising from behind Donnell's house. They had each nearly dressed during the night, when each awoke to pee and found the body colder than just a shirt could control. Now they fully dressed and ate the last of the food they had in the packs, and began climbing up toward Lucia Court.

"I love you," Beth said to Nathan.

"I love you too," Nathan said.

When they arrived halfway up the ridge to Greta's, they stood and looked out at the river valley. The world was green and golden in the rising sunlight. They saw tiny squirrels and heard birds and even car noises, airplane noises, voices. For a while they just stood in the sheer banquet of it all.

Then Nathan said, "Our lives are just beginning. Maybe we better begin them. There's still a lot to do today."

Beth lifted her backpack, taking a last look at Donnell's perch. She missed the visionary states she'd been in yesterday, but she felt glad, too, that this reality was all she could see right now. The other reality took people down into their fragile bones. She turned back, walking up the incline toward the black asphalt of the road, and the lonely, beautiful, normal human life that she, along with everyone else, had chosen.

★ ★ ★

If Beth had thought either that she would proceed immediately to the police station or that she would get a long rest from the events of the last two days, she saw differently as she and Nathan emerged upward from the river basin into Greta's backyard.

Though it was just dawn, everyone was waiting. The Romers were there, and the Svobodas. Annie was there, Greta and Trudy were there. Sally and her parents, Alex and his mother, and Sammy and his mother were there. They had all been talking and sharing experiences.

Greta cried, coming over to hug Beth. "You're all right! Thank God!"

Everyone spoke at once for a time, then Greta asked each person to speak briefly, in a circular fashion through the small crowd, as if a conductor guiding the orchestra, about their experiences of the last two days. Beth was glad the clamor subsided and each voice was heard individually. The Romers were almost convinced that their son's death had somehow precipitated a set of events, especially because everyone, now forty-eight hours later, had no doubts of Jeffrey's role in the illumination of light in the valley.

"He was a divine child," Greta said, and Marti, in tears, found herself repeating the words, hoping to replace grief with meaning.

Nathan told them about Donnell, and what part he'd played in the events. That he had taken his life, so close to Jeffrey's death, filled each heart with pain and yet, also, with a greater sense of mystery. Nearly everyone in the neighborhood revealed strange experiences and visions, and even parents who had not directly participated could see the light in all eyes, feeling the sense that something was now changed, here at the Spokane River.

Greta said, tears in her eyes, "We're part of the miraculous cycle of life, death and rebirth. Let's protect this, please. This feeling of love I have for all of you—can you feel how powerful it is?"

Heads nodded, "yes" murmured all around. As she listened and talked, Beth knew she was barely equipped to explain how she had been a part, as if guided to act by unseen forces, in the experiences they each described. She resisted revealing how she had participated, but Nathan told her story. It was in fact Alex's mother, an elegant black woman, who inspired her to open up. "We've all had a chance to discuss the . . . incidents," Mrs. Bass said. "I for one do not believe there were drugs involved, or the devil, or anything like that. I think, Beth, you know more than we do. Please tell us how we should understand all this."

Trying, first, to just tell the whole story in chronological order, from forty-eight hours ago to now, Beth reported what had happened in her. Beth talked until she was talked out.

As everyone spoke again, Greta said, "I think Beth and all of us have looked into the watery light that really surrounds and creates us. We don't understand it yet with our present brain systems. That's what you're saying, isn't it, Beth?"

Nathan agreed. "I hope one day to try to improve on our brains. I think that is why I've been called to neurology."

"We shouldn't control these experiences," Beth said. "We have to just be ourselves, speak our truth, and let happen what happens in the world. I'm convinced of that."

"What do we do if the media gets ahold of this . . ." Greta shook her head.

Beth found herself disengaging from the discussion, wanting not to "make a plan."

". . . Alfred Hecht will be here soon," Greta was saying. "He has spent his life studying these kinds of phenomena. We shouldn't do anything until we consult with him."

"I'll tell all of you what I know for certain," Trudy interrupted.

The discussion stopped to listen. She took off her sunglasses, in a symbolic gesture of sight, and said, "I haven't been a seeing person for twenty years. But through all of you these last few days I have seen more than I could hope for in a lifetime. I see that all of us here have known each other for more than the years of this lifetime. We are a cluster of united spirits. We will never be parted, and we will meet over and over. No matter what happens, I know that I'm loved in a million ways. This is what I know, and I don't want to talk now about how to control these things. I want to hear from everyone how they have loved. That is all I care about as I get older. Love."

Marti walked two steps over to her and hugged her. Beth felt moved in the same way. Annie followed. Greta came over and hugged Nathan. Sally hugged her father. Everyone found themselves reaching to someone else. Laura reached to kiss her husband, who lifted her gently in embrace. Landry and Marti embraced. Annie and Trudy rubbed their cheeks together on both sides, like Europeans kissing. Greta and Beth clung to each other.

The tableau, from Donnell Wight's house, must certainly have been one of light generated by the miracle of pure love among a community of like-minded souls. For some seconds it appeared as if the men stood back a little, protective like pillars—Landry, Nathan, Alex, and Harold—while the women embraced; but even their masculine protection was not needed for long, as they too dissolved into the vulnerability of affection on the grass there above the Spokane River. If from the Wight estate voices could have been heard, they would have been voices of connection as the breeze lifted the words on the wind, and chairs were brought out, and then iced tea and the neighbors found themselves in a communion appropriate to neighbors who have been united both by tragedy and the search for new innocence.

While the neighbors came to know each other in ways they had not done before, they did not notice the hawk, the osprey, the moth, the butterfly, the red-winged blackbird, and the other creatures of the air tied more to flight than to the grass and the earth, who formed their own congregation near the Sarbaugh yard. They cried out and they moved silently. They pecked and alighted and were flung about. Only from a certain view and a certain vision, only from a certain place and in a certain light did a pattern emerge among their flights, a pattern the neighbors themselves would have liked to see with their own eyes, but perceived instead with their own voices, and feelings, and immutable gestures of human love.

Epilogue

IN THE YEARS since that day, Beth has become a much-sought-after intuitive (preferring this name to "psychic" or "medium"). Trudy has died, but Greta is still alive, struggling with cancer. Annie did not become as crippled as her doctors had predicted. They have examined her a number of times, amazed that she is still walking. She knows that the miracle of that day kept her from becoming paralyzed. For a time, in 1993, she appeared on a number of talk shows to discuss her healing.

Nathan Wondreski opened a research institute in Los Gatos, California, to study the link between neurobiology and spiritual experiences.

Sandy and his family moved into Donnell's house soon after Donnell's death. Now two other large houses border the Wight estate on the cliffs above the river. Sandy sold off much of his father's land, including the shed and surrounding forest.

The mine shaft was given to the Army Corps of Engineers, who closed it for good.

Marti and Landry have had two other children, a boy and a girl, both of them healthy. Neither child has shown the gifts their deceased brother showed. Like all of the individuals who witnessed the light on that day, the Romers have been interviewed by the media, and, at times, believed.

Sammy and Sally are both in college. Sammy says he will major in psychology. He is convinced now, as a young adult, that even more happened to him and the others on that day in July 1992, and he aims to find out what.

Sally, mentioning the osprey as if it were a pivot in her life, has decided to become a veterinarian.

Alex and Brent have not remained in touch. Brent became a software designer for video games. One of his games involves a hooded watcher and a brave woman who fight beneath a huge light.

Alex and his mother moved to New Orleans, where Alex is a pastor in a liberal Baptist church. He often tells of the light above Jeffrey, and of his own feeling of infinite energy and connection on the cliff above the water. He has inspired a network of "miracle-seekers" who put out a newsletter of small and large miracles throughout the world. Alex has created a website, which gets 1,800 hits a day.

Laura Svoboda is the grandmother of three. Her son did marry his girlfriend. He reported to her that when his baby was born, he knew he must marry. He said he thought he heard a kind of low voice telling him to do it. The voice seemed to come out of a forest like the one near the river at his parents' house.

Harry Svoboda died just before Christmas of 1994. He was

known to have said very little about the events of the day, even about the visitation by his parents. But during the months following it, he created three scrapbooks full of geneological material, which he gave to his children and grandchildren.

None of the people involved in that day have forgotten it, and all those still living speak fondly of it. In Donnell's house, among his spiritual books, Sandy Wight found a collection of papers that appear to be pieces of writings of Ben Brickman's that Donnell brought back from India. No one has found the amulets and jewelry Donni Kozora spoke of.

Under the supervision of Dr. Adelle Tourtellotte, Beth was allowed to read a copy of Donni Kozora's journal. She, like the experts in charge, discerned a great deal about his everyday life, his hallucinations, and his beliefs. But if she thought to find some of the mysteries of the light solved in his written work—especially, how it was that she could do the things she had done over the forty-eight hours—she was disappointed. Whatever other records Donni kept, and the brain-plate he discussed, were destroyed in the explosion.

To the participants in Lucia Court of the two days' events, she ended up with little to report—the brilliant, abstract teachings of a madman were all that remained of his gifts; those, and the grief and pain he left behind along the Spokane River, as parts of bodies were dug up over weeks of police and canine immersion in the region, which Beth joined as best she could.

In the end, each person in Lucia Court who saw the light, whether young or old, had only their own experience to show for it.

And that, each learned, had to be enough.

For now.